Path of Sainthood
Miracles, Schemes, and a Perilous Journey to Truth in the Heart of Medieval Rome
Marina Pacheco

Marina Pacheco

Copyright © 2024 by Marina Pacheco

All rights reserved.

No portion of this book may be reproduced in any form without written permission from the publisher or author, except as permitted by U.S. copyright law.

contents

Offer		V
1.	Chapter 1	1
2.	Chapter 2	11
3.	Chapter 3	22
4.	Chapter 4	30
5.	Chapter 5	44
6.	Chapter 6	53
7.	Chapter 7	64
8.	Chapter 8	76
9.	Chapter 9	89
10.	Chapter 10	95
11.	Chapter 11	100
12.	Chapter 12	113
13.	Chapter 13	120
14.	Chapter 14	127
15.	Chapter 15	142

16.	Chapter 16	163
17.	Chapter 17	180
18.	Chapter 18	187
19.	Chapter 19	194
20.	Chapter 20	200
21.	Chapter 21	210
22.	Chapter 22	215
23.	Chapter 23	223
Get my short story collection Shorties for FREE!		227
Also By		228
About Author		232

Sign up for Marina Pacheco's no-spam newsletter that only goes out when there is a new book or freebie available and get my free collection of short stories!

Details can be found at the end of this book.

Chapter 1

A loud bang caused Alcuin to jump. It was a reflection of his frayed nerves as he waited for Galen's audience with the pope to end. A large cardinal, wearing the most heavily embroidered red-on-red robe he'd ever seen, was glaring at him, his hand still on the door he'd just slammed.

'You there,' he said, encompassing Alcuin and Carbo. 'What are you doing here?'

Alcuin was offended by his tone. It was even more arrogant than the usual Roman attitude. All the same, he stood and bowed, for the man was a senior cleric and respect was owed him. However, he wasn't going to simply buckle to the man's question either.

'The pope's secretary, Piccardo, told us to wait here.'

He noted Carbo's smirk at his reply. The big man wasn't fond of powerful men who abused their authority, although he, too, had stood up and was still in his deep bow. Which was just as well as it hid his grin.

'Why, damn it, why? Your answer is utterly nonsensical. Do they no longer require wits in our monasteries?'

Alcuin was quite astonished by the rudeness of this man. He sounded like someone who was used to getting his own way, which meant he had considerable power, so Alcuin had to proceed with caution, although he prayed that once Galen was finished with the pope they could start making preparations to get back home and wouldn't have to worry about the politics of the Church of Rome.

'The pope summoned my fellow monk, Brother Galen,' Alcuin said at his most neutral, keeping as much as he could from his face.

The cardinal leaned closer, running his eyes over Alcuin's face and clothes.

'You have an accent. Where are you from?'

'Enga-lond, Illustrissimo,' Alcuin said, being careful to use the correct form of address. He sensed this man would easily take offence, but at the same time he didn't wish to give away more than he had to.

His reply seemed to perplex the cardinal who looked like he was trying to recall something.

'Ah!' he said, after a moment's thought, 'That island far to the north.'

Alcuin bowed his head as a yes as Carbo shifted slightly closer to him. It was somehow touching to Alcuin that the big man was trying to provide some form of protective reassurance.

'It isn't usual to see a group of monks such as yourselves in Rome, let alone at the Lateran before the pope's council chamber.'

'We set off with Bishop Sigburt of Crowland, who sadly died en route,' Alcuin said, giving a vastly simplified explanation that caused Carbo's eyes to quiver.

'Why? Damn it. Why did you come to Rome?'

'I'm not in a position to say,' Alcuin said, growing increasingly uncomfortable with the man's probing.

'More importantly,' the cardinal muttered, more to himself than to Alcuin, 'why is the pope taking that young man as a saint?'

His words startled Alcuin for it seemed the pope had decided Galen was a saint and, worse, this cardinal didn't seem happy about it. But he had too little to go on and merely stared back at the cardinal.

'So you two are his minders,' the cardinal said, wagging his finger at Alcuin and Carbo.

'We are but fellow monks. Brother Galen doesn't need minders, he's perfectly capable of looking after himself,' Alcuin said, praying to God to forgive this lie while hoping Carbo's astonished face didn't expose them.

'Ha! He's a weakling, anyone can see it. People like that need someone to look after them. People like that,' he said again, flicking his thumb over his shoulder in the direction of the council chamber, 'are often puppets for others. You may have thought you'd hitched your cart to a useful source of power and income, but if the pope wants him, you won't be able to maintain your position. Not easily, at any rate.'

It took all of Alcuin's self-control not to roar at the cardinal that he was a fool, and a rude one at that. He was furious; not at the aspersions the man had flung at him, but at the awful words he'd spoken about Galen.

Carbo didn't have Alcuin's fortitude and gave an audible gasp, his face turning red.

'Brother Galen is a good man!' he growled.

Thank God he didn't have any eloquence to really go to town on the cardinal. Alcuin hastily grabbed his arm. Carbo's fists were already balled up and ready to punch the cardinal.

'We will be leaving soon, back to our home,' Alcuin said with another bow. 'There is no need to concern yourself with us.'

'You think you'll be leaving?' the cardinal said with a derisory laugh. 'Well... maybe you will, but the saint will be staying.'

With that he stomped off, looking somewhat like his ire had been relieved with his final remarks to Alcuin.

'Bastard,' Carbo rumbled, glaring at the cardinal's departing back. 'Who in God's name does he think he is?'

'A man with sufficient power to be talking to the pope,' Alcuin said, realising there was a tremor born of rage and frustration to his voice.

He was more shaken than he'd wanted to be by the cardinal, mainly because he had made it clear that being a saint might not be as simple as a confirmation and then being allowed to go home. It added anxiety to Alcuin's wait.

'All the same,' Carbo huffed.

'Let's just wait and see,' Alcuin said, returning to the bench. But his anxiety grew the longer they waited.

The silence felt heavy, with the solemnity of a church preventing further conversation. Not that Carbo ever had much of interest to say beyond grumbling under his breath over the cardinal.

All Alcuin could do now was look around some more. It was dark in the Lateran Palace. The floor and the walls were lined in large geometric patterns made from dark stones of black, deep red and green that gave a sombre quality to the light. He'd traced the lines in the highly polished stone to the point where he could hardly stand it anymore, while he prayed over and over again that it would all be over soon and, to calm his mind, worked on the plan to get them home.

Earlier, Alcuin had decided to leave Rome in June. That would give them plenty of time to reach the foothills of the Alps. They could build in rest stops along the way at the various churches and monasteries that accepted the regular flow of pilgrims to and from Rome. Then, come July or August, they could cross the Alps and make their way in easy stages back to Enga-lond.

With any luck, they'd be home before the new year. This would be as well, for it was a significant date: the year 1000AD. Alcuin shuddered at the thought. It seemed ominous, even if Galen was unperturbed by it.

Carbo gave a gusty sigh that sounded loud in the empty chamber and drew Alcuin's attention.

'It's taking a long time, isn't it?' Alcuin said.

Carbo nodded. 'But then, it is the pope talking to a saint, so it isn't surprising.'

Carbo was so much better at acceptance than Alcuin. The next minute, the pope's secretary reappeared. He was young for his position, with unusual light grey eyes that almost matched his ash blond hair. Even his tunic was a plain brown, but with an embroidered margin that gave an impression of luxury.

He nodded to Alcuin and Carbo before stepping in to see the pope and re-emerging almost immediately.

'His Holiness wishes to see you, Brother Alcuin.'

This no longer surprised Alcuin. After meeting Galen, people often became curious about him, probably because Galen always spoke embarrassingly highly of him. Doing so to the most senior man in the church hierarchy was another level, though. Still, he hurried after the secretary and bowed low before the pope.

He was of an average height, with white hair and a white beard. His piercing gaze could stop the words in a man's throat by sheer force of personality. The trappings of power - the throne atop a short run of stairs, the blood red canopy - added to his intimidating air.

'Welcome, Brother Alcuin,' the pope said. 'Brother Galen has told me a great deal about you.'

Alcuin flushed and said, 'Brother Galen is far too uncritical, Your Holiness. I'm sure he exaggerates my role.'

'Not at all. Now I suggest you help your friend down the stairs. I imagine our meeting has been a tiring one for him. Piccardo will show you to your new quarters.'

Alcuin was so stunned to be speaking to the pope that the mention of quarters barely registered at first. Then it hit him and he was filled with dismay. It seemed the cardinal had been right. He hurried up the stairs, took Galen's arm and, with a well-practised move, helped him to his feet and led him down the stairs.

Galen looked worn out, which was to be expected. He'd barely slept the night before, as always when he was worrying about the next day. They'd had a long walk to the Lateran, and then an extended audience.

It was a wonder Galen could get to his feet at all, and he now leaned heavily on Alcuin's arm. He turned the two of them to face the pope and they gave a deep bow and made to follow Piccardo out.

'Oh, wait, the codex!' Galen said and turned back. 'It was produced by the Abbey of San Agato from notes sent to us by Cardinal Gui. Fra' Martinus asked me to give it to you.'

Pope Sylvester waved for Piccardo to take the book, so all that was left was for Galen and Alcuin to give another bow and leave.

'This way, please,' Piccardo said as he led them out of the foyer and towards a dark corridor.

Alcuin gestured for Carbo to follow and he surged to his feet, wasting no time in taking Galen's other arm with his usual exaggerated care.

The trio followed Piccardo past an altar set against the wall at the end of another dark corridor. Although it was grand beyond anything Alcuin had seen thus far in Rome, the palace lacked light. The walls and extravagant carved columns flanking doors and propping up archways were quite a contrast to Hatim's white, sun-filled palace.

It was also surprisingly quiet. There was a hum of chatter coming from below via the stairs that led to the basilica, but it was almost as if they were the only ones on the current floor.

Alcuin looked down at Galen to see how he was doing, and what he might be thinking. His friend had his lips firmly sealed. The skin about his mouth was pressed so tight that his lips were white. He looked to be in shock. That was a bad sign. Alcuin itched to ask him what had happened between him and the pope, some of which had surely resulted in the two of them being given a room.

The corridor traced a square around the entire building. Piccardo turned a tight corner then stopped at one sombre dark door and took a key from his substantial ring of them. The door unlocked with a firm clunk that reminded Alcuin all too forcibly of his time in the Moorish jail.

'What is the meaning of this?' he asked as the three of them stood at the entrance of a large room that, aside from the marble walls, looked quite ordinary.

It had a single square window, two beds on either side of the room and two desks.

'Is this room not acceptable?' Piccardo asked in a neutral way.

Alcuin wondered whether he was irritated and assuming that Alcuin wanted something better. 'I thought we'd go back to the monastery.'

'Ah,' Piccardo said, 'did Fra' Martinus not say anything to you? The pope told him he would most likely be taking the two of you into his household.'

'What about me?' Carbo asked in a panicked voice.

'We didn't expect a third monk, but your presence isn't required. You may return to your monastery.'

Alcuin noted Galen's speculative glance up at Carbo. Piccardo probably assumed that the big man came from the Monastery of San Agato. Was Galen now wondering whether the monk would return to his monastery in the Pyrenees? Galen had already tried sending Carbo home once before and failed.

'I can't leave Brother Galen,' Carbo's mouth clamped shut as if that was the end of the conversation.

'We have no need for you,' Piccardo said. 'Brothers Galen and Alcuin will be assigned a servant to look after their needs and they will be perfectly comfortable and safe in the Lateran Palace.'

'Brother Galen doesn't like strangers,' Carbo said. 'If he is to have a servant, let it be me.'

'But you're a monk,' Piccardo said.

'I can leave my habit behind if that's what it takes.'

'Carbo,' Galen said softly, 'do you not think it's time you went home? Your fra' must be waiting for you, and I don't want you to drift so far from your calling.'

'You are my calling,' Carbo said and dropped to his knees before Galen, his head bowed. 'I will remain your faithful protector.'

Alcuin read Galen's dismay from his mobile face where a new emotion mingled with whatever had disturbed him during his conversation with the pope.

'Galen is too tired for this now,' he said. 'Piccardo, would it be possible to find work for Brother Carbo?'

Piccardo tilted his head in a vague acknowledgement and said, 'I will see what I can do. In the meantime, you are to remain here. You have been given quarters in the Lateran Palace so that you may be close to the pope and protected. Other options had been for you to reside in one of the nearby monasteries, but the pope decided against that.'

'I see,' Alcuin said and wondered whether the reason for that decision had been so that no other man, such as an abbot, could have authority over Galen.

'For now, it would be best not to be seen. Rest here and I will send somebody over with food.'

'I will bring the food,' Carbo said.

It earned him another one of Piccardo's blank gazes, but he gave in and said, 'Very well, follow me.'

'Say what you will of Carbo,' Alcuin said, watching the big man as he hurried after Piccardo, 'but he has a knack for getting his own way.'

'Mmm,' Galen murmured.

It was never a good sign when Galen became monosyllabic.

Alcuin guided Galen to the bed nearest the door and lowered him onto it.

'What's wrong?'

'We're never going to leave this place,' Galen said as his eyes flicked to Alcuin, reflecting the horror he felt at such a revelation.

'God's tears, did the pope tell you that?'

Ever since the run-in with the cardinal, Alcuin had been dreading such an outcome. He didn't want to remain in Rome, despite the elegance of their room and their new, apparently exalted, status.

'He said we would be seeing a lot of each other,' Galen continued in a low tone, 'but he said nothing about going home. He just assumes we'll stay.'

'Did he say why he'd be seeing you again?'

'He says I am a saint. At least… he thinks the power of public opinion will prevent anyone, even him, from gainsaying it. And he… I think he will find me useful. Although he also said… he said he would help me work out what is happening.'

Alcuin hadn't assumed that the pope would acknowledge Galen as a saint. Secular needs and the search for power frequently trumped the truth. Now he wondered what would happen to the two of them if Galen was revealed to the people as a saint sanctioned by the pope.

'Do you think he can help you?'

Galen shrugged. 'He is very clever… maybe he can. I just… I don't know. Oh Alcuin, he has a mind like a snake. It was twisting and turning about me, trying to work me out and trying to work out how he could use me. It was impossible for me to understand him!'

'He is a powerful man. He has risen to the position he has through guile, so we have to be as cautious with him as we would be with any king.'

'Yes,' Galen whispered and wrapped his arms around his trembling body.

'Time will tell.' Alcuin still hoped that his plan of leaving Rome in June would hold, although that only gave them a little over a month to convince the pope to let them go. Alcuin had his doubts that Galen would be able to convince him though, so it would be up to him to find a way.

'You should eat something when it arrives. You only played with your breakfast, and I know it was because you were too nervous to eat. But now it is well past midday and you haven't eaten properly since yesterday. Then you should rest and after that we will talk again. You'll see that you will feel better for having the food and the rest.'

'You're looking after me again,' Galen said with a wan smile.

'Well, I have to, my dear saint. If I didn't, you would wear yourself to death with your worries, and we can't have that.'

Galen gave a half-hearted laugh and said, 'But it would read so well in a book of my life. I was one so holy my fragile frame couldn't support the weight of earthly cares and I succumbed.'

'Nonsense! You've survived a lot worse than being set up in a fancy room in the pope's palace, and you'd have none but yourself to blame if you starved yourself to death here. Besides, you have to build up your strength if you're to make it over the mountains.'

'But we aren't going over the mountains,' Galen said, the light of appreciative amusement going out of his eyes. 'The pope won't allow it.'

'We'll see about that!' Alcuin said with a resolute set to his mouth. There was no way he was going to remain in Rome, and if he didn't stay, Galen wouldn't be staying either, pope or no pope.

Chapter 2

Galen didn't want to get out of bed, even though the crowing of distant roosters and the honking of geese added a loud domestic top note to the twittering of songbirds, the chirp of sparrows and the screech of swifts that had filled the air since dawn. Usually, such sounds brought him peace, but not this morning. He'd been so certain he was finally going to return home that he'd started feeling positively happy. Those hopes were now dashed and a grey depression had settled over him, making the ever-present pain in his guts feel more acute than it had for a while.

For all the time he'd been in Rome, Galen had tried to suppress thoughts of home. He worried about his family. Were they all still alive and well? They formed a part of his prayers every day to keep them safe.

He also feared they'd be suffering, not knowing whether he and Alcuin were still alive. He prayed that at least Penda, the bishop's shipmaster, had made it back to Lundenburh. If he had, he'd have to tell the king about the bishop's capture by the Moors. Then the rest would come out too and hopefully reach his father's ears.

How helpful that would be was debatable. At least his family would know he hadn't perished at sea. But after that? Would they give him up for lost? Would they assume he'd been martyred? Could his father do anything about it anyway?

Galen wasn't sure his father's affection for him would stretch to sending an offer of ransom. Even if it did, he'd have no way of knowing which group of Moors might have taken his son. Since then, so much time had passed anyway, and they'd lived through so much more.

Through all his hours of worrying, he'd held on to the belief that as soon as they'd spoken to the pope, they'd be able to get home and he could reassure his family that he was still alive and well. What a fool he'd been not to realise that there might be a lengthy process involved in determining whether one was a saint or not. And worse still, realising that a saint might be a useful tool for a pope. Now what was he to do about his family?

Galen sat up abruptly as a thought occurred to him. It was so simple he couldn't understand why he'd never considered it before.

'Alcuin!'

'So you're awake, are you?'

Alcuin was kneeling on his bed, his arms propped up on the windowsill, gazing outside.

'What do you see?'

Galen eased himself cautiously out of bed and made his slow, stooped way over. He'd been too preoccupied with other things yesterday to pay attention to his surroundings, but now it seemed more important than ever to take a look around.

Alcuin waved his hand to encompass the scene beyond, bathed in a golden light.

'Rome is such a strange place.'

Galen nodded, examining Alcuin. It seemed he was touched with melancholy too. Not surprising since he'd already made plans for their departure. Galen clambered onto Alcuin's bed and joined him by the window.

It really was an unusual sight. Their room looked like it was somewhere to the rear within the papal palace. Galen was now gazing out at an unpaved space from which two roads headed off in straight lines, one more or less to their right, the other to their left. Beyond that was a ruin-strewn wilderness-cum-farm. Closest to them were rows of grapevines, followed by a grove of apple trees losing the last of their white and pink blossoms, and, beyond that, an olive grove.

Some of the ruins still stood as high as a house. One had half a grand archway, but many were just stony piles or half their old height. All were covered in vegetation. An olive tree was sprouting from the top of the arch.

Above everything loomed an aqueduct. Further back, through the branches of oaks, pines, and dark, narrow cypresses, was the mighty Aurelian Wall that surrounded Rome. It was of a height Galen could barely fathom and must have taken decades of time and thousands of men to build. It was a necessary feat since it was needed to keep at bay the waves of barbarians that had assaulted Rome over the centuries.

It was strange to think that buildings had once filled the entire space surrounded by these mighty walls. Nowadays it was more than half empty. The people, their homes and churches had congregated around the Tiber River, the area that Galen and Alcuin had learned was called the abitato. The rest of what had once been ancient Rome had fallen into ruin and was dotted about with farms, farmhouses and churches. Some of the churches had been set up to chase away the creeping wilderness, or as way stations and points of safety that guarded key routes. Chief amongst these was the road to the mighty Lateran Basilica, where the pope was based. This wild space was called the disabitato.

Aside from the vast ruined Forum beside the Colosseum, the wilderness wasn't so obvious when one was on the road to the Lateran. But what buildings there were, tended to be clustered along the road's edge. The habitation was only two or three houses deep, though, which resulted in this view of ruin-filled countryside from the back of one of the most important palaces in the world.

'Wilderness but not wilderness,' Alcuin murmured. 'Everywhere you look, no matter how wild it appears, has been touched by the hand of man.'

'It is quite amazing how quickly nature has reclaimed the space,' Galen said. 'Even the tops of the walls are covered in grass. The ancient Romans would be astonished to see how their mark on the land is being obliterated.'

'Taken away by their descendants,' Alcuin said, pointing to a figure in the distance who was hacking away at a wall and transferring the bricks and stone blocks he freed to a cart with a donkey standing at the ready to roll it away.

'At least the materials will get a second lease of life.'

'Indeed,' Alcuin said and pushed away from the window to settle cross-legged at the head of his bed. 'What has cheered you up?'

'Was I very miserable last night?' Galen said, settling in the same position opposite his friend.

'Understandably so. We both thought we were about to go home.'

Galen nodded and tried to keep the depression from rolling back in. 'I thought... perhaps we could send a letter home.'

Alcuin blinked at him. 'A letter?'

'Well?' Galen said, smiling up at Alcuin's astonished face. 'The bishop sent one from Lundenburh to here, about us, and the pope sent one back, summoning Bishop Sigburt to Rome so... could we not send a letter?'

'Who would take it for us?'

'Perhaps we could ask Piccardo to add our letters to any that are being sent to Enga-lond in the future.'

Alcuin gave a thoughtful nod. This was one reason Galen liked him so much. He was always willing to entertain Galen's ideas.

'It's probably a long shot, but still,' Galen said.

'You've been worrying about your family, haven't you?'

'And you? You must wonder about yours and... and Emma?'

Alcuin laughed. 'I've been trying not to think about it. There isn't anything we could do from our distance. But I admit it was a blow to hear we'd be staying.'

Before Galen could dwell any further on such gloomy thoughts, there was a knock at the door.

'Brothers, it's me, Carbo.'

'Carbo?' Alcuin hopped off the bed and wrenched the door open. 'Oh! What happened to you?'

It was a fair question. Carbo was dressed in a simple brown tunic and slightly darker brown leggings.

He grinned at them both and stepped inside, putting the tray in his hands down on the first table he came to. It held two bowls of pottage, a plump cheese, a small pot of honey, a jug of wine and two cups.

'I finally convinced that secretary to make me your personal servant.'

'But...' Galen started, but couldn't think where to go from there.

'What of your abbot?' Alcuin asked. 'What will he say?'

Carbo was scratching his head as he gazed sheepishly at Galen and said, 'I went back to San Agato yesterday and spoke to Fra' Martinus. He has promised to send a message to Fra' Arnold to tell him I will stay with you.'

'For how long?' Galen said, feeling quite overwhelmed.

'For as long as you need me.'

Galen stared up at him, trying to work out how to shift the man's cast-iron conviction. He looked unmovable.

'But we have no money for a servant, and don't need one either,' Alcuin said.

'The church was going to provide you with one, anyway. I convinced that Piccardo fellow that I was perfect for the job because Brother Galen doesn't like strangers. Plus, I know how to keep my mouth shut, and it seems, for the time being, that your existence is being kept a secret.'

'Well...' Alcuin said, 'that's all true.'

Carbo grinned at him. 'You can rely upon me if either of you are ever in danger. In the meantime, I will look after you better than you've ever been looked after before.'

He seemed so happy, and he was a familiar face these days, so Galen found himself smiling back.

'Very well, if that is what you wish, then we are in your care, Carbo.'

'Then you should eat,' Carbo said, hiding his pleasure at having been accepted in a sudden gruffness to his tone. 'Piccardo said he'll come by today to talk to you some more.'

Galen was about to ask Carbo to join them, but the big man gave them both a smart bow, said, 'Enjoy your meal,' and withdrew.

'Carbo's been pretty active, hasn't he?' Alcuin said once the big man had left them alone to eat their breakfast.

'He puts me to shame. I was so shocked by the turn of events yesterday I could barely think straight.'

'Same here,' Alcuin said. 'But he is tenacious.'

'He adds to my guilt. When we were at San Agato I got the impression he missed his monastery too. Now he's determined to stick with us.'

'With you.'

Alcuin's smile took the sting out of his words but still made Galen burn with guilt.

'What have I done to him? Removing him like this from all he has ever known.'

'You have no need to feel guilty over Carbo. He has led a wandering life and is more adaptable than either of us. I can also plainly see that he is telling the truth when he said you are his new calling, for his former restlessness is gone.'

'Do you think that's true?'

Galen wasn't as convinced as Alcuin, but he felt there was at least some truth to his words. Then doubt made him wonder whether he was merely deceiving himself so that he'd feel better.

'He's like a dog - happiest by the side of his master, wherever that may lead him.'

It was an unflattering comparison, but Galen understood.

'I wish I could be the same. All I want is to return to my home, my family and all that is familiar to me. That is my comfort.'

'Don't give up hope, Galen.' Alcuin's expression flickered to another, less pleasant thought and he said, 'By the way, do you know who that overly flamboyant cardinal was who was with the pope when you arrived?'

Galen went blank for a moment trying to work out whom Alcuin meant.

'He came storming out of the council chamber yesterday,' Alcuin prodded.

'Oh, Cardinal Gui,' Galen said. 'He took instantly against me.'

'That's Cardinal Gui? The one who wrote the life of Gregory that you copied out and I had some hand in illuminating?'

Galen nodded. The work had been somewhat disappointing. He'd hoped to learn more about the recently deceased pope from the cardinal's dictated notes, but it was a hollow work, full of flattery, more designed to curry favour with the emperor, the former pope's uncle, than to enlighten.

'He's best avoided,' Alcuin said. 'He asked a lot of searching questions about you and I distrusted his tone.'

Alcuin watched Galen approvingly as he dipped the bread into the pottage. He needed to eat more, but he tended not to when he was distressed. The thought of sending a letter home seemed to have worked wonders for him.

Then Alcuin turned his attention back to the pottage. It was a richer dish than they were accustomed to getting at the Abbey of San Agato. It had a swirl of olive oil on top which he didn't approve of, and chunks of eel along with the onions, dried peas, barley and oats. At this time of the year there was always a bit of a dry patch when the stores of winter ran out and the new fruits and vegetables had yet to ripen, leading to rather boring meals. Still, the cheese was excellent, especially when combined with the honey, which was a rare treat at any time.

'So,' Alcuin said, aware that it was his role to cheer Galen up, even when he was feeling rather low himself. 'What should we do next? We may as well go back to San Agato to collect our stuff and thank the brothers for their hospitality.'

Galen nodded. 'I worry about Piero. He was getting the hang of Arabic, but he still needs supervision to fully understand it.'

'That boy will be sorry to lose you as a mentor, but as we're still in the same city, maybe you could continue to see him.'

'That boy?' Galen said, an amused smile playing on his lips. 'He's only three and a half years younger than me.'

'Good heavens! Is that so? I feel so much older,' Alcuin said as he dipped his spoon into the honey and then drizzled it over his slice of cheese.

'Well, you are a year older than me.'

'You feel like a grown man now. Piero doesn't. That's all I'm saying.'

'Perhaps our adventures have had an effect on us.'

'That must be it, because thinking back to when I had just joined the scriptorium, the slightly older monks didn't seem like grown-ups even then.'

Galen nodded but his eyes flickered uncomfortably and Alcuin realised it was because of the way Galen had arrived at Yarmwick. He'd been in no condition to notice what the other monks were like, no matter their age.

'Do you really think I could continue to teach Piero?' Galen asked.

Alcuin shrugged, glad that Galen had changed the subject.

'I suppose that depends on what the pope will want you to do. I can't imagine that keeping you hidden away is the full extent of his plan.'

'No,' Galen said. 'I'm sure it isn't.'

'Brothers, it's me, Piccardo,' came from the other side of the door, accompanied by a light tapping.

'Come in.' Alcuin was relieved that one as exalted as the pope's secretary was treating them with this much respect.

'I trust breakfast was to your liking,' Piccardo asked while tilting his head at the empty plates that had been wiped clean.

'It's very good, thank you,' Alcuin said.

Piccardo nodded as his gaze travelled from Alcuin to Galen and back again. 'You are looking more rested, so I can tell you more about your stay at the Lateran.'

'If this is going to take a while, you may as well sit down,' Alcuin said, gesturing to Galen's bed.

Piccardo gave a nod of thanks and settled on the edge of the bed, his back ramrod straight.

'For the time being, His Holiness has requested that the two of you remain within the palace and the basilica and keep your interaction with others to a minimum. At least until he has finished his discussions with Brother Galen.'

'His discussions?' Galen asked with an edge of nervousness.

'Pope Sylvester is an intellectual. At one point, he was the current emperor's tutor. He likes to test people.'

'I see.'

'When is that likely to be?' Alcuin asked.

'The pope is a busy man, but he will make time as soon as possible to see Brother Galen. You should be grateful. His Holiness rarely makes time to meet all the people that come to the Lateran claiming to be saints.'

Alcuin felt less than grateful. If they were such a nuisance, why didn't the pope simply send them home? It filled him with foreboding that Galen was still being tested.

'What should we do in the meantime?' Alcuin asked. 'I don't wish to be cooped up in this room with nothing to do.'

'Nobody is telling you to do that. I will take you around the palace and the basilica so that you may get your bearings. Then you will be free to look around whenever you like, except you are to stay away from the Lateran monastery. His Holiness requests that you be discreet for now. That is also the reason why you have been given a room in this part of the palace. It's the quietest and where you will run into the fewest people.'

'It is very quiet,' Galen murmured. 'Why is that?'

'The palace is large. The lower levels are used as offices and are where the pope's staff work, helping to run the church across the former Roman empire and beyond. The upper levels are used by the pope as his own quarters, but also to host visiting dignitaries and religious men, bishops from our own church and from other sects and religions. He tends to keep them in the rooms nearer him, so this particular section is usually empty and therefore deemed best for you.'

'And why should we stay away from the Lateran monastery?' Alcuin asked, for he wanted to confirm his guess. 'That seems suspicious.'

'The abbot of that monastery has a habit of taking ownership of talented people.'

'So the pope wants to maintain exclusive control over Galen,' Alcuin said and did his best to ignore the dismayed look Galen was giving him while another surge of anxiety washed over Alcuin. If naming somebody as a saint was a simple business, they wouldn't be kept hidden.

'What makes you think Brother Galen is the only talent the pope is protecting?' Piccardo said, gazing at Alcuin with an expression that was impossible to read.

Alcuin prided himself in being able to keep his thoughts hidden, but he was an amateur compared to Piccardo.

'What are you talking about?'

'Fra' Martinus also spoke highly of you, Brother Alcuin, both as a firm friend to Brother Galen but also as one of the most talented artists ever to visit his abbey.'

'Oh...' Alcuin said, lost for more to say because Piccardo had said something so flattering with such a flat voice it was hard to process it as a compliment.

'So you want us to stay out of sight,' Alcuin said, reflecting that Galen would probably prefer this, at least in the beginning. His friend, despite being shy, enjoyed getting to know people. He just preferred that it was singly or in small groups. It was crowds he struggled with, but they had both long since agreed that the life of a hermit was far from either of their ideals. 'We can do that, but when will you show us around?'

'This afternoon. I have a couple of delegations to manage for the pope this morning. You may as well go to your old monastery in the meantime and say your farewells. I will let Carbo know so he may show you the way out and protect you on your travels.'

Chapter 3

'Are you ready, Brothers?' Carbo asked, turning up shortly after Piccardo had left.

Galen admired the way he adapted so quickly to his new role that he looked like he had always been a servant at the Lateran. It was in stark contrast to Galen who was feeling all at sea again. Every time he became familiar with a place, his life was upended all over again.

'We're ready.'

Alcuin looked approvingly at Carbo who had arrived carrying a heavy-looking staff. Galen was glad that Alcuin was coming to accept Carbo. At first, he'd been the one who avoided Carbo, and Alcuin had seemed fine about having him around. But after Galen accepted him, Alcuin had become increasingly frosty towards Carbo. Whatever had been the reason, perhaps because he was a familiar face in the Lateran, Alcuin was back to being his usual friendly self and including Carbo.

'Just a minute,' Alcuin said as they approached their room's door. He opened it and looked to the left and right, 'All clear.'

'What's this?' Carbo said with a puzzled frown.

'We've been told to keep out of sight, so it's best if people don't know where we're staying.'

'What a strange place,' Carbo said, shaking his head. 'But never mind, I'll show you out. The Lateran is a warren. I'm still getting lost, but at least it's easy to find your rooms. All I have to do is go outside, then find the Lateran Palace entrance, come up the stairs that are right by the entrance, and then you're the third door along. Useful, huh?'

'Very,' Galen said as he took Carbo's offered arm and they headed down the corridor to the nearby stairs and out the door into the oblong square that they'd seen from their window.

'Just remember this route, if nothing else,' Carbo said with a big grin.

Now that they were outside they could blend in with the pilgrims and other visitors, many of whom wore the black robes of monks. It truly was easiest to hide a piece of straw in a haystack, Galen reflected. Which made it odd that, despite Piccardo's explanation, the pope was keeping them in his palace rather than leaving them at San Agato's or installing them at the Lateran monastery.

Still, now wasn't the time to wonder about that, as he had a walk ahead of him and that required his full effort and therefore attention. They headed to the left and the Via S. Giovanni in Laterano that Galen already knew led to the Colosseum.

'At least the spring is pleasant in Rome,' Carbo said while matching his pace to Galen's slow gait.

'It is a lovely day,' Galen murmured, looking up for the first time into a blue sky where tall white clouds were gradually falling apart as the sun intensified.

'Very nice indeed,' Alcuin said, coming up beside Galen. 'A walk was just what we needed. I'm not sure I want to spend all day from now on in that room.'

'It's not that different from a scriptorium,' Galen said as they passed a butcher's shop and then a money changer, 'or the hut we worked in when we were at the king's hall.'

'True, but I prefer working surrounded by people. It doesn't feel as lonely. Not that I'm saying your company isn't sufficient, Galen,' Alcuin added hastily. 'But I'm more inspired when I'm surrounded by other artists.'

'Perhaps, once we're settled, you can search out the master craftsmen and artists of the Lateran Palace. They must surely be some of the best in the world.'

Galen often regretted that he'd dragged Alcuin into this adventure. It had disrupted the time he could spend on his art, which was a loss to the world at large. He sincerely hoped Alcuin would learn something new here. Just as some of the Moors' endlessly repeating, interlocking patterns had found their way into the illustrations Alcuin had produced at San Agato.

'I'm sure there are masters I can learn from here too,' Alcuin said as they passed the booth of a shoemaker. He was doing a good trade from the pilgrims, who were lining up to patch shoes whose soles were worn through on their journey to Rome. A few more were gathered around the hostelries that served them and visiting dignitaries.

'I've been watching the palace guards at their training,' Carbo said. 'They're pretty good too. I'm sure I can also learn from them.'

'You're not going to take up the sword again, are you Carbo?' Galen asked while thinking his influence upon the big man wasn't the best.

'Never, Brother Galen. A staff is all I'll ever need or want to use. I may have changed out of my habit, but I haven't left my calling behind. I'll continue to follow the rules of St Benedict as closely as I may.'

'Once we get permission from the pope, we could join the Lateran monastery for their prayers, at least,' Alcuin said.

'I would like that,' Galen said. 'The rituals bring me comfort and keep me on the right path.'

'True,' Carbo said as they made their way down the hill, the Colosseum growing steadily larger as they approached, and the shops and hostelries thinning out.

Although this was the most abandoned part of the disabitato, even here there were people. Some had moved into the arches at the base of the Colosseum and set up shops, homes and warehouses, one per arch, alongside a small cluster of homes

'We must be getting nearer the river,' Alcuin said as he flicked his hand to drive away the flies and midges that were buzzing around them.

'Indeed,' Carbo said. 'It's as well we have moved to the Lateran that is on higher ground. I have heard from the other servants that a black miasma rises from the marshland around the Tiber and brings a sleeping sickness with it. At least on the hill we are less likely to come into contact with contagions.'

'A sleeping sickness?' Alcuin said, exchanging an alarmed look with Galen. 'Let us pray none of us contract it. As you say, Carbo, perhaps it is best that we've moved to higher ground.'

'It's cooler there too,' Galen said, for his black robe was absorbing the strong rays of the sun and he was getting steadily hotter.

'We're nearly there, Brothers,' Carbo said.

That was an exaggeration. Galen knew they were only halfway, but at least, once they reached the abitato, the buildings provided them with shade. And although Galen wouldn't say so to his companions, the crowds also slowed their walking speed which brought its own relief.

'What should we tell the brothers at San Agato?' Alcuin said.

'What do you mean?' Carbo asked.

'I mean, we can't tell them we're staying at the Lateran because the pope thinks Galen is a saint, can we? Not until the pope gives his permission.'

'Preferably not even then,' Galen said quietly. 'I don't have the courage to meet and converse with people who might come to me for miracles or for my wisdom.'

'You don't need to worry on the wisdom front,' Alcuin said gruffly. 'I know the miracle side of things can be trickier, but you could always use Marozia's technique.'

'Her technique?' Galen asked, pausing to catch his breath as he looked enquiringly at Alcuin.

'Tell them their faith isn't strong enough.'

Alcuin must have realised his reason wouldn't find approval with Galen, because he flushed and looked away as he spoke.

'How would I know that?' Galen said gently. 'What if their faith is stronger than yours and mine? How could I undermine them like that? No... I suppose I will have to fall back on a phrase I always found frustrating, but appears to be true. God truly does work in mysterious ways. I have no way of understanding when and why He acts or doesn't.'

Alcuin gave him a wry smile and said, 'And that's why you're the saint, rather than me.'

'Doesn't solve what we tell the people at San Agato, though,' Carbo said.

'Leave it to me,' Alcuin said as they arrived at the solid door to the monastery and he gave the bell-pull a hefty jerk. 'This will get Brother Donato all in a flutter,' he said with a grin.

Brother Donato's eye and one eyebrow, along with the bridge of his nose, appeared in the peephole after a short wait.

'Oh, it's you, is it?' he said and opened the door. 'Are you back?'

'Not for long,' Alcuin said. 'But we need to speak to the terrier and Brother Iacopo.'

'Sounds like you're moving out,' the old man said, making it accusatory, as if they couldn't stand the discipline of this monastery.

'Our visit was always temporary,' Alcuin said at his smiling best.

This was one of the things Galen admired so much about his friend. His ability to manage people, without upsetting them.

'Well, come on in,' Donato said, then pointed an accusing finger at Carbo. 'You will have to wait here. None but monks may enter the cloisters.'

Carbo looked like he was about to object, but Galen patted his hand before stepping away from his support and said, 'We'll be fine here, and we won't take long.'

Carbo muttered something under his breath but also nodded and took a seat on the bench by the door.

Alcuin then took Galen's arm and said, 'Are you ready?'

'I'll be sorry to say farewell to these men who have become brothers to me, too. I enjoyed my time in their scriptorium, where I arrived with a clean slate.'

'It was good for both of us,' Alcuin said as he led Galen through the cloister and to the scriptorium.

All the monks had their heads bowed when they arrived, and all that could be heard was the scratch of pens against parchment and one of the brothers sharpening his quill.

'Well, well, look who's back,' Brother Iacopo said as he looked up from his desk at the far end of the room that faced all his scribes and artists. His words had the rest of the monks swivelling round to see who it was. 'Fra' Martinus said it was possible you wouldn't be returning.'

Galen gave a sigh of relief, because everyone, including the armarius, was smiling.

'We weren't sure whether we'd be allowed back either,' Alcuin said. 'But as it happens, we're just here to fetch our things and thank you for your hospitality.'

'Oh no! Are you not coming back?' Piero asked.

'Are you going home?' Iacopo jumped in.

'No... at least, not yet,' Alcuin said.

'Who would want to make such an enormous journey, anyway?' Brother Luca said, while smothering a yawn.

'Well, we know you wouldn't,' Brother Feo said. 'But what is the delay? Surely you have told the pope all about your bishop. Why would he keep you here after that?'

Galen's grip tightened on Alcuin's arm, but he just shrugged and said, 'I assume the pope has a few more things he wishes to know. How can I pretend to know what he is thinking?'

'It's not about the saint business, is it?' Feo asked.

'Feo!' Iacopo snapped, as his brows beetled together into a fearsome scowl.

'Ah,' Alcuin said. 'So you know?'

'There have been rumours. You know how it is,' Iacopo said. 'Fra' Martinus dismissed it all as idle gossip, but now it seems it isn't.'

'That is still to be determined,' Alcuin said at his most absolute.

It usually prevented further questions. Galen hoped it would this time too, because the monks' speculative gazes that all settled upon him made him deeply uncomfortable. Their opinions of him were shifting. That saddened him because he'd liked that they had treated him as an equal before.

'In the meantime,' Alcuin continued, 'the pope has ordered that we say nothing on the subject, and the same must apply to you.'

'Of course,' Iacopo said, nodding his head meaningfully at each one of his scribes. 'Now, I believe your books are still on the shelf under your desk, Brother Galen. Please help yourself. Oh, except the Moorish book on numbers. Brother Piero has been working on that one.'

Galen glanced down to Piero's desk, the one closest to the door, and realised the young man was staring at him with wide, surprised eyes.

'I was hoping,' Galen said, turning back to Iacopo, 'that I could continue teaching Piero and Brother Bosso to read Arabic. At least... at least while we are still in Rome.'

'If you would do that, I would be grateful,' Iacopo said.

'You don't mind? They'd have to come to the Lateran to do it.'

'They can go together every morning, if that suits you, Brother Galen? It is wonderful enough that we can enhance the skills of two of our brothers, but for them to learn from a saint... at least, a good man such as yourself, is even more of an honour.'

Galen felt his face growing warm at the comment, but he suppressed that and the shaking from having so much attention on him, because he was glad that he could continue to teach his pupils.

'Would it be possible to see Fra' Martinus as well?' Alcuin said, jumping in as he often did when Galen spiralled into incoherence.

'Ah, I'm afraid our abbot has taken to his bed again. The signs aren't good this time.'

'I'm sorry to hear that,' Alcuin said.

'We will pray for his recovery. It wouldn't be the first time we have all but given up hope for our abbot to pull through. I just fear this time...' He gave an expressive shrug and the rest murmured in sorrowful agreement.

Galen reflected that a man could be a godless heathen, but still gain the respect of his people if he did the right thing and treated them well. Fra' Martinus was a strict abbot, but it seemed he had his people's respect.

Chapter 4

Alcuin was pleased with the outcome of their trip to San Agato. His gain had been a bundle of parchment Brother Iacopo had given him for his art, along with the loan of the pattern book Alcuin had been working through during their stay.

The triumph for Galen had been that he would continue to teach Arabic to Piero and Bosso. This had sufficiently cheered him up to momentarily forget that they were now unsure of when or whether they might ever get home.

Carbo had left them at the door of the palace, with a hurried, 'I must fetch your lunch,' while Alcuin helped Galen up the stairs and back to their room.

'Do you think Piccardo will indeed come back today?' Galen asked as he settled on his bed with a relieved sigh.

'Who knows, but at least now you have your books and pen and ink, so you'll have something to occupy your time. And I have pen and parchment, so I'm happy too.'

'You need paints,' Galen said, his eyes roaming about their still unfamiliar room.

'I'm sure I'll find a craftsman to make me some.'

'And how will you pay for it?'

Alcuin shrugged. 'I'm sure I'll find a way.'

Galen smiled at him. 'You're always so confident.'

'But generally right,' Alcuin said, his grin making the comment less obnoxious.

'Yes,' Galen said, 'you are often right, and your optimism keeps my spirits up.'

'And you are disarming in your honesty. Another man would just have laughed at me, or teased me and told me not to be so full of myself.'

'Brothers, here's lunch.' Carbo's voice came through the door, accompanied by the thump, thump, thump of his boot.

'What is this?' Alcuin said once he'd leaped up to open the door and stared down at two steaming pies and a jug of wine.

'I bought it from the baker across the street,' Carbo said. 'It's a pigeon pie, and it's delicious. I've had several already.'

'Several?'

'Do you have money, Carbo?' Galen asked, rising from his bed to examine the pies. 'You shouldn't be spending your money on us.'

'Well... Piccardo gave me the money. He said as a servant of the Lateran Palace I should be paid, and he gave me extra to buy you food and anything else you may need.'

'So all the food we've had so far was bought by you?' Alcuin asked.

'Yep,' Carbo said with a big grin. 'Aside from the first meal you had here, actually.'

'Why?' Galen said. 'It makes no sense when this palace has a kitchen.'

'You'll have to ask Piccardo about that,' Carbo said. 'Now eat.'

Alcuin broke off a corner of crust and chewed on it. 'It is good.'

Galen followed his example and smiled. 'Very good.'

'I'll also get you some new robes so we can get yours cleaned. There's a nunnery nearby that does laundry,' Carbo said.

'Good heavens, must we fend entirely for ourselves?' Alcuin said, growing irritated. 'If the pope is making us stay in his palace, should he not treat us as guests and provide for us?'

'That's what he is doing by giving me money,' Carbo said. 'Don't worry about the plates, I'll come back for them. The baker will give me back some of my money if I return the plates to him.'

'Goodness,' Galen said as Carbo left. 'I've never handled money. Have you, Alcuin?'

'Never. We never needed to at the abbey.'

'I wonder what new wonders we will experience here.'

'As long as it's more things like this pie, then I'll be happy,' Alcuin said and tucked in.

Piccardo arrived shortly after they'd finished eating and said, 'I see your man has been looking after you properly.'

He glanced at the plates where even the crumbs had been gathered up and eaten by Alcuin. The pie was so delicious he might have been tempted to eat whatever Galen left behind, but even he'd eaten the entire thing, leaving only crumbs for Alcuin to scavenge.

'Why is he having to buy food for us and even arrange for our laundry to be done?' Alcuin asked.

Piccardo barely reacted to Alcuin's comment. This was unusual for a Roman because they were a proud bunch and easily took offence and set to cursing anyone who questioned them.

'Your situation is a bit different from most guests. In fact, most of the people who come to see the pope have to find their own lodgings. That's why there are so many hostelries near the palace. The privileged few who are invited into the palace include the emperor, kings, and visiting bishops, and they always bring their own staff.'

'I see,' Alcuin said, feeling embarrassed, for he and Galen were clearly not such exalted guests.

'On top of that,' Piccardo said, barely acknowledging Alcuin's comment, 'the pope wants to keep your presence quiet for the time being, so I can't tell the kitchen to provide your meals. There are no greater gossips in all the palace than the servants.'

'Right, fine, that's all explained.'

'You would probably also feel uncomfortable eating in the triclinium with the pope himself, and whichever august guests he has to entertain.'

Alcuin felt Piccardo was now deliberately ramming his point home.

He hung his head, nodding. 'Alright, understood.'

'I will explain further as I show you around,' Piccardo said, turning back to the door. 'Please follow me. I will take you outside again, and around to the basilica.'

'Can we not reach it from inside?' Galen asked.

'You can, but this is the route I am choosing to show you.'

Rather than taking it as a snub, Galen just smiled up at Alcuin as he took his arm and the two of them followed Piccardo out and around towards the front of the palace. This took them through the Lateran square, although that was the wrong word for the irregular shaped space whose bare earth had become muddy with spring rain and churned up by the passage of hundreds of people and livestock. It was far busier here, too. Clusters of mostly men, many of them in ecclesiastical garb, stood about chatting. A couple of hawkers were working the crowd with the offer of fresh bread and olives.

Piccardo stopped in front of a dark bronze statue on a pedestal before the basilica. It depicted two children reaching up to the teats of a wolf.

'The founders of Rome: Romulus and Remus,' Piccardo said. 'As children, they were abandoned in the woods and a wolf suckled them.'

'How extraordinary,' Galen said.

Piccardo nodded, but as one who'd told the story many times before and no longer found it interesting. He turned towards the basilica, a rather plain-looking building of reddish tan bricks that made up for the lack of ornamentation with its immense size and the two towers that stood to either side of the pointed roof.

Piccardo walked past the disorderly queue that snaked its way into the basilica, into the portico and turned left.

'St Tomas's oratory,' he said of the small chapel.

Alcuin suppressed a laugh as he realised that what he'd just thought of as a small chapel was the same size as the church in Galen's burh. Truly, Rome was changing his perspective on things. For Rome, the chapel was simply decorated, with marble walls and frescos of the saints at the small altar. Piccardo only paused long enough for them to get a glimpse of this chapel before he headed for the first of three doors that opened into the basilica. This was the only door that was guarded, and the liveried soldier stepped aside at Piccardo's approach, which caused some murmurs and speculative looks from the people jostling to get in through the central door.

Piccardo was rather interesting to Alcuin. His dress was unassuming, making people not in the know ignore him. Although he was the pope's secretary, none of the dignitaries trying to get inside seemed to recognise him. But the staff, like the guard at the door, did know and treated him with respect.

'The basilica,' Piccardo said in his usual deadpan voice, although a bit softer in reverence to the sanctity of the space.

Pilgrims were walking up and down the basilica gawking and pointing out features like the double run of columns along the two side aisles. Crimson and black-robed clergymen stood in huddles in the nave, deep in conversation. A susurration of prayer filled the air, coming from the crowd on their knees before the pulpits, choir and altars.

It wasn't the first time Galen and Alcuin had been in the basilica, but their first impression had been rushed, and their minds focused on meeting the pope.

'The basilica is approximately 325 feet long and 180 wide,' Piccardo said, walking briskly to the far end, weaving around the people. 'Constantine the Great built the basilica and during his time the apse vault shimmered in gold. This was later replaced by the mosaic we have now of Christ and His apostles. You may come and visit here whenever you like.'

'Thank you,' Galen murmured.

Alcuin was of the opinion that Piccardo wasn't interested in engaging with them, for he barely acknowledged the thanks.

Still facing the apse, he pointed to a staircase to his right, guarded by two men armed with spears. 'The entrance to the palace that leads to the council chamber where you met His Holiness. As you know, that is also a way into the palace, but not one that you can take without an escort or a pass.'

'So that's why we didn't come out that way,' Alcuin murmured to Galen.

'On your left,' Piccardo said, waving his arm, 'is the entrance to the monastery's cloister. There is another entrance further along up the stairs in the apse. Again, you are to avoid going into the monastery until His Holiness gives you permission.'

'Of course,' Alcuin said, feeling that he and Galen were being treated like children.

He helped Galen up the stairs into the apse where they barely had a chance to take in the silver and gold candelabra, the statue of Christ, the apostles and angels and the seven altars, as Piccardo headed for a door to the right.

'We'll have to come back another time to take a proper look,' Alcuin said to Galen as they followed Piccardo through the door and out into another large square enclosed on three sides. On the right was the Lateran Palace. The open side faced the disabitato and three roads led from it.

'That collection of buildings before us are remnants of what was here before,' Piccardo said of a grouping of five buildings of vastly different styles: a tower, three simple church-like buildings and one more ornate that stood just off centre in the square.

'That's the library, which you are free to use,' Piccardo said of the church-like buildings.

He was walking so quickly that Alcuin could feel the strain it was putting Galen under.

'Should we walk slower?'

'No, it's fine,' Galen said. 'I need to walk more, anyway.'

Piccardo made a diagonal across the square, heading to an octagonal building that stuck out from the third wall.

'The wall is part of the monastery,' Piccardo said. 'This large octagonal building protruding from the end with the dome is the baptistery, also built by Constantine the Great. He built it on top of another existing building. That is the nature of Rome. It is either built on top of old Rome, or using bricks and stone from older buildings.'

'So the basilica and this baptistery are both nearly 500 years old,' Galen said, coming to a stop so that he could speak while catching his breath.

Piccardo looked like he was doing some mental arithmetic before he nodded. 'That's about right, yes. You may also visit the baptistery and the attached chapels whenever you like. You might find them more conducive to prayer. The basilica tends to be noisy.'

Alcuin wondered whether Piccardo also meant that they'd be more out of sight if they used these less popular chapels. Although even here the occasional traveller and pilgrim was peeking inside to see what fresh wonder they might discover.

'Now for the last bit,' Piccardo said, veering back towards the palace and, Alcuin realised, the main entrance that was already growing familiar. 'The palace is the largest building and where most ecclesiastical administration is done. Here you will find those who work in the papal chancery: bishops, cardinals, lawyers, notaries, canons, clerks, as well as servants, retainers and those who have business with the pope. It's a vast and complicated mission to support the church across the known world.'

'I imagine it is,' Galen said, blinking in surprise. 'I had never considered that before.'

'There was no reason to,' Alcuin said, 'for it had no impact on our lives.'

'And that will most likely continue to be the case,' Piccardo said as he led them back inside, but this time, not upstairs. 'But I will show you around so that you don't get lost and know which places to avoid. We'll start at this chapel. It forms the easternmost corner of the palace. If we continue from there, we reach the pope's triclinium, where he hosts the most important guests.'

'I can see why,' Alcuin said, aware that his mouth was hanging open in amazement. The hall was massive. 'This is bigger even than our king's hall, and reserved only for dining?'

'Amazing indeed,' Galen said. 'And far more ornate than any hall in Enga-lond.'

He was right about that. Alcuin counted five niches each fitted with a semicircular bed, along both long sides of the hall, plus another at the bottom end. There was a polychrome marble floor and in the centre was a fountain with a purple porphyry stone basin. There were frescoes in the ten side-niches and a beautiful mosaic, bright with gold, in the bottom one.

'This is where the pope eats,' Piccardo said, coming to a halt before the end alcove.

'On a bed?' Alcuin said.

'It is the style of ancient Rome, and still copied for banquets here. This is a very political space. The pope has to demonstrate his power through the decorations and the meaning of the images, as well as the food he provides. There is always lots of meat,' Piccardo said with a wave of his arm to take it all in. 'The mosaics also tell a story and provide a warning. So you see in the mosaic above me a clear explanation of the division of power between the emperor and the pope. For here, on one side, Christ gives the keys to St. Peter and the flag with the cross to Constantine. On the other side, the Prince of the Apostles gives to Pope Leo the Episcopal pallium and to Charlemagne the flag. The pope and the sovereign jointly share the care of the

Christian people, and both answer exclusively to the authority of the church.'

'I see,' Galen said, gazing wide-eyed up at the image that sparkled with thousands of gold mosaics, and the colourful figures lined up along the bottom.

'Are you giving our little saint an introductory tour, Piccardo?' a voice said from the doorway, causing the secretary to swing about, a frown snapping his eyebrows together.

'Cardinal Gui! His Holiness has ordered that no one calls Brother Galen a saint until his claims have been properly investigated.'

The sudden appearance of the cardinal took Alcuin aback. He was a big man, tall and heavy, and his red cardinal's robes made him look extra sinister.

Galen's grip on his arm also tightened as he jerked back, but his expression of horror mingled with disgust surprised Alcuin. Galen could never hide his thoughts, which was always a problem, but Alcuin had never seen such a negative response towards anyone from his friend.

'So there is still some doubt, mmm?' the cardinal said, coming up to Galen and looming so close that Galen bent backwards to create some distance.

'You aren't very impressive,' he murmured, almost to himself.

Alcuin was about to step in when Piccardo said, 'If there isn't anything more, Illustrissimo, I shall continue with my tour.'

'Of course, of course,' Gui said with a dismissive wave.

He then clasped his hands behind his back and strolled off. Piccardo gave an almost inaudible tut, his scowl lingering.

'Neither of you like him very much, do you?' Alcuin said. 'I can understand Piccardo, because you must surely have known the cardinal for a long time, but what about you, Galen?'

'Me?' Galen said.

'You looked repulsed.'

'I did?' Galen said. He flushed.

'Yes...' Piccardo murmured. 'Why did you react in such a violent way to a man you barely know?'

'I'm embarrassed to say his horrific visage startled me. I shouldn't be so easily swayed by something that no man has control over.'

Piccardo and Alcuin shared a puzzled look.

'Describe him to us,' Alcuin said.

'He was just here,' Galen said, looking puzzled. 'He's very fat and his purple pockmarked face, with those livid red veins poking through, seems to speak of corruption.'

'Pockmarked face?' Alcuin said.

'Livid veins?' Piccardo asked.

'Yes?' Galen said, stepping back from the intensity of the gazes fixed upon him.

'My friend, while you are correct that the cardinal is a big man, his face is nothing like you described. It's quite unexceptional. Some might even describe it as handsome.'

'No,' Galen said, his eyes flicking to Piccardo.

'I'm afraid I see what Brother Alcuin sees,' Piccardo said.

'But... how is that possible?'

'It's happened once before, remember?' Alcuin said. 'With Pope Gregory. You said his face looked skeletal, when it looked ordinary to the rest of us.'

'Oh no, what can be the meaning of this?' Galen asked.

'Ask His Holiness,' Piccardo said, but he looked intrigued now.

'When?'

'When he calls for you. For now, I will continue your tour. There isn't a lot more to see.'

Picardo led them back out of the triclinium, through a couple of chapels and into a large, cloistered space bisected by a covered walkway and surrounded by three stories of what he called offices.

'It's where all the work gets done,' he said as they passed one open doorway where, in a room the same size as their bedroom, three clerks were bent over their work at large, dark brown desks. Scrolls and codices were piled up on the desks and chests against the walls and even on the floor.

'If this is where they work, where do they sleep?' Alcuin asked, noting that there seemed to be a mixture of clerics in red or black robes, and lay people in a variety of robes amongst the workers they passed.

'They rent houses or rooms outside,' Piccardo said with a gesture in the general direction of Rome's abitato.

'Oh,' Alcuin said, sharing yet another surprised look with Galen. 'No wonder the palace is so quiet at night.'

After the grand tour of the Lateran complex, minus the monastery, Galen was so exhausted that Alcuin put him to bed. Combined with the morning walk to and from San Agato, it was hardly surprising that his friend was worn out. Especially when he added what they were going through with moving to a new place, meeting the pope and the uncertainty of their future. It all weighed heavily on both of them.

'I'm going to look for Carbo,' Alcuin said. 'One place Piccardo didn't show us was the kitchen. They should be willing to give us some hot water, at least.'

Galen nodded, but didn't open his eyes, which reflected how worn out he was.

'Don't worry, I'll make you a good, reviving tea,' Alcuin said as he hurried out.

He wasn't sure where he would find Carbo, but as the man was large and his scarred face distinctive, it wouldn't be too difficult a task. As it happened, Carbo was sitting on the floor, right by their door, his head bowed over the staff he'd taken to carrying everywhere he went.

'Carbo?'

'Oh, Brother Alcuin,' Carbo said as he looked up, a grin on his face.

'What are you doing here?'

'Just being ready should you or Brother Galen need me.'

In Enga-lond the servants, thralls, thanes and masters all lived together, sleeping in the great hall. Alcuin had noticed that in Rome, many of the servants slept at their master's doors. It looked like Carbo was prepared to do even that. At least he had a decent cape to wrap around himself for comfort. Alcuin wondered whether he should invite Carbo into their room, but he didn't like the idea because it would prevent Galen from speaking freely with Alcuin. He felt Galen would agree with him. Even though Galen had accepted Carbo, the man wasn't a friend.

'I'm looking for the kitchen,' Alcuin said. 'I want some hot water, so I may make tea for Galen.'

'Is Brother Galen feeling unwell?' Carbo asked as he rose to his feet, a worried frown settling on his face.

'It's just been a more active day than he's used to. So, how about getting me to the kitchen?'

'I can fetch the hot water,' Carbo said. 'There's no need for you to trouble yourself.'

Alcuin felt that now familiar twinge of jealousy whenever Carbo tried to take away his role of looking after Galen.

'When I need it, and you are at hand, I will ask you for the hot water. But I still need to know where the kitchen is on those occasions when you aren't around. After you've shown me that, you can also take me to the market. I need to top up my supplies of the herbs Galen needs for his teas. I hope Piccardo has at least given you sufficient funds for that.'

'He has been generous, and he told me whenever I need more to just come to him. The pope wants Brother Galen to be comfortable.'

Alcuin noted that he wasn't included in this comment and wondered whether that was because he was a low priority for

Carbo or, despite Piccardo's words, if the pope wasn't really interested in him either. It was a blow to his pride that he, a formerly renowned artist, seemed to have sunk into obscurity while Galen was in the ascendency. He shook the thought away as unworthy. Galen already felt guilty enough having dragged him into this adventure. The least he could do was make good use of his time.

'Alright,' Carbo said, 'let me take you to the kitchen and then the shops. Before that, did you know that this room,' Carbo gestured at the door of the next-door room, 'is actually a chapel?'

'Can we use it?' Alcuin asked, setting off after Carbo who didn't hang about when he wasn't supporting Galen.

'What else is a chapel for?'

Alcuin nodded. There was certainly no shortage of chapels in the palace. There were even more altars dotted about, including one at the end of their corridor.

'Perhaps that was why we were given the room beside it,' Alcuin said.

That way, they could be kept hidden, working in their room and praying in the chapel beside it. It gave Alcuin a sense of unease to be so invisible. What was the pope doing? That was unanswerable at the moment, but at least he and Galen could resume the seven divine offices.

The kitchen was on the ground floor, and boiling water was easily procured. It seemed that Carbo had already made his presence known to all the servants and the normally argumentative and often downright contrary Romans had accepted him. Being big and having the looks of a retired warrior probably worked wonders for him.

After making the tea for Galen, Alcuin followed Carbo out into the small conurbation that surrounded the Lateran and on to an apothecary. Thankfully, he stocked almost all the herbs listed in the now extremely worn letter Brother Benesing had given Alcuin so long ago, detailing what medications to give Galen and when.

'Thank you,' Alcuin said, emerging from the shop well resupplied. 'Now, lend me your purse for another project, Brother Carbo, for I need paints and brushes.'

Chapter 5

Galen listlessly flipped through his Moorish book of numbers. He'd just finished yet another morning lesson in Arabic with Brothers Piero and Bosso, their fourth since Galen and Alcuin had taken up residence in the Lateran Palace. It was always good to see them, but life felt flat after they left.

At least Alcuin had procured paints. Now his head was bowed over a piece of parchment, working on a design of Christ and the apostles, similar to the one he'd seen in the pope's triclinium. It was the beginning of a new pattern book for him. He'd be able to refer to it in years to come for his own work, and it would also provide inspiration for fellow artists. That was if they ever went back to life in an abbey.

Galen pushed that sombre thought away and glanced out the window. The sun was already high, and almost as hot here as it had been in Al Andalus.

'If you're alright with it,' Alcuin said without raising his head, 'I'm thinking of taking Carbo out on another trip to the abitato. I want him to take me to a marble worker so I may observe their craft.'

This was something new for Alcuin. He'd started taking an interest in artisans and their crafts. They'd already been to visit a dye maker, and Alcuin was experimenting with the effects of dyes on his parchment, along with his new inks and paints.

Galen wasn't feeling up to the walk and felt he got too much in the way. Alcuin was forced to look out for him, rather than going clambering through the workshops as he so obviously wished to do.

'I think I'll just stay here and work on my letter,' Galen said.

It was his letter home, and it was growing by the day. He had so much to tell his family.

'Brother Galen,' Piccardo said, standing as still and expressionless as a statue at the door. Since the place was so quiet they'd taken to leaving it open for the slight breeze that created. 'His Holiness will see you now.'

'Finally!' Alcuin muttered.

Galen agreed. Usually he was fine with putting things off and delaying confrontation, but this wait had been unbearable.

'Do you want me to go with you?' Alcuin asked.

Galen desperately wanted to say yes, but shook his head. 'I'll be fine.'

He was at least warmed by the virtuous thought that he'd done the right thing. Furthermore, Alcuin seemed to think he would be fine, too, for he neither looked dismayed nor worried and he didn't argue either.

'This way,' Piccardo said as he led Galen back in the direction of the council chamber, but turned at the last minute to a door on one side. 'The pope is in his study today.'

'Oh… right,' Galen said, and followed Piccardo into a large room.

'Brother Galen,' Sylvester said, jumping up from his desk after Piccardo announced him and bowed himself out. 'Welcome to my study.'

'Thank you, Your Holiness,' Galen said, unable to stop his eyes from roaming the room.

It was rather full. At one end stood a massive marble desk covered in manuscripts and scrolls. There were several comfortable-looking chairs, also bearing books, and, dotted all around, a number of gadgets whose applications Galen couldn't fathom.

'My study interests you?'

Galen nodded. 'So many books.'

'Items close to your heart, hmm? But what about these devices? What do you make of them?' the pope asked, pointing at one after another.

'I don't know what they are.'

'Let me show you.' It seemed the pope was eager to show off and equally curious to see Galen's reaction. 'Will you be horrified, as so many are, or will you be intrigued? I hope you are intrigued, but either way, there is no need for nervousness. It's unsettling.'

'I beg your pardon,' Galen said, trying to smother his feelings.

He did worst with impatient, outgoing people and the pope seemed to be of that nature.

'This over here is an abacus,' the pope said as he took Galen's hand and led him to a table in which a series of grooves had been cut. Set along each groove were several smooth white pebbles. 'It's a device for assisting calculation,' Sylvester said, and went on to explain how it worked.

Galen's eyes widened as he listened.

'What an ingenious device,' he said as he shifted the stones as directed and added two unfeasibly large numbers together. 'It would have taken me hours to do that using Roman numerals and writing it down.'

'Don't I know it!' Sylvester said with an indulgent smile. 'Now, how about this device?'

Galen looked up at a circular plate of metal etched with numbers and set in a wooden frame. Two arms were set on a pin in front of it and dangling through the frame was a rigid brass rod which held yet another featureless brass plate at its end. The rod swung ceaselessly back and forth, producing a loud click each time. 'What is it?'

'This is my own invention. It's a mechanical clock,' Sylvester said. 'If you look at the two hands, you can see that it tells us the time. It is now ten hours since midnight.'

Galen's eyes flicked to the window, taking a reading from the height of the sun and said, 'This device breaks time into small segments with each tick, does it?'

'Something like that,' Sylvester said. 'I am both amused and pleased that my little saint checked my clock and my assumptions against his own knowledge of where the sun should be at this time of day. It denotes a questioning mind.'

'I... um...' Galen started, not knowing whether he should or even could explain.

The pope waved away his attempts and led Galen to another table.

'This is my pride and joy. I discovered it during my time studying in Seville and Cordoba,' he said of a small sphere suspended on a rod in the centre of five parallel circles and one broader diagonal band. 'This is an armillary sphere. I refined it when I realised heavenly bodies move diagonally across the sky. It has a multitude of uses. I use it as a teaching aid, and I've added sighting tubes so that I may fix the position of the pole star and record measures for the tropics and equator.

'It's a circular model of the astrolabe really,' the pope said, pointing to a flat bronze disc lying beside the armillary sphere, its face engraved with a grid, as well as numerous concentric circles and numbers at various intersections. Screwed to the centre was a large arm with a smaller one above it. 'With this device, a user can calculate astronomical positions and measure the altitude above the horizon of a celestial body. It can also be used to identify stars or planets and to determine local latitude given local time, or divine local time if you have the latitude. It's useful on land and on calm seas. Finally, it can be used to survey or triangulate. A truly useful device!

'But this big machine in the corner, I can explain. It's an organ,' Sylvester said, pulling Galen along more rapidly than was comfortable.

He pushed down on an ivory key and a note of pure brilliance filled the air. Sylvester smiled, no doubt because Galen's eyes, already wide, now felt like they might pop out.

'Hah! You are amazed. Good, good.'

Galen got the impression that the pope was enjoying himself tremendously. Perhaps he didn't get many opportunities to show off. He played a few more notes, then plunged down several fingers to produce a chord.

'Sweet Mother of God!' Galen said. 'Music using just one hand.'

'Indeed, although it is better using both,' Sylvester said and played a sequence of chords with both hands.

'You would normally need an entire band to get so much sound,' Galen said, overwhelmed by the brilliance and loudness of the organ.

'You appear not to have heard an organ before, but this is not one of my creations. This is merely a refinement. The other organs I have seen had to be hand pumped. I created one that is powered by the flow of water. The first of my experiments was built in Riems. This is my second: a smaller version that is powered by water from the aqueduct.'

'I see,' Galen murmured, his eyes drifting across the room.

'Your translation of the Moorish treatise on numbers impressed me,' Sylvester said as he let go of Galen's hand, rounded the abacus and flopped into a chair while motioning for Galen to take the seat opposite. 'It was elegantly worded and the explanations were clear. It gave me the impression that you know something about mathematics.'

'Oh yes, well, when I was a boy, my teacher, Father Pifus, made me work through the Venerable Bede's book, *On the Reckoning of Time*. It awoke in me an interest in numbers and I have tried to manipulate them from time to time, but—'

Galen stopped abruptly. He shouldn't run on and waste the pope's time.

'But what?' Sylvester said as he traced his finger down the groove of his abacus, as if he was distracted, which Galen doubted.

'I have always enjoyed working with languages more,' Galen said. 'Rhetoric, logic and grammar all form a strong basis from which to work and which inform my—' Galen stopped and blushed a fiery red. 'Please forgive me, Holy Father, this can't interest you.'

'Oh, but it does. What does the trivium inform for you?'

'My poetry,' Galen said, blushing so that his face felt as if it was aflame as he stared down at his toes.

'Poetry,' Sylvester said with an amused smile. 'So it always is with you people from Enga-lond. You delight in the play of words sometimes to the exclusion of all else.'

'I believe you are right,' Galen murmured.

'But numbers still interest you?'

'All learning interests me. I translated Boethius's deliberations on rhetoric into Englisc a while back.'

'Did you indeed?'

Galen gave a quick nod and said, 'I still have the original Latin version.'

'Have you read his most famous work, the Consolation of Philosophy?'

'Yes, in Englisc, quite a long time ago.'

'Does it not provide you with inspiration on how to lead your life? After all, it teaches how to accept hardship by a process of philosophical detachment, does it not? Surely that would be useful for you?'

Galen looked dubiously up at him and said, 'I... don't seem able to achieve the detachment Boethius argues for. It is a fine philosophy but... difficult to put into practice.'

'As are so many words of the wise,' the pope said with an accepting nod. 'Tell me, is much of your poetical work written in Englisc?'

'It has a better rhythm and structure than Latin for poetry.'

'Is that so? Well, that is an assumption I must test,' Sylvester said as he leapt to his feet again and made his way to a book-filled desk where he rifled through the manuscripts which littered it till he came upon an ancient-looking codex. 'The poetry of Publius Ovidius Naso. You take it away, read and translate it into Englisc if you wish. Then you come back and tell me which is better for poetry, Englisc or Latin, for I doubt you could turn a prettier phrase than Ovid.'

Galen took the book with a hasty bow and said, 'Forgive me, Your Holiness, if I have offended you.'

'Offended me? Nonsense! I just believe that every assertion should be tested, that is all, and I am making you do the testing. For your translation, you will doubtless require parchment. Talk to Piccardo. He will supply all you need.'

'He already has, thank you, Your Holiness,' Galen said with a deep bow, clasping the codex to his body. 'He has also provided the funds which enabled Alcuin to buy some paints as well. Alcuin is a very fine artist and he shouldn't be left idle. It isn't good for him.'

'As bad as for you to sit idle, little monk?'

'Idleness isn't good for anyone,' Galen said, flushing. 'Perhaps... you could give Alcuin a project too, Your Holiness. I'm sure you will be impressed by his work.'

'That's an interesting challenge,' Sylvester said, stroking his white beard. 'I do believe I have something... something that will stretch your friend.'

'What is it?'

'Wait and see,' the pope said, looking entertained. 'Now, we must speak of other things. I understand you had a curious meeting with Cardinal Gui a few days ago.'

'Ah... yes.' Galen should have realised Piccardo would report such a thing to the pope.

'Did Cardinal Gui always look the same to you? Did he look as corrupted when you first saw him speaking to me?'

'He hasn't changed,' Galen said, but nerves made his voice faint. 'I don't know for certain that he is corrupted.'

'Ha! I do,' the pope said with a dry laugh. 'I know the man well. He is worse than you can imagine. Aside from him, it seems you saw the late pope in a different light too?'

'He… he looked unwell the first time I saw him, dangerously thin, and even more skeletal the second time. Then… he died.'

'How fascinating. Has this ever happened with other people?'

'Not that I know of.'

'Mmm, we shall have to come up with a way to test it,' the pope said, then gave Galen a sharp look.

He jerked back, aware that he'd probably given himself away again with his face.

'If you are dwelling on the death of Gregory, don't. I am aware I didn't dispel your doubts at our last meeting, and for a man to die in his bed at the age of 27 is rare, but let me give you two more arguments that I pray will convince you that I had nothing to do with it.

'First, I was the emperor's tutor in his youth, and I knew Gregory well. If I was involved in bringing him down, or even suspected of it, do you really think the emperor would have supported my selection as pope?'

Galen could see the strength of the argument as well as a counter that even family members had killed each other off in an individual's quests for power. But he gave an accepting nod, since the pope was watching with his hawkish eyes.

'Second,' Sylvester said, apparently amused that Galen was yet to be convinced, 'I have found during my long life that nothing is predictable. Our lives are dangerous. Even the food we put on our tables is not always safe, as you know from the ergot in the bread incident that swept through Rome last year. I have also seen cases where poison was blamed for a natural death, and cases where a natural death was recorded when the person was clearly poisoned. It is beyond the wit of man to solve this, but I am sure God in heaven will know His own and offer a final judgement.'

'That is true.'

Galen had felt much the same way about Septimus after the rape. Sometimes all a man could do was pray an evildoer came to justice at the end of his life. At least Septimus had been found out and stopped during his lifetime.

'Now, go and do what I have asked of you,' the pope said, his voice softer and kinder, like a beloved teacher. 'We will talk more later.'

'Yes, thank you,' Galen said, scrambling to his feet, despite the pain it caused him.

He still had no answers to his questions. In fact, the pope had only grazed the surface when talking about Cardinal Gui. But he was tired physically and mentally and ready to go. Until he remembered one important point.

'Your Holiness, might I ask... do you ever send letters to Enga-lond?'

'I have yet to do so, but my predecessors certainly did. Why?'

'I was wondering... would it be possible to send a letter home? Our abbot and our families don't know that we've arrived in Rome. For all I know, they may believe we perished at sea.'

'Mmm, yes, I see. Speak to Piccardo. He will let you know when we next send a letter to any of your bishops or the king. You may add your missive to our bundle. It may take a while, though.'

'I understand, thank you,' Galen said, giving a deep bow.

At least the pope was willing, even if he didn't know when that might be.

'If you are in a hurry,' the pope said as Galen was heading to the door, 'it might be quicker for you to find a group of Anglo-Saxon pilgrims and have them carry your letter for you.'

Chapter 6

Galen walked as quickly as he could manage through the palace, clutching the pope's book of ancient Roman poetry to his chest and keeping a wary eye out for people. The pope's warning to keep out of sight was uppermost in his mind, especially as the palace was bound to be a hotbed of intrigue that dwarfed King Aethelred's court.

Galen had no wish to figure as a pawn in it by being caught by some disgruntled Roman noble or cleric. He was especially wary of anyone wearing a red robe. The last person he wished to run into again was Cardinal Gui.

Despite that, Galen didn't go straight back to his room. The pope's suggestion that he find a band of pilgrims to take his letter was an idea of such brilliance that he made a beeline for the basilica. Since he was unaccompanied by Piccardo, rather than go through the front door with its long line of visitors and where he'd look too conspicuous as a solitary monk, Galen took the stairs directly from the palace into the basilica and flashed his newly acquired pass, a letter with the pope's seal, at the guards.

He stuck to the darkest outer aisle and moved cautiously from one shadowy space to a pillar, to the next shadowy space. He was being as discreet as possible as he skirted around clusters of pilgrims, observing their mannerisms and their clothes before moving closer to listen in on their conversations. His heart hammered in his chest in combined fear and anticipation while he tried to guess where each group was from.

'My, you are a very busy young man,' a rough, gravelly voice murmured from the shadows.

It made Galen jump and he swung round to find the speaker. The man facing Galen was older than he'd expected and short, but with a powerful enough build that he could easily have been a warrior. His black hair was peppered with grey and he had a prominent growth of stubble. His eyes were deep, with the heavy lids common amongst the Romans. Despite his tonsured head, he was wearing a plain cream-coloured robe that didn't look like any order Galen was familiar with.

'No need to jump,' the man said with an easy smile. 'I am fond of people-watching and you slipping from one group to the next caught my eye. Are you looking for someone?'

'Not exactly,' Galen said.

'Perhaps I can help. I'm a regular to this basilica.'

Galen had his doubts, and, although the man seemed friendly enough, Galen could tell he wouldn't simply let him go without an explanation.

'I don't suppose you've come across any pilgrims from Enga-lond?'

The man's face took on that blank expression Galen had become familiar with. It seemed not many people in Rome knew of his home.

Then the man gave him a regretful shrug and smile and said, 'I'm afraid on this occasion I can be of no help. Perhaps next time.' He gave Galen a nod and strolled away.

Galen had lost track of time on this quest but finally realised that it was getting late when the light shining through the large basilica windows grew dimmer and his shakes now had more to do with tiredness and pain than excitement.

Alcuin would be alarmed that he hadn't already returned to their room. Galen reluctantly started making his way back when, just before he reached the stairs, his ears picked up a now unexpected but longed for sound: Englisc!

It was coming from a trio of men, dressed more like thanes than pilgrims, who were making their leisurely way down the middle aisle.

Galen peeked around the pillar to take a closer look and his heart leapt with joy at the sight of their familiar clothes and hairstyles, just as it twisted in sorrow to see these men and be reminded of how far he was from home.

Without giving himself a chance to back out, Galen left his hiding place and hurried after them.

'Excuse me, sir,' he said, his voice coming out at only a whisper. It was so soft the men didn't hear and Galen had to take a deep breath and try again. 'Excuse me, are you from Enga-lond?'

The three men stopped and slowly turned round. The biggest looked Galen up and down, his grey eyes indifferent as they swept across Galen.

'Why do you want to know, little monk?'

'I just.... I was just wondering,' Galen said, aware that his voice was trembling with nerves which would disgust these obvious warriors. He licked his lips and said, 'Have you come from Enga-lond recently?'

'We left a few months back in weather that was foolhardy to attempt, but my mission couldn't wait.'

'Is something not well in the land?' Galen asked, alarmed by any news that implied a hurried flight.

'It is as well as it has ever been,' the man said impatiently. 'Now you must leave us, for we have to try to see the pope.'

'Oh,' Galen said, feeling powerless to prevent the men from turning away from him. 'Please, sir, my name is Galen, I... I am the son of Ealdorman Hugh. You don't happen to know how he is doing, do you?' Galen cried after them.

He hoped he wasn't dishonouring his father by claiming their relationship when he was certain he was creating a miserable impression on these men. But the effect of his words was nothing short of miraculous. They froze, then all turned around again.

The leader said, 'You are Brother Galen? The Saint of Yarmwick?'

Galen took a surprised step back and said, 'Um... well, I am Galen of Yarmwick.'

'By God's eyes! Can it be possible?' the man said, coming closer and staring so intently at Galen that he took another step back. 'You set off to Rome with Bishop Sigburt, the Bishop of Crowland?'

'We did.'

'Is he here? Can we see him?'

'He died.'

Galen had never regretted the fact more, for the bishop would have been a great help here.

'Oh,' the man said and flung his head back to examine the ceiling, apparently deep in thought. After a moment, he looked back at Galen and said, 'Can you get us in to see the pope?'

'I... I don't know.' Galen said. 'I can ask his secretary for you. He may be able to ask the pope.'

'You don't have the ear of the pope, then?'

'Who me?' Galen said, blushing with embarrassment. 'No.'

'Does he not think you are a saint?'

For a breathtaking moment Galen considered saying no, but it was a lie and he knew the truth would come out, eventually.

'He does, but there are many saints in Rome.'

The man spat, a great gob which glistened on the polished basilica floor and drew Galen's horrified gaze. How could the man behave like this in Rome? How could he make himself look like such a barbarian, acting as if he was at home in his own hall?

'We have been trying for days to see the pope, but he is hemmed in by protectors who block our every attempt.'

'He is very busy,' Galen said sympathetically.

'Do you think this secretary would get us to see the pope?'

'He will certainly tell the pope that you wish to see him.'

'Huh,' the man grunted and looked thoughtfully at Galen again. 'That will have to do, I suppose. How do we find the secretary?'

'I can take you to him.'

'Very well, then lead on,' the man said with a wave of his hand.

Galen led the men upstairs into the palace with only a slight qualm about whether he was allowed to do such a thing. After all, it was the pope himself who'd said he should find pilgrims to transport his letter. Of course, he'd said nothing about bringing them into the pope's own house. But a force greater than his fear of authority drove Galen on. Thank goodness he knew where Piccardo's office was. He prayed that the usually busy man would be in.

He was walking as quickly as he could, since he didn't want to look like a small, weak man before his compatriots. Although he could walk faster than in the past, he couldn't maintain the pace and had to stop, his hand against the wall for support as he fought to catch the breath that his pain had robbed him of. He squeezed his eyes shut as nausea threatened to overwhelm him.

'Are you alright?' the big man asked.

'Yes, I'll be fine,' Galen said as he forced a smile.

The big man tilted his head in acceptance and said, 'I'm Ealdorman Bregowine. This is Elfwig and Swithred.'

Galen nodded a quick hello and, as he was still trying to catch his breath, he asked, 'Do you know whether Ealdorman Hugh and his family are well?'

'He was when I last heard of him. As for his family, I can't say. If you get me in to see the pope, I'll take a letter back for you if you like.'

'A letter,' Galen murmured.

The man had brought the subject up himself, thank God. It acted as a tonic, strengthening Galen's resolve. He pushed his body more upright and headed in the direction of Piccardo's office once again.

'I would be grateful for that. Thank you.'

As Galen approached Piccardo's office, he sent up a heartfelt prayer to God that the man would be in. It was late now, and Galen had no idea when Piccardo went home. It was still a strange idea to him that the men who worked in the palace lived separate lives in homes removed from their place of work.

Thankfully, a pale flickering light spilled from the open doorway to the office, and Galen screwed up his courage to approach.

Piccardo was the sole occupant of an office filled with even more paperwork than the pope's own study, but in a smaller space. He had his head bowed low over the parchment, but it seemed that he didn't see it, for his gaze was unfocused.

Galen tapped too lightly at the door to be heard, getting no reaction, so Bregowine reached over his head and knocked considerably louder on the open door.

Piccardo's head snapped up and he glared at the interlopers. Then his gaze fell upon Galen.

'Brother Galen, what is the meaning of this?' he asked. His tone was flat, but not the neutral tone of a disinterested man, rather, it seemed to Galen, he was trying hard not to show that he was in pain.

'Perhaps this is a bad time,' Galen murmured and started backing away.

Bregowine wasn't willing to let this opportunity slip by him. He stepped into the office and went down on one knee, bowing his head while his two companions did the same.

'Please, sir, we've come a long way. Would you give us a moment of your time?'

He spoke in Englisc, and Piccardo merely looked taken aback before glancing at Galen. It was as well he'd come after all. Galen translated, gaining a grateful smile from Bregowine.

'What do they want?' Piccardo asked as a frown formed.

Galen took a deep breath and asked Bregowine the question, praying he didn't get into trouble for what was happening now.

'I am in a serious dispute with my bishop,' Bregowine said, and Galen translated again. 'I have come to petition the pope over this matter. I did send a letter over a year ago but have heard nothing. The matter being urgent, I have come in person this time.'

'He wishes to see the pope?' Piccardo said in that same, disconcerting, flat voice.

'In exchange, I will do whatever the pope wants,' Bregowine replied upon Galen's translation. 'And I can make a substantial donation to you and the church.'

'Bribery won't work with Pope Sylvester,' Piccardo snapped.

'I apologise if I have caused offence,' Bregowine said without waiting for Galen. It was easy enough to see when a man was angered, even if it was Piccardo. 'I have already offered to take a letter home for the Saint of Yarmwick. It isn't intended as a bribe, merely paying my dues.'

'Do you think you'll be able to do it, Piccardo?' Galen asked, at the end of his translation. His voice was soft, for he feared what getting on the wrong side of this secretary might do.

'Perhaps, but as even this barbarian has said, nothing comes for free in Rome. If I'm to get them in to see the pope, then you must do something for me.'

'Me?'

'You are a saint, are you not?'

'Maybe?' Galen said warily.

'I have a wife,' Piccardo said and for the first time showed a trace of embarrassment mixed with desperation. 'She is very ill. Her parents don't believe that she will live.'

'Oh,' Galen said faintly.

'If you visit her and give her a blessing, then I will get your countrymen in to see the pope.'

'Piccardo...' Galen raised his arms and then dropped them helplessly to his sides. 'In all my life, I know of only four times when a miracle could be said to have occurred. I have very little chance of doing anything for your wife.'

'All I ask is that you try.'

'I will try,' Galen said, 'to pay for a favour or for nothing at all but, I beg of you, don't put all your hope in me, for I can make no promises.'

Piccardo nodded. 'Tell your countrymen to wait. I will get back in contact. And I will come and find you this evening to take you to my wife.'

'Galen! Where in all that's holy have you been?' cried Alcuin when Galen came staggering into the room.

Galen, though, was so excited he could feel his face glowing.

'What's up?' Alcuin asked, obviously surprised. 'Don't tell me the pope has said we can go home.'

'Oh... no, I'm sorry, it's not such momentous news,' Galen said, and his smile faltered. 'But it is good news. Alcuin, I met some people from home! Ealdorman Bregowine is their leader. Do you know of him?'

'I can't say that I do. But come and sit down. Drink this spiced wine and have some bread, for you've had a long day.'

'You're looking after me again.' Galen settled on his bed, cross-legged and took a too large bite of the bread. Still chewing, but eager to continue his tale, he said, 'Well, Bregowine has come to petition the pope to get involved in a local argument with his bishop. I don't know what the full case is. He didn't want to mention it and, to be honest, I wasn't that eager to know either, but he said that my father was alive and well when he left Enga-lond.'

'That's good.'

'There's better,' Galen started, then realised something. 'Oh, Alcuin, I didn't think to ask about your father.'

'It's no matter,' Alcuin said with a laugh.

Alcuin would be aware of how overwhelmed Galen felt with his own news, but it filled Galen with guilt for having been so selfish.

'What was better than hearing that your father is well?' Alcuin asked.

'Bregowine has promised to take a letter home for us and ensure that my father gets it.'

'Has he indeed?' Alcuin said. 'That would be a fine thing.'

'Wouldn't it?' Galen said with a beatific smile and took a more leisurely bite of the bread.

He was so happy that even his tiredness and associated pain had no effect on his appetite. In fact, the bread tasted delicious.

'When does he intend to go back?' Alcuin asked.

'As soon as he's spoken to the pope. He came by boat and intends to return the same way. How I wish we were going with him!'

'The pope made no mention of your leaving, then?'

'He behaves as if I'll stay here for the rest of my days.'

'Have you actually asked him whether you can go home?'

Alcuin had probably already guessed that Galen hadn't dared to do so, which made Galen feel bad for both of them.

'He wants to work out more about my being a saint, and as nothing has happened since we've been in the palace, I doubt he is ready to let me leave.'

Alcuin looked like he was about to speak when his gaze flicked to the door where Piccardo had appeared. He gave a slight bow.

'Have you already managed to get Bregowine an appointment with the pope, Piccardo?' Galen asked.

'Not yet,' Piccardo said, casting a dispassionate eye over Galen. 'First, you must do what you have promised.'

'You've been making deals?' Alcuin said.

'You're surprised,' Galen said, because this really wasn't his usual style.

Alcuin was always nagging him to not just give people what they asked for, but to try to benefit from the situation as well.

'Brother Galen is going to bless my wife,' Piccardo said.

'Now?' Alcuin said. His tone had hardened as it always did when he sprang to Galen's defence.

'Time is of the essence,' Piccardo said.

'Galen?' Alcuin said, fixing him with a stern glare.

'It's alright. I want to do this,' Galen said and downed the wine. Not because he wanted it, but because it would make Alcuin feel better seeing him do so.

'Where will you be taking him?' Alcuin asked.

'My house is near the Colosseum,' Piccardo said.

'I'll come with you.'

'No, Alcuin,' Galen said as he stood and put a restraining hand on Alcuin's arm. 'I can do this on my own.'

'But you don't have to.'

'I want to.'

It was such a simple phrase that it failed to convey Galen's full thoughts and emotions. Part of him always wanted Alcuin's company and support. But increasingly he felt he should be more independent. He felt guilty enough dragging Alcuin to Rome, so he was determined to stand on his own two feet now. Besides, there wasn't much to this mission.

'I will stay with him at all times, and ensure he returns safely to the palace,' Piccardo said, correctly reading Alcuin's dubious expression.

Alcuin shook his head. 'If you won't take me, at least have Carbo. He can protect you should anything go awry.'

'Nothing is going to go awry,' Piccardo said, sounding irritated.

'All the same,' Alcuin said firmly.

Galen could tell he wasn't going to let this lie. The fact that he wanted at least Carbo to go along spoke volumes about how worried he was about sending Galen off on his own. It touched Galen's heart, but also made him wonder whether he was so weak that Alcuin couldn't believe he could look after himself?

Chapter 7

Galen, clutching Carbo's arm for support, followed behind Piccardo along the dark Via S. Giovanni in Laterano towards the Colosseum. It was so dark that they only had the lights coming from the houses to guide them on the first bit and then the light of the moon once they left the little conurbation that clustered around the Lateran. Fortunately, the road was one that was made by the ancient Romans and thus straight, paved and relatively easy to navigate, even in the dark. After only a few minutes, they could see the lights coming from the cluster of houses around the Colosseum and beyond that, the denser lights of the abitato.

They travelled in silence, which gave Galen far too much time with his own thoughts. Alcuin would have been talking to distract him, but Carbo was a quiet sort who spoke when another initiated conversation, and Piccardo was unlikely to do so at the best of times. When he was as distressed as he currently seemed to be, he clammed up. Not that they were friends, so conversation would be awkward anyway.

Galen prayed to God with every step they took that he could be of service. He hadn't had the courage to ask Piccardo what ailed his wife. He'd find out when he arrived. It was a moment he dreaded, for he had no way of knowing what would happen next. His mind moved back and forth between him being able to produce a miracle and being of help, or failing miserably.

Perhaps the best would be if the wife was sufficiently recovered by the time they arrived.

They skirted around the bulk of the Colosseum and Galen nearly lost Piccardo in the deep shadow it cast.

'Slow down,' Carbo had said in his deep low voice.

Galen wasn't sure whether that was aimed at him, for he'd tried to put on a turn of speed to catch up with Piccardo, or if it was aimed at Piccardo who, nevertheless, did slow down. At this reduced pace he led them up a small side street. Galen was surprised by how modest the houses were. He'd expected one with such noble features and the secretary of the pope, to live in more luxury.

Was Piccardo really leading him to see his sick wife? Or was it a trap, a way of luring him out? He was so naïve he'd assured Alcuin that he could do this alone. Now, with darkness all around them, Galen was thankful that Carbo, with his vast bulk and sturdy staff, had come along.

Piccardo stopped before a building with two stories and a covered staircase that cut diagonally up the outside of the building in the style of many Roman homes. He gave the simple wooden door beside the stairs a short, sharp knock. It was swung open instantly by an old woman, a shawl wrapped over her head and body, holding a lamp in her right hand.

'Is that him?' the woman whispered as she held up a lamp to examine Galen's face.

'It is,' Piccardo said, his expression giving away nothing of how he felt.

Some of the tension left Galen's body because the woman looked like a worried mother.

'This way,' Piccardo said as he turned and led Galen up the stairs.

'Wait down here, Carbo,' Galen said.

'Are you sure, brother?' Carbo said, looking far from happy.

'We are about to visit somebody on their sick bed. It would be best not to alarm her.'

It was to Carbo's credit that he understood. 'I'll wait right here. If you need me, just shout.'

'Thank you,' Galen said, but in a distracted way.

His mind was focused on the sick woman he was about to see as he followed Piccardo up the stairs.

The old woman followed, anxiously wringing her hands and saying something in a breathless, urgent voice in the peculiar dialect of Rome, from which Galen could only pick out a few words, the gist of which seemed to revolve around God's will.

Piccardo ignored her chatter as he opened the door at the top of the stairs and motioned for Galen to enter.

The room was simple and lit by a single lamp. A woman lay still as death in the middle of the bed, the blankets pulled up to her chin. Another woman, kneeling on the floor beside her, turned from her prayers as they entered.

'This is my wife, Zenobia,' Piccardo said as he knelt before the bed and fiddled with the lamp to make it burn more brightly. The woman didn't even react to the brightening of the flickering light. 'And her sister,' Piccardo said of the other woman who rose to her feet in the way of one whose knees had stiffened from being down for so long.

'What happened?' Galen murmured. 'She's so pale.'

'She gave birth to a boy. It was a long and painful labour and she lost a lot of blood.'

'I'm sorry,' Galen whispered.

Then he noticed the small, wrapped up bundle the sister was holding.

'My son, Paulus,' Piccardo said, seeing the direction of Galen's gaze. 'He is also struggling and won't suckle from his aunt. We were hoping, if we can save his mother, that he will take sustenance from her.' Piccardo was a proud man and he spoke dispassionately, but he couldn't hide his pain. 'What will you do now?'

'I will pray for your wife. That is all I know how to do,' Galen said and sent up yet another heartfelt plea to God to help him, Piccardo, and his wife and son.

'Very well. I will stay here with you,' Piccardo said and pulled up a chair.

The child's aunt lay the baby boy beside his mother. He appeared to be fast asleep, but too pale and silent for a newborn.

Galen took a deep breath to fortify himself and knelt beside Zenobia. He placed one hand on her head and the other over the baby's chest, then closed his eyes and prayed. The situation reminded him of the time he'd prayed so desperately over Alcuin, and he begged God to give him a similar outcome.

Galen was barely conscious of the room around him, and only partially emerged from the trance-like state of prayer he'd dropped into when he heard an agitated discussion between an older man and the woman who'd let them into the house. They stood in the open doorway arguing in hushed tones until Piccardo got up and closed the door on them.

Galen sank back into prayer and continued throughout the night. The room ceased to exist around him. His body became meaningless. He couldn't even feel his knees on the floor. All that was left were his hands on mother and child and the prayers he sent up to heaven, one after the other, pleading for God's mercy.

By dawn, Galen wasn't certain whether he was still awake or whether he'd dropped into sleep. Strange dream-like images drifted past his half-closed eyes. Fragments of conversations, so real that it seemed they were in the room, assailed his ears. Once he was convinced his mother was standing at his right shoulder speaking to him. He didn't have the energy to turn around to look and just kept up his whispered prayers.

Galen's stamina was waning, but he became aware of the light which gradually grew in the room with the rising of the sun. His chin rested on his chest, too tired to raise his head, but his lips moved ceaselessly.

Zenobia opened her eyes and murmured, 'Piccardo?'

It startled Galen out of his trance and he looked up to check whether this was yet another hallucination.

'Zenobia!' Piccardo cried. 'Oh my dear, you're awake!'

'What happened?'

'You were ill,' Piccardo said.

'My baby,' she whispered, as her eyes took on a look of panic.

'It's alright, it's alright, he's here,' Piccardo said. 'Our son.'

Perhaps it was from his touch, or the sounds in the room, but the baby set to wailing. It was a feeble sound, but more encouraging than the silent, motionless child of the night.

Galen forced himself into wakefulness and blinked at the brightness in the room. 'She is still weak. You must give her some gruel,' he mumbled.

'Yes, yes, of course,' Piccardo said. He put his son beside his mother, hurried to wrench open the door and set to shouting for Zenobia's mother.

The old woman came, wailing as if anticipating death.

Piccardo stopped her with a sharp word and presumably ordered her off to fetch food for her daughter. With that, all tranquillity was gone.

Galen was so tired that the people who rushed into the room and bustled about Zenobia appeared in a confusing blur of colours and a cacophony of unintelligible words. As he was no longer wanted or even noticed, he made his way slowly down the stairs. He stopped two thirds of the way down because Carbo's broad back was blocking the exit. He was snoring so loudly, his head resting against his staff, that it felt like he shook the stairs on each exhalation.

Galen wondered whether he should wake the big man and return to the pope's palace, but there was no way he had the energy to even make the attempt. Instead, he eased himself onto the step behind Carbo and, grateful for the man's reassuringly broad back, closed his eyes to rest them.

'Brother Galen?' The words, along with a gentle shaking of somebody gripping his shoulder, made Galen jump as his eyes flashed open and he looked about in panic.

'It's alright, it's only me,' Piccardo said. 'I've brought you some food. You must be starving.'

Galen looked about blearily, noting the bright light and the people strolling past in the road and Carbo hovering behind Piccardo at the bottom of the stairs.

'What time is it?'

'It's late morning. I'm sorry that I just left you here. I'm afraid we've all been focused around Zenobia and Paulus.'

'How are they?'

'Still very weak, but now... now I have hope.'

'I'm glad,' Galen said and looked down at the bowl of pottage Piccardo was holding.

'I beg your pardon,' Piccardo said and thrust the bowl into Galen's hands. 'It appears my abilities as a host have entirely left me.'

Galen gave him an answering smile and took a mouthful of food. His mouth filled with water as his hunger took over and he wolfed down another couple of spoonfuls. Seeing him eating seemed to reassure Carbo, who took up a guard-like position, leaning against the wall of the house and watching the passersby. They gave him a wary but curious look. Galen had the feeling he'd be the talk of the neighbourhood in no time.

Piccardo looked very tired, but relieved that his wife was alive. He no doubt was eager to return to her and his son, but he stayed beside Galen.

'You don't belong here,' Galen said.

'You are astute.'

Galen watched him for a moment more, then shrugged and went back to his food.

'Your face is very mobile,' Piccardo said. 'You have obviously decided I won't speak to you, and yet you don't mind.'

Galen flushed and said, 'My face has ever given me away, try as I might to hide my thoughts.'

'You are right. I don't belong here. I was once a priest and the son of a noble family. At the time, I was Pope Gregory's secretary, but then I met Zenobia. She was a servant in the Lateran Palace, and we fell in love.'

'You gave up your calling.'

'I love Zenobia more than life itself. I wanted to do the right thing by her, not turn her into yet another clerical concubine.'

'Pope Sylvester has condemned that.'

'And I agree with him. A vow of celibacy is a vow of celibacy. When I met Zenobia, I had two choices. I could either renounce her or renounce my calling. I chose her. And for my honourable purpose, my family disowned me.'

'Oh,' Galen said.

'You look pained. Why is that?'

'I was disowned too,' Galen said, growing more embarrassed. 'It was... it was very difficult to bear. But... they took me back after a few years. Perhaps the same will happen for you.'

'I don't require them to do that. They threw me out and I won't go crawling back.'

Galen's eyes widened in dismay and caused Piccardo to give him a slight smile. 'I don't mean anything about your situation. I know nothing about that. But you don't know my family either. They are not worth wishing to rejoin.'

'I see,' Galen said, but still felt sorry for Piccardo.

'I doubt you understand. Family life in Rome is complicated, with feuds inside and out and a fierce battle for dominance. I am relieved that my son will never be dragged into that hell,'

Piccardo said. 'However, despite being disowned, one of my uncles brought my existence to Pope Sylvester's attention and, to my surprise, he called me in and took me as his secretary. He said he wanted a man of integrity. One who would stick to his beliefs. As I'd chosen to leave the priesthood for my wife, he thought I set the right kind of example.'

'Oh.' This piece of information on the pope was strangely reassuring to Galen.

'I have left you with nothing to say. And I have been a poor host. You saved my wife's life—'

'Are you sure?' Galen broke in, feeling uncomfortable that everyone was rushing to praise him when the recovery had been far from complete.

'I am certain. Zenobia is still weak and will require careful nursing, but she is no longer dying and my child has already suckled from her.'

'I am glad.'

'So another miracle for you.' Galen shrugged and must have looked so unhappy that Piccardo said, 'You don't wish me to speak of it?'

'Not really, no.'

'You astound me. Why in God's name not?'

Galen sighed and put down his spoon, gathering his tired thoughts to see how he could explain.

'I fear this... this ability. I fear it when it works, and I fear it all the more when it fails. You were lucky last night, for your wife came back to you. How would you feel towards me this morning if she had died? And if your son had followed her not long after?'

'I don't know, but I begin to understand your dilemma.'

'Mmm,' Galen said, and his mind drifted, noting the bright chirp of the sparrows hopping about on the thatched roof of the house opposite.

It all seemed too mundane a scene for the deep conversation they were having.

'Having said that, I watched you as you pleaded with God to save my wife. It impressed me that one who looks so frail could have the stamina to pray all night. I had my anxiety for my wife and child to keep me going. You didn't. My dread robbed me of my ability to sleep and tipped me into a nightmare that I would lose all that is most precious to me. In fact, I'd all but given up hope, especially when Zenobia's mother gave up and decided that her daughter would die,' Piccardo said, looking more awkward than Galen had seen him before.

'But a certain train of events came to my aid. A series of mini miracles. The first was that I vet all the pope's correspondence and filter out anything the pope doesn't need to see. I read Fra' Martinus's letter. Little did I know as I read the descriptions of the miracles attributed to you that I might need to call upon you. At that time, I'd been anticipating the birth of my first child with the same excitement as Zenobia.' Piccardo scratched his head as if embarrassed.

'The second miracle was that you were willing to come to my house and pray for my family, even though I used your own desperation against you, for which I am sorry. Especially because I now realise you would have come anyway. You are very kind and that makes you vulnerable to others who might want to use you. Nonetheless, I am grateful to you and thankful to the Lord that He led you to Rome.'

It was strange to hear so much from such a reserved man. Especially when he wasn't used to this kind of conversation with anyone other than Alcuin.

'Oh!' Galen said and surged to his feet. 'Alcuin!'

'What of him?' Piccardo asked, retrieving the bowl that had clattered down the stairs.

'He'll be wondering what happened to me, as will Brothers Piero and Bosso. I have to get back right away.'

'There's no need to worry,' Carbo said. He'd been silently listening to the two men, his eyes as round as saucers. 'Brother

Alcuin will see that I'm not back either, so he'll know you are safe.'

'All the same... my duties,' Galen said.

Piccardo laughed, which was a surprise coming from a man who had never even smiled before.

'Don't worry, only let me wash my face, and I will accompany you back. No doubt the pope is also wondering what has happened to me.'

'Will you get into trouble if you go missing?'

'I have so much to do and so many places I have to visit that people rarely know where I am. Besides, His Holiness will understand once I explain. It will be useful for you too, since he's still making a decision about you.'

'All the same, we should get going,' Galen said.

'Are you alright to return alone?'

'I have Carbo,' Galen said, looking up at the big man.

'Very well,' Piccardo said, waving them off. 'You have my eternal gratitude, Brother Galen.'

Galen nodded, then took Carbo's proffered arm and allowed himself to be led back to the road that would take them to the palace.

'Carbo... Are you sure you wish to remain by my side?' Galen asked as they made their slow way home under the baking sun.

'If not me, then that smooth secretary fellow would assign somebody else to look after you, and they could be a spy,' Carbo said, tilting his head back to Piccardo's house.

'A spy? For the pope?'

'Maybe him, maybe somebody else. There are always rats sneaking around in places like the Lateran Palace.'

Galen nodded. Power attracted intrigue, and the last thing he wanted was to have somebody bought off by one of the factions in the palace. Cardinal Gui sprang instantly to mind.

If he was intent on pulling the pope down, he'd find it useful to learn more about somebody the pope might declare as a saint.

That brought its own dangers but provided some inspiration for Galen's other concern: giving Carbo enough to do.

'Carbo, if you mean to stay, you need to maintain your fitness too.'

'My fitness?'

'You can't sit beside our door day after day, hour after hour, only rising to buy us food and clean the room.'

'But you have to be able to find me whenever you need me,' Carbo said, his jaw setting the way it did when he meant to stand his ground.

'And you need to take at least an hour a day to maintain your fighting fitness.'

'My fighting fitness? Why do I need that? I gave up being a warrior years ago.'

'Do you not think people might come after me one day and try to do away with me?'

'I wouldn't let them,' Carbo said, back to his stubborn look.

'But you would do it better if you were fit,' Galen said. 'And if you always train in the same place, Alcuin and I could find you if we needed you.'

Carbo looked momentarily stumped. Then a smile dawned on his face.

'You truly are a saint, Brother Galen. You're always looking out for people.'

'So you saved both mother and child,' Alcuin said when Galen finally got back to their room. 'I'm glad.'

It was a brief comment, and what Galen expected now. He never encouraged talk about miracles and ever since his life had been saved, Alcuin also spoke less about saints and miracles. It was the strange effect miracles had when they impacted a person directly. It was much easier to talk about miracles when they happened to others.

'Aside from that, I have news of my own,' Alcuin said, his expression one of happy pride. 'The pope came to see me this morning, grumbling that he couldn't find Piccardo.'

'What did you tell him?'

'It was nothing to do with me so I feigned ignorance. It's for Piccardo to tell His Holiness.'

'So was he looking for me?' Galen asked.

'No, to my surprise, he came with a commission for me,' Alcuin said.

'That's wonderful news.' Galen was relieved that the pope had done this. Alcuin was a self-confident man but playing second fiddle to Galen had left him feeling less important and Galen didn't want that for his talented friend. 'What did he want from you?'

'He's commissioned an image for a stained glass window.'

Galen blinked at him. 'A stained glass window? Is that appropriate for an illustrator?'

Alcuin laughed and said, 'His Holiness told me that a talented man should think more broadly, when I asked him the same question. Apparently he also knew that I'd been to the marble workshop and he approves. That was why he gave me this commission.'

'Well,' Galen said, considering the pope's words, 'it is certainly a challenge and one I am sure you will rise to.'

Chapter 8

Galen had no idea how long it would take Piccardo to get Bregowine in to see the pope. His Holiness was a busy man, after all. Nonetheless, Galen had faith that Piccardo would do it. In the meantime, he continued his routine.

Galen taught Arabic to Piero and Bosso in the morning, after having apologised profusely for vanishing for one of those mornings. Thankfully, neither they nor Alcuin had chided him much for his absence.

Once his students had departed - it was so strange for Galen to think that nowadays he had students - he spent some time composing his letter home. This had grown to epic proportions.

The rest of the time he spent translating the poetry of Ovid. It had come as a shock to discover that the pope had given him rather explicit love poetry. He found himself blushing at times over the descriptions he was reading and then over the words in Englisc he needed for a faithful translation.

Why had a holy man had given him such an explicit book, written by a pagan? Galen suspected it was purely because the pope admired Ovid's skill. But perhaps it was also a test to see what Galen made of the theme.

At his darkest moments, he wondered whether the pope was testing to see if he might stray. It was unfair to do so, since Galen was all too aware of how easily he slipped from the path of righteousness, although the form of temptation the pope had put before Galen was a poor choice, since he had no experience with women. At least, not that kind of experience.

Or perhaps it was what he'd said to Alcuin about the stained glass window design: that talented men should broaden their experience.

In between the teaching, writing, translating and drawing, Galen and Alcuin said their prayers in the chapel beside their room. The monastery bells aided their endeavour as they rang for each of the seven divine offices. Alcuin even rose in the middle of the night for Matins, although Galen had been exempted from that and slept through.

Each day, after working on his design for the pope, Alcuin took himself off to learn more about the arts. Over the last few days, he'd been spending time at a workshop that produced the mosaics that decorated many of the churches of Rome. Of course, he'd invited Galen to go with him, but Galen turned him down. His friend deserved some time to pursue his own interests unencumbered.

While Alcuin was out, Galen took to visiting the basilica. He'd found the perfect spot in a quiet corner near the stairs that led from the palace. From here he could see all the activity in the choir and the nave. It was amazing to watch the flow of humanity that came daily to pray and mingle with the highest members of the church. Thankfully, people took no notice of a solitary monk perched in the shadows on the edge of a marble bench.

He'd taken to bringing his notebook, a quill and a small horn of stoppered ink of the kind monks used when they travelled, for there was so much to note, especially now that he had hopes of communicating with his family. He wanted to record all the wonders to make sure he didn't forget them and could relay everything in his letters.

Everyone fascinated Galen: what they looked like, the wide diversity of languages spoken, their clothes and gestures. But he spent most of his time searching out people who could be from home. He'd had a moment of excitement when he'd picked up something that for one thrilling moment sounded like Englisc, but then he'd realised it was a group of Danes.

The language wasn't quite right, and the men were dressed in the far more relaxed way that typified them, their shirts hanging open. He judged them to be Danes from the mainland, and therefore not worth bothering about as they were unlikely to know of his family. He drew back a bit, though. It was always best to be cautious with the Danes.

While he watched, he considered his time in the Lateran Palace. Strangely enough, being here was giving him time to think. Watching the great ebb and flow of humanity in the hall and the rich variety of people that came from all around the Christian world, his mind fell to considering the matter of belonging.

He'd never entirely belonged anywhere, not even at home. Not that he'd considered it then. It was the only experience he'd had of life and, as boys did, he hadn't given it any thought.

Then he'd landed up in the monastery for reasons that still made him feel ill to think about, as pain stabbed through him as a physical reminder. He'd not belonged there either, not for a long time. After Alcuin arrived, he felt he had a friend. But he dragged Alcuin out of belonging, rather than that he'd been allowed in.

Strange that he wanted to go back there. Or perhaps he didn't. Maybe he just wanted to go home to see his family. He shook that thought away. There was no point in bringing on melancholy.

He moved on, considering King Aethelred's Great Hall. There, too, he'd not belonged, but he'd understood it. It had familiarity. It was a great Anglo-Saxon hall filled with the finest warriors of the land. Of course, they wouldn't be interested in a small man such as himself. But there, at least, he'd had a place as a craftsman for the king.

Hatim's palace, on the other hand, had been utterly alien with an unfamiliar way of living, an unknown language and a different religion. Even if he hadn't been a prisoner, he'd have had no hope of belonging since there were too many differences.

Finally, two monasteries: one on the frontier and one in Rome. Alcuin had fitted perfectly happily in both of them, making friends and joining in with their activities. Galen, too, had felt a certain degree of comfort, for it was familiar and he knew the role expected of him.

The Lateran was entirely different. It was a mixture of a great hall, a monastery and Hatim's palace. It was filled with supplicants begging for favours from the pope, and an army of clerics administering to the needs of the church. Each man within it manoeuvred for his own personal gain, be it wealth or power. In amongst all of this, mingled the local nobility forming and breaking alliances and trying to gain influence with both the pope and the royals and the nobles inside and visiting Rome.

Galen watched this world of power-broking with interest. Having long ago realised that to become part of a world you had to belong, or, at the very least understand it, Galen started categorising the people. He listened closely to names and was gradually building up a picture of the structure of political Rome.

'Well, well, if it isn't my inquisitive young friend,' a gravelly voice murmured as the stocky, grey-haired man Galen had met before emerged out of the shadows and settled on the bench beside him. Thankfully not too closely. 'Have you not yet found your compatriots?'

'Oh...' Galen murmured, noting that the man was still in the simple cream robe of their first meeting. 'No... I found them.'

'Ah, that's good. There's nothing more comforting than mixing with your own kind.'

That was true so Galen nodded and then wondered what he should do next. It would be rude if he jumped up and hurried away now.

'So what have you found to fascinate you today?'

'Fascinate?' Galen asked, hitting a blank.

'You looked to be in deep and satisfying thought as your gaze skipped from one group to another.'

'The wide diversity of creation is amazing.'

The man beside Galen seemed sophisticated despite his modest clothing and Galen's words felt foolish even to his own ears.

The man just smiled and said, 'Our Lord certainly seems to have a fondness for variety.'

'And He gave us free will to express ourselves however we see fit, which leads to a wide diversity of clothes, customs and languages as well,' Galen said, happy that they were in agreement.

'So you value free will, do you?'

'Of course. It is a gift from God, after all.'

'And yet, our church, and your order, severely restricts that will,' the man said while pointing at Galen's black habit.

'Not really,' Galen said, 'for I freely chose to join the order and take my vows.'

'Well, I suppose that is also true,' the man said, nodding along. 'So what do you make of the actions people are taking to protect themselves for the coming millennium? That is something even men with free will can't avoid.'

With the year 1000 AD fast approaching, Galen had heard much talk about it in the cathedral. He'd also frequently overheard the servants and local clergy saying that the number of pilgrims to all the holy sites of Rome had greatly increased owing to people's dread of what the new year might bring.

'Surely, if the millennium will herald the coming of Christ, that would be a good thing, wouldn't it?' Galen asked.

'Ha,' the man said with a dry laugh, 'you must have led a saintly life indeed to have no fear when we could all be facing a final judgement.'

'I can hardly claim that,' Galen said, but he was taken aback by the man's bitterness. 'But if you confess all your sins, with sincerity, God will forgive you.'

'I wonder...' The man was shaking his head and looked far from convinced. 'I just wonder how far our Lord's mercy extends.'

Doubt was a powerful thing and Galen could tell that the man was so deeply concerned that he could not be reassured by words alone. Galen also had nothing more he could say and wondered whether he could politely take his leave now.

As he stood up, a man standing at the edge of those praying before the altar caught his eye. He looked surprised for a moment, then leaned across and whispered something to his friend. The friend looked over to Galen too and another man turned around, all three of them staring at Galen.

What was this? What was happening? Galen was used to people whispering to each other about him. He didn't like it, but he'd grown accustomed. This was different. These men looked pleased, excited even.

The man who'd first caught Galen's eye made straight for him, cleaving a path through the crowd, his friends in tow. He stopped a respectful distance from Galen and gave a deep bow.

'Forgive me if this is impertinent,' the man said, 'but do you happen to be Brother Galen of Enga-lond?'

Galen was tempted to deny it but he couldn't bring himself to do so. 'Yes?' he said and glanced down at the bench. For some reason he didn't want the man he'd been talking to previously to hear his name. But he was already gone.

'You are!' the man cried, and his face was suffused with a warm, friendly smile as he fell to his knees. 'You are the saint, Brother Galen! O please, Brother Galen, will you give me your blessing? I have heard that anyone who gets your blessing may forever travel without harm coming to them.'

'You have?' Galen said, as a demon of thought wondered why this miraculous ability had failed to make his own journey an easy one.

'Please, Brother Galen, will you bless such a miserable one as me?'

'We are all equal in God's eyes,' Galen murmured, as he held his hand up and made a sign of the cross over the man.

His actions opened a flood gate as the man's friends fell to their knees, also begging for a blessing. Curious glances from the rest of the room changed into thoughtful ones as the implications of meeting a saint dawned on every person in the basilica. They swarmed towards Galen, who staggered backwards.

'Brother Galen, the Holy Father wants to see you,' Piccardo said, materialising at Galen's elbow.

He took Galen's arm in a firm grasp and, looking down his nose at the people clamouring to get to him, led him past the pope's guards and into the quiet corridors of the palace. The guards crossed their spears over the door so that the crowd was left still crying out to Galen for his mercy, but incapable of following him.

'Thank goodness you came, Piccardo,' Galen said as he passed a trembling hand over his face, trying to recover his composure. 'Only let me catch my breath and then I'll be ready to see His Holiness.'

'There is no need for that.'

'For what?' Galen said vaguely.

'The pope doesn't want to see you. I only said that to get you away from the mob.'

'Oh,' Galen said with a relieved laugh. 'Well, I'm glad you did. Thank you.'

'It would appear that word of your being a saint has got around. I have said nothing on the subject, but Zenobia's parents, no doubt, have told everyone they know.'

'How... how are your wife and son doing?'

'They are growing stronger by the day, thanks to you.'

'Thanks to God,' Galen murmured. 'I'm glad. I suppose the pope was right. He said any whisper of a miracle was bound to get out.'

'And it did, even down to a description of you, apparently.'

'What will I do?'

'What can you do? I wouldn't pay too many more visits to the basilica on your own, though.'

'You noticed I am there frequently.'

'The pope employs me to notice things. Since I have found you, though,' Piccardo said, 'I am actually on my way to see the pope. Along with these letters he needs to review and sign, we can speak to him about your countrymen.'

'Oh... right.' Galen couldn't work out why he might be needed. He wasn't the best at convincing people. 'If you think it might help.'

Piccardo actually smiled, not anything extravagant, but so astonishing that Galen was taken aback.

'You underestimate yourself, Brother Galen,' Piccardo said.

Galen mumbled something so garbled even he wasn't sure what he said and hurried after Piccardo.

'I don't really think I undersell myself,' Galen said, working up the courage to speak, since Piccardo seemed to be in a good mood.

'The pope likes you. That's often enough to sway a person who has a decision to make.'

'He likes me? Me? Not what I might be?'

'Being a saint is useful, of course. But saints can also be difficult. Their word carries weight and it isn't always used in support of the church.'

'Really?' Galen said, while trying to speed up to remain beside Piccardo. This was easier than usual. Either Piccardo was in no hurry or he was being considerate of Galen.

'Have you heard of Nilus of Rossano?' Piccardo asked.

'Yes, he also warned Pope Gregory that his path would lead him to danger.'

'He is, without a doubt, a holy man. But one who isn't afraid to speak his mind and with sufficient supporters to keep him safe from criticism or attack.'

'But I would never be like that.'

'I don't know. You've already started attracting followers. I don't mean the people who just flocked to you for a blessing in the basilica,' Piccardo said, as if reading his mind. 'But people who genuinely admire you, like Carbo... and me,' he added more softly. Then he laughed and said, 'But that isn't why the pope likes you.'

'It isn't?'

'Gerbert d'Aurillac, rather than Pope Sylvester, is a teacher at heart. He loves to learn and to teach and is beloved by his students. He corresponds with many of them to this day, no matter how long ago they left his care. I think he sees you in a similar light.'

'As a student?'

'Did he not give you something to work on?'

'He did... a book of poetry to translate.'

'Ah, poetry and translation are your strengths, are they not?'

'Yes, I suppose they are,' Galen said, much struck.

The only experience he had of teachers was Father Pifus, who had used rote learning and punishment for any failings. It was such a different style that Galen hadn't even recognised what the pope was doing.

'Your Holiness,' Piccardo said as he stepped into the pope's study.

'Ah, Piccardo, bringing me more work I see, and trailing Brother Galen,' the pope said, looking up from his paperwork. 'To what do I owe this pleasure? Especially after I've been given the silent treatment for days.'

Thankfully, the pope's eyes held a twinkle, which reassured Galen that he wasn't complaining to his secretary.

'Forgive me, Your Holiness,' Piccardo said as he laid his pile of documents before the pope. 'You have been busy, and I have had a great deal to think about.'

'Have you?'

'I fear I shouldn't bring it up.'

'But you will, for why else is Brother Galen here? Anyway, it is always best to tell me what is on your mind, my son, otherwise you will irritate me by withholding a mystery. And sit down, both of you, else my neck will freeze in this position.'

Galen sat stiffly on the edge of the chair opposite the pope's desk.

Piccardo looked more leisurely but still on edge and said, 'This concerns Brother Galen.'

'I thought it might.'

'You are aware my wife was pregnant?'

'Was?' Sylvester said softly, and his expression grew more concerned.

'My wife nearly died giving birth.'

'I am sorry to hear that.'

'She was so ill that I asked Brother Galen to come to our house, to bless her.'

Sylvester sat up straight and fixed his gaze on Galen. 'She was healed? Did Brother Galen produce a miracle for you?'

'He did. For my wife and my son, who was born weak and sickly.'

'Are you certain?'

'My wife was so far gone that her mother had begun work on a shroud. After Brother Galen came to visit, she and my son got better, although their recovery is slow.'

'You are certain it was down to Brother Galen?'

This was such an awkward question, and the pope's gaze, fixed on Galen, was so intimidating that he could no longer keep eye contact and stared at his toes instead.

'There is no doubt in my mind that Brother Galen saved my wife and child,' Piccardo said. 'He prayed over them all night and in the morning she woke. We hadn't been able to get her to wake in three days.'

'And young Brother Galen just went along and did this at your request, did he?'

'I believe he would have if I had simply asked, but he presented me with an opportunity because he had a favour to ask of me.'

'Did he?' Sylvester said, settling back in his chair and apparently enjoying dragging the information out of his reluctant secretary.

'There is a group of his compatriots here who wish to see you, and Brother Galen said he'd speak to you on their behalf.'

'Why would Brother Galen wish to help them with their aim?'

'They have promised to take a letter home for him if he gets them in to see you.'

'My, what a long tail of favours this is turning out to be. The problem being that you have extracted your favour before you have provided Brother Galen with his. It leaves him in a rather weak bargaining position.'

Galen's head snapped up. Would the pope really turn down the request? He prayed not.

'He saved my wife's life,' Piccardo said stiffly. 'I owe him far more than this favour.'

'And yet I haven't seen this bunch of Anglo-Saxons.'

'I've been waiting for the right moment.'

'From that, I gather you disapprove of Galen's countrymen.'

'Their quarrel is trivial, Your Holiness. They are unhappy with their local bishop.'

'Trivial to you perhaps, but to them of the utmost importance or they wouldn't have undertaken such an arduous journey. I will see these men, Piccardo, and then Brother Galen may be at ease, for his letter will be delivered. I might even suggest to the men that they would do well to ensure delivery.'

'Thank you, Your Holiness,' Galen said before he could stop himself. 'I am deeply grateful.'

The pope smiled benevolently at him, and Piccardo cleared his throat.

'Now, we need to speak of something else, don't we?' the pope said. Galen and Piccardo exchanged a look of 'what now?' while the pope continued. 'The guards told me there was a disturbance in the basilica.'

Galen was impressed that this news had reached the pope even before he and Piccardo had.

'Ah,' Piccardo said. 'That may be my fault. I suspect my in-laws have spread the story of Galen's miracle around and somebody recognised Galen from that.'

'It may not have been you, Piccardo. Ealdorman Bregowine asked if I was Saint Galen of Yarmwick when he met me. So... so it seems that all of Enga-lond has already decided what I am. Just as you said they would, Your Holiness,' Galen said, his words growing softer as he spoke. 'It only needs Bregowine telling everyone that they'd met me and their entire hostel would be abuzz with the news.'

'Well, it was only a matter of time,' the pope said, sitting back in his chair. At least he didn't look perturbed by this turn of events. Then again, he had thought this an inevitability. 'I had hoped to keep things under wraps for a while longer, and I believe I will still do that for now. But sooner or later, I am going to have to introduce you to the world as a new saint, Galen.'

'Yes, Your Holiness,' Galen said. He couldn't suppress the tremor in his voice.

'But first, I want you to complete the work I have given you. How is it going?'

Galen felt his face grow hot with a blush and said, 'It's... it's a bit challenging.'

The pope actually chuckled. 'Nevertheless, you will persevere. You may leave, Brother Galen. Now I have to complete the irritating work that Piccardo insists on piling onto my desk.'

After bowing out of the pope's study, Galen took a slow walk back to his room, his heart in the tumult he was growing accustomed to. The good news was that he now knew his letter would eventually reach his home and family. The bad news was that the pope was going to confirm to the world that he was a saint. It still made Galen squirm to consider that.

He wished he knew why God had chosen him and why everything remained so unclear. He felt unprepared, but in that perhaps the pope could help him.

Chapter 9

Alcuin watched Galen scribbling away at his letter and said with a laugh, 'What are you doing? Writing an epic?'

It was a fair question considering the hours and hours he'd put into it.

'I am just getting down everything that happened to us since we left home,' Galen said, looking up with a shy smile. 'It turns out it's been quite a lot, but I am nearly finished. I've reached the point in the tale where we met the pope. Would you like to read it?'

'I'm not sure I dare. Does it say nice things about me?'

'Of course.'

Alcuin arched a quizzical eyebrow, pleased that his friend was so happy and, because curiosity was his abiding sin, he took the proffered, tightly written pages.

'Brother Galen, Brother Alcuin, good morning,' Brother Piero said from the doorway.

He had an air of suppressed excitement, as did Brother Bosso, who was looming behind him. His hairy arms were in full view as he'd rolled up his sleeves because of the heat.

'Welcome,' Galen said, beaming at them. 'Let's continue our Arabic, shall we? You're progressing well.'

'Before we do,' Bosso said, also looking like someone trying to hide his emotions, 'we should tell you what we saw and heard on our way over.'

'What you saw?' Galen asked.

Alcuin, who'd retired to his desk to read Galen's letter, also looked up, because Bosso sounded like he had something urgent to tell them.

'In the habitation near the Colosseum,' Piero said, nodding in agreement to what Bosso had said.

Alcuin and Galen exchanged a look before Galen asked, 'What did you see?'

'An old shrine by the side of the road suddenly has hundreds of offerings laid before it. Inside the shrine, next to the image of the Virgin Mary, they have placed a small figure of a monk in black robes.'

'Ah,' Galen said, and his face lost some colour.

'We stopped to ask what the shrine was about from one of the crowd that was gathered there to pray. They said that a few days ago a young woman died giving birth to a stillborn child. Then a saintly monk paid the house a visit and prayed over the bodies and as the sun came up, the woman and child rose too.'

'Did that really happen, Brother Galen?' Piero asked, looking awed.

Galen sighed and Alcuin could tell he was more disconcerted than usual.

'She and her child weren't dead, just very ill,' Galen said. 'I did pray over them all night, and they woke in the morning. But they were still weak and in need of convalescence. To be honest, it could have just been a matter of time before they woke of their own accord, with no help from me at all.'

'Oh,' Piero said, but there was something to his expression and Bosso's that made it clear they still thought it a miracle.

Galen gave them a wry smile. Their attitude towards him had shifted from mere friendship to awe.

'But...' Piero said, 'if you could heal this woman and child, perhaps you could do the same for Fra' Martinus.'

'All I can do is try,' Galen said. 'I can make no guarantees for anyone. But in the case of Fra' Martinus... he has already turned me down.'

'He turned you down? Good Lord, why?' Bosso asked.

'He said he was old, and that old people grow sick and die. It is the way of the world.'

'That sounds like him,' Bosso said with a sorrowful nod.

Alcuin got the impression there was more to the Fra' Martinus situation than that. He'd always sensed that Galen had a sadness about the abbot that had nothing to do with his illness.

'But enough of that,' Galen said. 'Shall we return to our studies?'

'Oh, yes, of course,' Bosso said, picking up faster than Piero that Galen didn't want to carry on the conversation. 'Let's get to work.'

Alcuin watched them for a while. Usually, he'd slip out during the lesson and find some craftsman or master to learn from, but today he had some thinking of his own to do. He bent his head over Galen's letter, but the words just drifted before his eyes as his mind ran riot with speculation.

It amazed Alcuin that Galen's visit to Piccardo's house had resulted in a modification to a local shrine and such an outpouring of reverence. He didn't know what to do about that and he was certain Galen didn't either.

Galen had shared with him that the pope knew of this new miracle and was intending to introduce Galen to the world as a saint. Thankfully, at some as yet undecided time in the future.

But with a shrine popping up, Alcuin wondered how much longer the pope could delay. That prompted Alcuin to think about what their lives would be like once the announcement was made. Until now they'd lived... well, no, until they'd left Yarmwick, everything had been quiet for Alcuin, with nary a ruffle nor bump on his path. Even that wasn't true for Galen, though. His travails had begun when he was attacked. Nothing after that could have been said to be normal.

Every time they thought things had calmed down and a new pattern established for their lives, it got upended all over again. It was as if God had set Galen upon a path of continuous testing. When would it ever end?

Not anytime soon. Once Galen was officially proclaimed as a saint, his life would change again, and Alcuin got a glimpse of that from Bosso and Piero. They'd always treated Galen simply as another monk, albeit grateful to be learning from him and admiring his skill with languages. But now they were treating him with awe. It created a distance between them.

Alcuin realised, as the closest person to Galen, that his life would change too. It was already more different than he'd ever imagined.

'Ah,' Alcuin sighed and sat back in his chair. Galen and his students looked up at him, waiting. 'I beg your pardon. That was louder than intended.'

The trio nodded and went back to their work. Alcuin watched them for a bit before he turned his attention to Galen's letter and forced himself to focus. It was an astonishing tale and Alcuin had even more to consider by the time he reached the end.

When Alcuin had set off for Yarmwick, he'd assumed it was his final destination. That he'd remain there illustrating manuscripts until he grew old and his eyes failed. Then he'd enter semi-retirement, teaching younger illustrators and working in the abbey.

If he hadn't befriended Galen, his life would be poorer for it and he would have lost a friendship of the ages. But, dear God, what upheaval, and for such a small, frail man as his friend. Why was God testing him to breaking point?

Or maybe He was testing them both, for if Alcuin hadn't picked Galen as his scribe, the two of them would never have gone to King Aethelred's hall together. Miracles might not have occurred, at least not within sight of the king and his bishops. They might never have been summoned to Rome, been shipwrecked, captured by Moors, seduced by a cult and caught up in political intrigue.

In all that time, he and Galen had survived, and occasionally thrived, which they could be proud of.

'Well done, you two,' Galen said, beaming at his students.

That, too, wouldn't have happened, Alcuin thought. Galen was a teacher now, and a scholar, for the pope himself had given Galen a translation to work on.

'Thank you, Brother Galen,' Piero and Bosso said, rising and giving Galen a deeper bow than usual. 'See you tomorrow.'

Galen nodded and waved them off before he turned back to Alcuin. He was so easy to read that Alcuin already knew he didn't want to talk about the shrine. They would have to face the whole saint business eventually, but not today.

'Well?' Galen asked, looking meaningfully at the handful of parchment clutched in Alcuin's hand.

'God in Heaven, Galen,' Alcuin said as he put the stack down on his desk and tapped it, 'you make me out to be a hero.'

'Well, you are.'

'Hah! If only. I'm just a man struggling to get through the world in one piece.'

'And you manage that while, at the same time, you keep me in one piece, too.'

'But you don't make yourself out to be a hero. You just say, and then I did this, and then I did the other, and then Alcuin came riding to the rescue.'

'As you always do.'

'Not always. In the end, you saved my life. That was a section that made uncomfortable reading, I can tell you!'

'I can take it out if you don't like it.'

'And leave out the only bit of the tale where you allow yourself some glory? No, I won't hear of it. The whole thing stays in, miracle and all.'

'You don't think it's too vain of me to speak of such a thing?'

'It really happened, didn't it?'

'Yes?'

'Then it stays in. To leave it out would be to hide God's work and that would be wrong.'

'That's true,' Galen said, looking relieved to have that pointed out.

'I'll tell you something else,' Alcuin said of something he at least felt truly enthusiastic about. 'This is a fine piece of writing. I lived through it and I was gripped by what you had to say. If *I* had to do the retelling, it would be a muddle and very boring. You have a pretty turn of phrase. We should make a copy of it before you send away the original. And if you like, I'll illuminate it for you.'

Galen turned pink with pleasure. 'You would illuminate something I wrote?'

'Certainly, especially something this good.'

'You really like my writing?'

'You'd be wasted as a mere translator. You should turn your hand more to writing.'

Galen flushed even deeper red and shook his head in disbelief as he looked back down at his letter.

Alcuin laughed, pleased that he'd left Galen so happy while he felt equally embarrassed over the glowing terms Galen had used to describe him in his letter.

The mood was too good to spoil it with talk of shrines, so Alcuin stood and said, 'I'm off to the stained window makers. I need to understand how they put the glass together before I can refine my design. Do you want to come with me?'

Chapter 10

'Here, the copy of my letter,' Galen said, handing it over while looking shyer than usual.

Alcuin could understand why. It felt strange making a record of a life when they were both still such young men. Still, Galen had spent days on the letter itself, and a fair few hours making the copy. There were a few scraps of parchment on his desk that had been discarded as he made tweaks and changes.

Alcuin rubbed his hands together enthusiastically and said, 'I've been dreaming up designs to complement these pages. I'll be putting some of what I've learned in Rome into the pictures. Their style differs from ours, although it's not without similarities.'

'I'm glad it gives you something to do,' Galen said. 'Although your talent is wasted on a mere letter. You should work on some grand masterpiece for the pope.'

'Hopefully the stained glass window design will be to his liking.'

'It's shaping up nicely,' Galen said, for Alcuin had shown him some preliminary sketches. 'But when I get a chance, I'll show some of your work to His Holiness so he may understand what an exceptional talent he has living under his roof.'

'Ha! Galen, you are my greatest admirer,' Alcuin said. 'Meanwhile, I have seen such magnificent art in Rome that I am feeling quite humbled.'

'There's no need to be. I have eyes of my own and I know how good you are. Even Hatim said you were on a par with the best he had seen in Al-Andalus.'

'I'm not sure he went quite that far,' Alcuin said, then paused at the sound of voices.

Carbo's was the one he recognised. The others were speaking loudly and slowly in Englisc.

Galen sat bolt upright. 'It's Ealdorman Bregowine!' he said and rushed to the door. 'It is him and he's come with Elfwig and Swithred.'

'Ah, Brother Galen, thank God!' Bregowine said as he spotted Galen leaning through the door. 'I didn't think this big lug had understood us.'

Alcuin jumped up and hurried forward. He'd regretted not meeting his countrymen before and was glad of the opportunity now.

'My friend, Brother Alcuin,' Galen said, waving his hand to encompass Alcuin and the room. 'Have you had a chance to speak to His Holiness, Bregowine?'

'We have indeed, and I have his reply to my damned bishop safely tucked away,' Bregowine said, tapping his chest and a lump discernible through the tunic. 'Now all that remains is for me to take charge of your letter too, Brother Galen.'

'It's ready,' Galen said and hurried to his desk to seal the bundle of parchment before bringing it over.

In the meantime, Alcuin looked these men over. They were all tall, taller than the average Roman, lean and muscular and fair. Elfwig was so fair he'd been burned by the harsher southern sun, and his forehead was blotched where burned skin was peeling off. Considering how obviously they looked like thanes, it amazed Alcuin that Galen wasn't only pleased to see them, but quite relaxed about it. Maybe it was because he was older and had lived through more. Or maybe it was because of how extremely polite the men were that set Galen at his ease.

'Are you heading straight back home now?' Alcuin asked.

'We will leave at dawn tomorrow. Before that,' Bregowine said, turning back to Galen and looking surprisingly hopeful, 'we were wondering whether we could take you out for a feast? You and Brother Alcuin, of course.'

Galen looked so surprised by the invitation that he turned to Alcuin to see what he thought.

'Ah, if you can't, or if your calling or... I'm afraid I'm not too knowledgeable about what monks can do. Or perhaps, such as we aren't worthy—'

'No, I'd like that,' Galen said. 'Thank you for the invitation.'

Bregowine looked relieved. It was so strange to see this behaviour: warriors not only being polite but awed. This, Alcuin realised, was what Galen's life was going to become.

'Excellent! There's an eatery nearby that does tolerably decent food. We intend to eat our fill, in readiness for our journey, and we hope you will do the same. I can't tell you what a relief it is to have people who speak the same tongue as us for company.'

Alcuin knew exactly what Bregowine meant. He'd had all his schooling from a young age in Latin, but even for him it was like taking a mental rest to speak Englisc. It also wasn't as if he felt uncomfortable with Roman people now, especially the brothers from San Agato who had become friends, but it just felt so much more comfortable with his own people.

The modest establishment Bregowine had mentioned turned out to be attached to the best hostelry by the Lateran that seemed to cater mainly to bishops and nobility from all around the world. Alcuin even noticed a couple of turbaned Moors and did a double take to see whether Hatim might be one of them.

To the side of the building was a wide patio, shaded by grapevines. The host led them to one of about a dozen tables there and then hurried off to fetch the food. Bregowine had made him exceedingly happy by ordering roast meat.

'I know you're supposed to live pious lives, but I hope you can occasionally partake in a feast,' Bregowine said as he settled with a happy grunt at the table.

'We can,' Galen said, beaming happily.

'Brother Galen?' Bregowine said, growing more serious while his companions leaned in too, as if to share in a secret.

'Yes?' Galen said immediately, more wary.

'Forgive me if this is too prying, and we may have misunderstood since we barely have any Latin between us, or whatever the devil the locals speak, but... have you performed another miracle?'

'Oh, that,' Galen said, blushing.

Alcuin wondered what he'd say. It seemed there really would be no escaping the rumours.

'Vox populi, vox Dei,' he murmured.

It was essentially what the pope had said: the voice of the people is the voice of God.

'There was something minor... no.' Galen stopped and took a deep breath. 'There was a young woman who nearly died in childbirth. I prayed over her and her son and they have recovered thanks to God's intervention.'

'Good Lord!' Bregowine said, crossing himself as his companions followed. 'It is an honour to be in your presence.'

Alcuin held his breath waiting for their request for a blessing, certain they'd want one, especially as they had a long journey ahead of them. They didn't ask, perhaps distracted by the great steaming suckling pig the tavern owner placed in the centre of the table, along with several jugs of wine and the lightest, palest bread Alcuin had ever seen that turned out to be soft and delicious and perfect for mopping up gravy.

While he ate, he and Galen asked Bregowine and his companions for all the news from Enga-lond, and Alcuin mulled over Galen's response to Bregowine's question. It was the first time he'd not turned down such a question, batted it away or ignored it. Instead, he'd acknowledged it and thanked God. That was quite a change.

At the end of what turned into a couple of hours of feasting, by which time Galen and Alcuin could barely move for the food, the expected request was made.

'Brother Galen, saintly Brother Galen,' Bregowine said, slurring his words as he'd consumed heroic quantities of wine. 'Give your poor servants a blessing, would you? If for nothing else than to ensure your letter gets home swiftly and safely.'

'Of course,' Galen said as he waved his hand to encompass the trio. 'May God fill your sails with wind and may you have a safe and trouble-free return home.'

'Nicely put,' Alcuin said with a benevolent, alcohol-fuelled smile. 'Farewell, my fellow compatriots. Thank you for everything.'

Alcuin helped Galen to his feet, intending to assist Galen's walk back to the palace, but for once, it was Galen providing Alcuin's staggering steps with direction, rather than the other way around.

Chapter 11

Alcuin pulled at his collar in a vain attempt to get a bit of air circulating. The Lateran Palace was a fine building but nothing could keep out the blistering heat. It was hard to believe that they'd already been in Rome for two months. During that time summer had rolled in and it was insufferable.

It wasn't as roasting as Al-Andalus, but it was close. It was so hot that Alcuin had pulled the shutters closed, so that only a line of light was left. The sun was so bright that this stripe was sufficient for him to continue his work. This was so different to Enga-lond, where such bright days were rare and the light never seemed to have such force.

Still, he had plenty of time to work on his illuminations, so he couldn't complain. He was rather enjoying working on Galen's story, although his friend was frequently absent.

Since Bregowine's departure, Galen had barely been able to sit still as he waited for a reply. Alcuin teased him that no message could get to Enga-lond and back instantly, but Galen gave his shy smile and a quick nod and set off to the basilica. At least it gave his friend something to do as the hot days ticked past at an interminably slow pace.

Alcuin understood his restlessness. He had less of a family attachment, but he felt he could compete against Galen in his desire to return home. He had added a clause in his daily prayers, always done with Galen and Carbo in the chapel next door, begging God to get them home.

Not that he regretted the time he was spending in Rome. It was far, far better than being a prisoner in Al-Andalus. Here he could wander around, discovering not just the art of the monastic scriptoria but even venture further afield.

He'd been forced into it by not being able to join the Lateran monastery, which would have been his natural home. But they were still prohibited from making themselves known there. So Alcuin had instead spent his time discovering a vast new pool of inspiration from the craftsmen of Rome.

His musing was interrupted by a rap at the door and the pope walked in.

'Your Holiness!' Alcuin said as he jumped to his feet and swept a low bow.

'I see your young friend isn't here,' Sylvester said.

'No, Holiness, he's… well, he's probably gone to see whether there are any visitors come from Enga-lond.'

'Why would he do that?'

Alcuin grimaced in embarrassment, unwilling to tell the pope and reveal Galen's restlessness. Then he shrugged. He had no choice, and perhaps it would help Galen.

'He's hoping one of our countrymen will arrive bearing a letter from his family.'

'Surely his letter has not had a chance to get to Enga-lond yet? Not to mention finding his father and then getting a message back. I shouldn't expect to see anything in under four months.'

'True, but he hopes his family has written to him previous to that.'

'He is very close to his family, is he?' the pope said and settled on Galen's bed, avoiding the stripe of light that fell across it.

It appeared this was going to be a long visit. Since Alcuin wanted to gauge how likely they were to be allowed to go home, he was quite pleased to have the pope's ear. He was more likely to ask the important questions than Galen was, after all.

'Family loyalty is a powerful force in my country and Galen feels its pull, for yes, he is close to his family.'

The pope nodded thoughtfully and asked, 'How is his work on my translation going?'

'Oh!' Alcuin said and grinned. 'A bit slowly, Your Holiness.'

'You smile. Why is that?'

'Galen is very shy, and it has to be said a very good, obedient person. Your Roman love poems are embarrassing him.'

'They are?' Sylvester said with a returning smile.

'It seems that sometimes he is squirming as he reads them, and as he writes them out.'

'But he continues with his task.'

'You ordered it, so he will do it.'

'Do you think he at least likes the poems?'

'I believe that is part of his difficulties with them. It disturbs him that he admires the words and the craftsmanship of the writer, but he probably feels guilty that he likes any part of poems that he suspects, despite you giving them to him, are inappropriate.'

'And what of you, young man? Have you read these challenging works?'

'I have, Holiness, both in the original Latin and in Galen's translations.'

'And?' the pope asked, waving for Alcuin to sit down.

He settled on his bed, so that the two were now facing each other. 'I like the poems... but I'm afraid I'm more worldly than Galen.'

'He is a strange combination of wisdom and innocence. As a saint should be, I suppose.'

Alcuin recognised that the last bit of what the pope had said was more to himself than part of the conversation, so he felt safe enough not commenting.

'Do you speak Englisc, Your Holiness?'

'Why do you ask?'

'I wondered whether you'd be a good judge of Galen's skill as a translator. At the risk of trumpeting his abilities, I think he is doing an excellent job of translating Ovid.'

'I'm glad to hear it, although I sense a but.'

'Not really a but, Holiness, just something else I wanted to tell you,' Alcuin said and hesitated, waiting for a sign from the pope that he could continue speaking.

Sylvester smiled and said, 'You know what I realise when speaking to you rather than to your friend? You are more careful about what you say and how you approach me. Your friend sometimes manages to hold back his words, but all too often he just blurts out exactly what he thinks.'

'That sounds like Galen,' Alcuin said. 'It seems to win him friends, though.'

'His openness has a certain charm. Now, what was it you wanted to tell me?'

'It's about his writing, Your Holiness. Galen's an excellent translator, no doubt, but he's also a talented writer.'

'He is?'

'Yes, look at this. It's his letter home,' Alcuin said as he held up the first page of Galen's writing.

'Illuminated by you?'

Alcuin blushed and said, 'I once drew a few episodes of Galen's life for the Moor, Hatim. I thought I did an adequate job, but I longed to do it properly, so I am drawing images along the edge of all the pages, but also on a couple of leaves I'm inserting between Galen's pages.'

'You have a very fine hand,' Sylvester said, examining the illuminations closely.

'Thank you, Holiness, but read the words. You'll see, they're wonderful.'

'It's a good thing that I am, after all, something of a scholar of languages, or I might not have bothered learning your rather obscure Englisc.'

'A good thing indeed, Holiness. Very few people this far south seem to know anything about our language at all.'

'Your images give me a good idea of the content, without having to read it, along with my knowledge of what Galen has already told me.'

'But not an idea of how well Galen writes.'

'Not yet, but once he has finished with Ovid, I will have another commission for him. I'll ask him to write the complete tale of his life in Latin and you shall illuminate that one too.'

'His whole life?'

'Mmm, it is a requirement for being named a saint, you know? The people may already say that he is one, but we have a procedure in the church. The one who is nominated as a saint must write down his life. That then has to be reviewed by a local bishop. That bishop will also interview as many witnesses as he can about the saint's life and the professed miracles.

'Only after that can the bishop make a ruling on whether he believes the nominated person is a saint or not. At that point he sends his recommendations to the pope, who will make a final declaration,' Sylvester said with a gentle smile as he placed his finger on his chest. 'But whether or not it is procedure, it would be good to get down Galen's life in his own words.'

Although Alcuin had already guessed that the pope planned to proclaim Galen as a saint, he'd had no idea that there was such a rigorous process to go through. He was also stunned to hear that these concrete steps had already been considered and were about to be put in motion.

'It may not be that easy for Galen to write a history of his life, the rape, the ostracism, the—'

'Ostracism?'

'He didn't tell you that part?'

'It appears that way. Are you referring to when his father disowned him?'

'No, I mean the monks of Yarmwick. When I arrived at the abbey Galen had already been there for two years and, because he'd been raped and they thought him a catamite, he was shunned.'

'I see. All he told me of that episode of his life was that his mother sent him to the abbey so that his uncle could save his life, and that he'd become a scribe.'

'It was a difficult time for him, and for much of it he was still in shock.'

'No doubt. It explains why he is so shy.'

'From what I heard from his uncle and mother, Galen has always been shy. It was what made it impossible for him to force his presence onto the monks and what made it so easy for them to keep him out of their company.'

'So his charm doesn't always win people over.'

'He didn't have a chance to try. Nobody would speak to him.'

'I see. And what about here? Has he made any friends?'

Alcuin tilted his head thoughtfully. 'He has, but not many. Galen isn't outgoing, so unless someone approaches him, nothing will happen.'

'Even though he spends time in the crowds of the basilica?'

'He isn't a very memorable person, and he never makes the first move, so people are unlikely to notice him. At least, that used to be the case. I worry about what he will do once he is proclaimed a saint. Ealdorman Bregowine, who appears to be an honest and decent man, wouldn't have given Galen the time of day had they met anywhere else. Yet now, because he thinks of him as a saint, he was very friendly and even took us both out for a meal. I am so accustomed to being feted by people I scarcely notice it anymore. But to Galen, being mobbed and having people push friendship on him might be problematic.'

'Indeed,' Sylvester said.

The sound of the crowds and the calls of the shopkeepers outside drifted through the window in that pause.

'Your Holiness…' Alcuin started and then paused to gather his courage. 'Will… will we ever be able to go home?'

'Go home?' Sylvester said as he tilted his head. 'Why would you want to? There are far more opportunities available to men of your talent in Rome than in your far-flung abbey.'

'Both of us?'

'Do you intend to abandon Brother Galen? I find that hard to believe. I am aware that Galen values your friendship greatly and relies heavily upon you. It is a fact that Galen is both grateful for and regrets.'

Alcuin nodded because he knew how guilty Galen felt about their relationship.

'On the other hand,' Sylvester continued, 'you benefit a great deal from Galen too, don't you?'

'I do, but most people, most of all Galen, don't realise this.'

'Well, I've been around for a long time,' the pope said.

'Then you must know, Your Holiness, that sometimes the pull towards home is intense, especially when you've been away for a long time, or are very far from home.'

'Mmm, it has been a very long time since I experienced homesickness. I enjoy travel, you see, and meeting new people. I got the impression Galen was the same.'

'More so than me,' Alcuin said. 'But Galen is also strongly attached to his family and misses them greatly. Which is why… if I could give him hope that he will see them again, I would be grateful. After all, when we set out on this journey we firmly believed that we would return home soon.'

'Life is full of surprises,' Sylvester said. 'And at this point, there is much that Galen needs to know, so I'm afraid you too will have to wait and make the most of your time in Rome.'

'Well? Galen asked cautiously of Carbo after their midday meal.

This was something Galen insisted upon. He didn't actually want Carbo to join Alcuin and him and live in their room, but they had returned to the rules of St Benedict, regulated by the Lateran monastery's bell, which meant they prayed together for most of the divine offices and ate together at the times the rule decreed. Since it was summer, their largest meal was after Sext. Although, rather than having somebody read from Benedict's rules during dinner, they ate together in silence, and then read a short passage to each other after the meal.

Once that was done, they had a moment to chat and Carbo told them all he'd learned at the Lateran. Since he was no longer officially a monk, although he was still keeping to most of the rules, Carbo had a degree more freedom and brought back interesting titbits of news that helped Galen piece together a picture of life in the Lateran.

Carbo ran his fingers through the somewhat shorter hair that had regrown from his tonsure. It was a sparse patch as his baldness moved his hairline ever towards the rear.

'There is talk of a new saint. Linked to the shrine near the Colosseum. The story seems to be growing and becoming ever wilder.'

'Wilder than a woman and her son rising from the dead?' Alcuin said, shaking his head.

'Sometimes the story includes more people, sometimes they say the woman and child had already been shut up in a tomb for three days.'

'Dear God,' Galen murmured. It wasn't the first time descriptions of his actions had been exaggerated. The successful defence against the vikings at Hasculf's village of Wodenshurst had been attributed to the fact that Galen had prayed for them the whole way through the battle. Galen firmly believed it had been due to the men's valiant defence, but he was given the credit nonetheless.

'There's more,' Carbo said.

'More than that?' Alcuin said with a laugh. He looked uncomfortable, and that was probably because of the miracle that had brought him back from the dead. 'There is more, and we know it, but the people around here don't.'

'It isn't that, it's worse,' Carbo said slowly and seriously.

'Why is it worse?' Galen asked.

'The staff in the kitchen tell me that Cardinal Gui is investigating this miracle.'

'He must know it's down to you, Galen,' Alcuin said.

'Maybe,' Galen said. 'Although I doubt Piccardo would say anything to the cardinal about the event, or to the pope, so... all he has to go on are the rumours that everyone else is listening to.'

'He could go to the parents,' Alcuin said. 'They'd be easy to track down. Then he'd see the connection with Piccardo and straight to the pope. You can bet he'll make trouble if he puts it all together. Or even if he doesn't, he'll keep digging.'

'Oh dear,' Galen said, because that sounded all too probable. 'I should tell the pope.'

'As if that will be easy,' Alcuin said with a laugh.

'Well... I shall find Piccardo and ask him,' Galen said.

It had been his intention to do so immediately, but despite what he now knew about Piccardo it took a few days for him to work up the courage to seek out the pope's secretary. When he finally did, he found the man hard at work at his desk, with a hopeful queue of men standing before him in silence, praying he'd eventually look up and ask them why they were there.

Galen joined the back of the queue, his gaze drifting about the room with its cubbyholes filled with scrolls, and the multitude of codices. It spoke of decades' worth of work. At that moment Piccardo glanced up, spotted Galen and shot to his feet.

'Brother Galen!'

'Hello, Piccardo... I was wondering whether I might have a moment of your time.'

'Of course, Brother,' Piccardo said.

It gained him some black looks from the men who'd no doubt been waiting for hours. The rest looked deeply curious as to what made Galen so special. He flushed because it was best they didn't know.

'Out,' Piccardo said to the other men, shooing them with his hands as he walked to the door and shut them out so that it was only him and Galen. 'Please, take a seat.'

'Thank you,' Galen said and settled on the chair with the embossed leather base. 'How... are your wife and son doing?'

'Very well,' Piccardo said. He smiled and it transformed his face so completely Galen was left blinking in astonishment. 'Paulus has now been baptised. I hope you don't mind, but we gave him the additional name of Galanus.'

'Oh!' In the past, Galen would have said he wasn't worthy of having such an honour bestowed upon him. But he'd realised that people wouldn't care, and also it denied God's hand in the miracle. 'I hope he will prosper with it,' he said.

Piccardo nodded, his soft gaze fixed on his thoughts of his wife and son.

Then he shook himself and asked, 'What can I do for you, Brother Galen?'

'I was wondering, Piccardo... I heard the shrine near your house has—'

'Ah, I'm sorry about that,' Piccardo said, throwing up his hands in that expressive Roman way. 'I warned my in-laws, but I couldn't stop them or the servants of the house from running away with gossip. It was too great a miracle to keep a lid on it. I've already informed His Holiness about what's happened.'

'What did he say?' Galen asked as he perched on the edge of one of Piccardo's chairs.

'That it was too great a miracle to be hidden and that we shouldn't be trying to hide God's grace anyway.'

Galen nodded. Hiding God's grace had never been his intention, and he did worry about that.

'But you must have heard that the rumoured miracle speaks of your wife and child rising from the dead?'

'I did, and I promised the pope that I would correct that rumour, but he said it would be a waste of my breath and that tales invariably get augmented.'

'So he isn't displeased?'

'On the contrary, he was chuckling to himself over the whole matter. The Franks have a strange sense of humour.'

Galen found himself in complete agreement with Piccardo on this matter, for he could find no cause for amusement.

'Was that all?'

'There was one other thing, related to the miracle... Carbo hears a lot of gossip and he has told Alcuin and me that Cardinal Gui has been asking around about this miracle too.'

Piccardo swore under his breath but said, 'I suppose that, too, was inevitable.'

'Yes,' Galen said hesitantly. 'Because of him I wanted... I wanted to know a bit more about the situation in Rome. If I'm going to be a pawn here, I should know what I am facing.'

For the first time in Galen's acquaintance, Piccardo actually looked disconcerted. 'Do you have any idea how vast a subject that is? I have lived in Rome all my life and worked in the Lateran for most of that time and I still don't know all there is to know.'

'I see,' Galen said. 'Perhaps you could tell me of the ones I should be most wary of. Cardinal Gui, for instance.'

'Ah yes. Well you know he is a dangerous man and best avoided. But since he has also shown an interest in you, I will tell you what I know. The cardinal has no interest in becoming pope. What he wants is to be the power behind the throne. It's great to have all the influence without the associated risks. He's outlived quite a few popes already with this strategy.'

'So he's trying the same with His Holiness?'

'That would be impossible. Gui has multiple concubines and lives a luxurious life. He doesn't even try to hide his hatred for the current pope, although he is being careful to not make his machinations too obvious. He also has an advantage because the people of Rome prefer one of their own to be pope. An outsider, installed by an outsider emperor, is at an immediate disadvantage.'

'I see,' Galen said. He was starting to understand why nobody took his warnings for Pope Gregory seriously. Life here truly was precarious. 'So what is he doing?'

'He's trying to undermine the pope so that he will be unseated and replaced by someone Gui can manipulate. To do that, he is attacking Pope Sylvester's virtue.'

'His virtue?'

'Ironic, isn't it? A pope who wishes to clean up the church is being accused of an alliance with the Devil.'

Galen was so surprised he blinked. 'Is this because he can rapidly add up numbers in his head?'

'That is one of the so-called pieces of evidence Gui is using against His Holiness. All he wants is to introduce a more effective way of recording and manipulating numbers. So he demonstrated its effectiveness and for that he is accused of fraternising with Satan.' Piccardo shook his head. 'But don't worry,' he added, probably because he saw the alarm on Galen's face, 'he is a resilient man. He has survived living at the emperor's court. He can win against Gui as well.'

'How?'

'By researching the cardinal and watching him as much as Gui watches the pope. He doesn't slander the man, but one day I wouldn't be surprised if Gui finds himself in court, or stripped of his office and his power if he continues to flout the pope's laws.'

Galen fervently hoped that would happen quickly.

'What should I do if he comes looking for me?'

Piccardo gazed thoughtfully at him and Galen guessed he was trying to work out how much resistance Galen might be able to put up.

'If he does try to speak to you,' Piccardo said, 'tell him that he needs to address his questions to the pope.'

'Would that work?'

'His Holiness has ordered you to live quietly and not become known. That would apply doubly when it comes to Cardinal Gui.'

Chapter 17

Galen hurried down the stairs that led to the pope's study, clutching his translation to his chest. He hoped that his work would find favour. It had taken nearly four months, but he was pleased with the result. Aside from the bawdy nature of the poems that sometimes embarrassed him and sometimes resulted in lots of questioning and more complicated, difficult to explain feelings, he had enjoyed doing the work.

He prayed the pope would be pleased with his efforts and allow him to translate something else. For if he did, and Galen established himself as a translator, then, God willing, if he ever got home, he might be able to continue with translations rather than just being a scribe. But there were too many 'what ifs' in those dreams and Galen tried to banish them as he knocked on the study door and heard the pope's energetic voice calling him in.

'Ah, Brother Galen,' Pope Sylvester said, looking up from a large page of parchment that covered his desk. 'Come in and take a look at this!'

'At what, Holiness?' Galen asked, coming closer.

'This design by your friend Brother Alcuin for the stained glass window,' Sylvester said with an expansive wave of his arm that took in the entire parchment. 'I now have the images from all the artists I commissioned. What do you think?'

Alcuin, unusually for him, had not let Galen see his window design, so this was the first time Galen was seeing it. It was unmistakably in Alcuin's style and looked to be Saint Luke, as he was accompanied by an ox.

'It's a very fine image. How does it compare to the others?' Galen said, trying to remain neutral so that he didn't undermine Alcuin's chances.

The pope seemed to understand his intentions and gave him a knowing smile. 'It is amongst the best I have received.'

Galen couldn't suppress a smile of pleasure mixed with relief as he nodded. 'Where do you plan to put this new window?'

'In the council chamber to the right of the cathedra. I have a south-facing window that is perfect for stained glass, and I will have a superb view of it.'

'I'm sure it will look wonderful, Holiness.'

'Now, on to other things. Piccardo tells me you have finished translating Ovid.'

'I have, Holiness,' Galen said, thinking that the pope really was like the best of encouraging teachers as he handed over his manuscript.

'Well, let's take a look,' Sylvester said. 'Feel free to wander around in the meantime and test out any gadget that takes your fancy while I see what kind of translator you are.'

Galen's heart gave a kick of fright to think he'd remain in the room while the pope analysed and dissected his work. As he had no choice, he made for the desk furthest away, where he could keep his back to the pope. He didn't have the courage to watch the man's face, lest it show disappointment.

The table he stopped at had more sheets of parchment, all of which appeared to be alternate designs for the stained glass window. They all looked very fine, and quite different, one from the other. None, in his opinion, looked better than Alcuin's.

Galen couldn't work up much interest in them though, as his mind alternated between worrying about the pope's verdict on his work and wondering whether Bregowine had made it back home safely. So much was riding on one man. It seemed like a fragile thread that could so easily be snapped on its way home.

It didn't help to remind himself that he had contingencies. If he didn't hear anything from home within four... no, make that six months, he could send another letter. Writing the letter had been helpful in organising his thoughts. He'd started to face the reality that he might actually be a saint. At the very least, he'd have no choice in the matter.

That being the case, he had to work out how he responded to this challenge. It wasn't exactly new, but he'd always tried to slip away from what it meant, and not think too deeply about it. That was no longer an option.

People treated him differently once they heard he was a saint. Some of that could have left him feeling cynical, but he realised that most people were responding to the presence of God. For them, Galen was a symbol of the divine and therefore the respect they were showing him was actually respect for God. That was right and proper.

Others had baser instincts. Cardinal Gui, for example, who, Piccardo had told Galen, watched everything the pope did and dripped poisonous words into people's ears against him. Since Sylvester was supporting Galen, he realised the cardinal was a danger to him, too. It made Galen shudder.

'It isn't that bad,' Sylvester said.

Galen's head snapped up, his mind a confused blank. What was the pope talking about?

Sylvester grinned and said, 'You were either shuddering over my designs for the window or your translation. I may be immodest, but I think the designs are easily as good as any produced by an expert.'

'They are very beautiful,' Galen said.

'Then it's your poetry you are worried about. Don't be. I knew my instinct was right to give this translation to a poet. You have a sense of the rhythm of language. You have done a much better job than a mere translator. Your version has soul.'

Galen flushed with gratitude as he mumbled an incoherent thanks.

Sylvester laughed and said, 'Now I have another challenge for you. Your friend Alcuin tells me you are also a talented writer. I intend to test that too. I want you to write something for me.'

'You do?' Galen was stunned by this request, this glimpse into a world he'd only dreamed of but never believed he'd actually be allowed into. 'What... what do you want me to write?'

'A story of your life, in Latin, from the very beginning to now with you at the Lateran.'

'My life?' Galen said, as his dream evaporated.

This wasn't what he wanted to write about.

'The whole thing, leaving nothing out,' Sylvester said and then, noting how Galen's shoulders slumped, and the hopeful spark faded from his eyes, he added more gently, 'This is only the start, Brother Galen. After this you may write about any topic you please. But I must and I will have your life because I believe it is important. And, more prosaically, because it is a requirement when judging whether or not a man is a saint.'

'It is?' Galen was surprised, not only about the requirement but that the pope was asking him to move forward to that next step. It seemed the inexorable march to sainthood could not be slowed. 'There is much... there is much I would rather the world didn't know, Your Holiness,' Galen said, aware that his voice held a note of pleading.

'I know, my son,' Sylvester said. 'And if it makes you feel better, aside from its official use, I will hold on to the manuscript and keep it private till after your death. But I would fail in my duty to God if I didn't get a record of your life and make your position official.'

'Why?' Galen whispered.

'Because it is already clear to me that you are a saint. Your life should be recorded so that others may learn from it.'

Galen's thoughts flashed to how unlike a saint he was in his daily life, and he said with some difficulty, 'I... my life has been nothing special... nothing exemplary. It is... it is only the miracles.'

'Only the miracles? My son, what else besides miracles do we have as proof of our Lord and God living among us and working through you? As for your life, perhaps it seems ordinary to you now, but in later years, when scholars examine your deeds and your words, other significant meanings may emerge.'

Sylvester stopped and no doubt read Galen's inner struggle play out across his face. He couldn't gainsay his pope, but he was having difficulties accepting his words as an obedient son of the church ought to.

'Here,' Sylvester said and handed over a thick tome. 'Something of mine for you to contemplate.'

'What is it?'

'A record of some of my debates. I have a high reputation in that field, and I thought that interested you. When I was the Bishop of Ravenna, I once held a debate against my peers that went on for the whole day. This codex records some of what was said.'

'Do you want me to translate it?'

'I merely want you to read it. If you are going to be an informed commentator on life, you should be well educated.'

'Oh.'

Sylvester gave Galen a benevolent smile that he felt far from worthy to receive.

'You have a good mind behind all your insecurities, Galen. I know, for I have been testing it in the same way as I have tested a host of young men who have passed before me over the years.'

'You have?'

'Why do you think I showed you my inventions, got you to work with them, talked to you about Moorish numbers, gave you difficult poetry to translate, and questioned you on your thoughts? It was all a test. One you passed far more easily than many a youngster who has been brought up to believe himself an intellectual,' the pope said, waving his arm to encompass his office.

'Part of your charm is that you don't swagger about, puffed up with your own conceit. But know this: yours is a far stronger mind than most. It has the potential to be up there with the great minds of the past. You could easily be another Venerable Bede, given time, but you must unshackle yourself from your own low expectations.'

Galen blinked at the pope in amazement and became aware that his mouth was hanging open.

'Yes, Your Holiness,' he whispered.

'Good. Now, how long should I give you for this task? Will two months be sufficient?'

Galen blinked at him. Two months felt too soon; not for the work itself, but for the assessment and what felt like the foregone conclusion that would follow.

'Two? I suppose I can write everything in two months. I already have the part from our departure from Lundenburh written, so that just needs translating. As for the rest… yes, two months will be fine.'

'Good. I like that you're a fast worker. I will get Cardinal Gui to conduct the review.'

'Card… Cardinal Gui?' Galen said. Now his head was spinning.

How could this be?

'Ha, you are probably aware that he doesn't like me, but that will work in your favour. There is so much evidence that you are a saint that he won't be able to deny it. So he, a man known to be my enemy, will have to accept you as a saint. The church will then accept it too, for two enemies will have come together to proclaim you as such.'

'Do you think there is so much evidence?' Galen asked.

Pope Sylvester smiled at him and said, 'It all starts with the letter from your Bishop Sigburt, outlining two, or possibly more, miracles. Having the word of a bishop is powerful enough, but your king and his entire court witnessed that same miracle. I have written to the king and the two men named as recipients of God's mercy, Ealdorman Maccus and the thane called Uictred, for their witness statements. It was rather convenient that Ealdorman Bregowine came to see me, for I sent my testimony requests via him. I also asked that he gather whatever additional information he can.'

Chapter 13

Galen sighed and, because he'd reached the point where he had to describe the rape, put down his pen. This was such a difficult section that he'd skipped over it and written everything else. It had taken the two months the pope had given him and he was in daily expectation of Piccardo turning up to summon him back to see the pope. More even than the letter, writing his whole life down from the very beginning had prompted a lot of soul searching.

He'd even added his thoughts on certain events, looking back at them with the benefit of hindsight. Like the time when he turned seven and went to the burgh's training field in the expectation that his father would start teaching him to become a warrior. He'd been terrified at the prospect and hopeful at the same time. He knew he was small for his age, and he was quivering with dread to stand at the edge of the field with so many thanes and older boys around him. But his father hadn't even glanced in his direction.

He'd thought perhaps he'd not noticed him. His nerves had caused him to select a rather far-flung log upon which to perch, and he'd used the pile of gear the men discarded when they trained, along with the spare weapons, to partially hide himself. So the following day, he'd tried to stand out more and, after that got him nothing, ever closer, his heart thumping so hard in his chest he could hardly breathe.

Day after day he'd waited, until one day, when his father, mid-sword thrust, had looked directly at him. It felt as if the air froze around them as Galen held that gaze, incapable of moving. His father had seen him, surely now…

But that mighty warrior had merely continued the thrust and turned back to his men. Galen had waited until the end of the training, but even when everyone had washed, pulled their clothes back on and returned to the burh, never a word was said to Galen. Then he understood, or at least had thought he did.

His mother had sent him to Father Pifus the next day to start preparing him for life as a monk. It had been a deeply hurtful time, which had made his father's later acceptance, and even apology, doubly strange when it had happened.

Writing it down now, he could see how a mighty warrior couldn't have trained a tiny, shy child like him. He added his own commentary in his text to fathers everywhere, though, to at least explain things to their children, for their hearts could be so easily crushed. It was strange how that episode still hurt after all that had happened.

Anyone else writing his life's story wouldn't even have bothered to put it in. Or, if they did, might have framed it as Galen learning that his true place was in the church, through that lesson, as if it were ordained by God. Galen had his doubts.

He believed that God's gift to human beings was true free will and that everything his father had done, and everything he had done, was through that will. It laid far more responsibility on his and his father's shoulders, but that felt right to Galen.

Another section that had given him great difficulty was the miracle that saved Alcuin. It had been such a shocking moment, being on the brink of losing his best friend. The agony of that night still haunted his dreams. But then the astonishing miracle that once and for all proved that God was indeed working through Galen.

He'd avoided thinking about it in part because it was such a painful moment. But also because of the enormity of what had happened and the hysterical relief and joy he'd felt when Alcuin was completely healed. It had shaken him to his core and caused a crisis of indecision he was only now overcoming.

That was his own fault. His own stubbornness to accept that God might want to use him as an instrument of His mercy. He felt entirely unworthy. How could somebody that most people looked down upon, be someone Almighty God would favour?

Favour was perhaps the wrong word. The people around Galen, not those closest to him, but the rest, thought being able to perform miracles was something any man would rejoice over. If he could perform them at will, Galen might have agreed. But he couldn't. That filled him with the dread of disappointing desperate people. That was God's will though, and Galen had no say, but he was the one left facing the disappointed supplicant.

He'd written extensively upon this point. Emphasising again and again that miracles weren't his will but God's. Warning people they had to prepare their hearts and minds for disappointment. He wished he could explain why, but he didn't know, and once he'd started writing about it, he couldn't stop. That, at least, was his will. He was uncertain of how the pope would take it.

Now, this was all that was left: writing about the rape. His mind couldn't focus enough to start though, so he stood, stretched and headed to Alcuin's desk to look at his illuminations. They always brought him a modicum of peace.

Alcuin had just gone off to buy more paints. His passion for the colour blue hadn't waned and he was using, according to his thrilled supplier, an inordinate amount of that most expensive of pigments. To Galen, it looked wonderful. The deep azure skies Alcuin was painting with their dusting of stars looked so much like the night sky that if one gazed at it for a while, it felt as though you were looking up on a light, cloudless night.

A forceful knock at the door jarred Galen out of his introspection and with his heart hammering in his chest he said, 'Who is it?'

'It is I, Bregowine.'

'Bregowine?!' Galen cried as he wrenched open the door.

The big man grinned at him and said, 'Hello, Brother Galen.'

'You came back!' Galen said, assimilating the man's dusty clothes — he must have come straight to the Lateran without stopping to wash.

'Yes, well, my problems with my bishop haven't been resolved. The man continues to be difficult and to bar my family from the church despite the letter the pope gave me to give him. So I'm back to renew my pleas to the pope to have the bishop removed.'

'I'm sorry your last visit didn't achieve what you wanted.'

'Don't be,' Bregowine said with a grin as he removed a thick sheaf of pages from his tunic. 'Else I wouldn't be bringing you this.'

'A letter from home!' Galen breathed, his heart quickening. Would it all be good news? Was everyone well — alive, even? 'Did you... did you speak to my father?'

'I was fortunate that he was in Lundenburh when I got back. I gave him your letter and left, thinking I had completed what I'd set out to do. But when I formed the intention of returning to Rome, I dropped back in on your father to offer to carry any message he might have for you. It turns out he'd written and then sent your brother back home in a hurry to get your mother to write to you too, hence the size of the missive.'

'So they are all well?'

'I believe so.'

'Thank you,' Galen said as he took firm hold of the bundle, his hands trembling with the emotion of getting this letter. 'Thank you so much.'

'The way I see it, I have much to thank you for, too, Brother Galen, for my journey home and back to Rome has been swift and unremarkable.'

'I'm relieved to hear it.' Galen had been afraid Bregowine might feel let down if his journey had been difficult. 'Might I ask... the pope told me you also took a couple of letters back for him.'

'Oh yes, I have become quite the messenger, and to the most exalted people too. The king, the Bishop of Lundenburh, and some of the highest men in the king's court. I've brought their replies too.'

'You have?'

'I thought it would help get me back in to see the pope again. I can't keep relying upon you, can I?'

'I suppose not,' Galen said and wondered whether Bregowine had any inkling of what the letters might be about. It didn't seem that he did. Then again, perhaps Galen was being too self-absorbed. No doubt the pope had much to hear from some of his most far-flung flock.

'Well, I'll be off,' Bregowine said with a grin. 'I'm overdue for a rest and I can tell you are dying to read your letter. But I'm probably in Rome for a while now, so if you wish to send another letter back, I'll drop in before I leave and take it for you.'

'You are very kind.'

Bregowine laughed and said, 'For befriending a saint? Believe me, Brother Galen, I'm getting more out of this than you realise.' Then, with a wink, he was gone.

Galen gazed after him in surprise, uncertain of what he'd meant. Not that it mattered now. Galen shut the door with a firm click, cast himself upon his bed and with trembling fingers, broke the seal on the letter and started reading.

His heart was in his throat for fear that he might receive bad news. But his father, anticipating this, opened with the line that all was well. Considerably relieved, Galen devoured the rest of the letter and then read and reread it, trying to get every ounce of meaning from it and drawing considerable comfort from the missive.

When Alcuin arrived, Galen was sitting on his bed, the letter in his lap, tears dripping down his face.

'Good Lord, Galen, what's wrong? Are you alright?'

'I'm fine,' Galen said as he smiled up at Alcuin and wiped away his tears. 'It's a letter from home. It finally came, and everyone is well. Oh Alcuin, we've been away from home for so long! Cwyneth is expecting her third child already.'

'Phew,' Alcuin said as he dropped into a chair, suddenly shaky himself at the length of time they'd been away.

Galen said a little more hesitantly, 'My father asked yours if he wanted to send a letter too, but he... he didn't.'

'That's alright. I wasn't expecting anything from him,' Alcuin said.

'He's still alive but... but a little more eccentric.'

'I fear you mean that he's gone quite mad.'

Galen gave a quick, uncomfortable shrug and looked down uncertainly. Then, from amongst the folded pages of his letter, he pulled out a slim, still-sealed missive. 'It's from Emma and addressed to you,' Galen said and handed it over with a trembling hand.

Alcuin snatched it away and tore open the seal, suddenly overwhelmed by his own emotion. His eyes flicked through the words at speed, looking for all the important information.

He sighed with obvious relief and said, 'She's alright. She's well. And I... I have a son.'

Galen nodded. He'd already had that information from his father, or at least the news that Emma had delivered herself of a son. He continued to watch Alcuin's face. He had far more understanding of what his friend was going through now that he had read the poems of Ovid, and his heart ached all the more in sympathy.

Alcuin sighed and started on the letter again, reading it more slowly this time, taking in all the information Emma had sent, all the minute details of his son.

'She named him Edmund.'

'Yes.'

'She tells me he is a sturdy little boy, and he has my curly blond hair and my charm.'

Galen nodded.

'You don't mind that I speak of him, do you?'

'Not if it makes you happy. If it hurt you to think of him… of them, then it would sadden me.'

'You really are a good man, Galen, not to have taken this as a slight to your family's name.'

Galen smiled and said, 'I never liked Eni. I was always sorry Emma had to marry him.'

Alcuin laughed and said, 'That's rather lucky for me. But it will always be a source of regret that I can never acknowledge my son, and that he will call Eni Father.'

Galen couldn't imagine a worse fate for anyone than that and said, 'He is a great comfort to Emma. I'm certain that one day she will tell him about his real father. A man he can be proud of.'

Alcuin gripped Galen's shoulder in a powerful grasp, unable to come up with the words of thanks he felt overwhelmed by. 'As I said, you are a good man.'

Chapter 14

After the incident in the basilica when he'd been mobbed, Galen was more cautious when he went there now, and made sure to keep his hood up to hide his face. Still, rumours had got around that a saint had been seen in the basilica and, even though he chose dark shadows within which to rest and watch, people still slowed as they walked past him to try and guess whether he might be the fabled saint.

It was worse in the library that Galen had visited to see what types of manuscripts they might have. The space was smaller and full of the religious - monks rubbing shoulders with clerks and bishops - who all turned to examine Galen when he walked in. It was sufficiently intimidating for him to flee and not return.

The baptistery was impossible. Although it had plenty of dark nooks, it was filled with pilgrims who eyed Galen with distinct curiosity. He'd left that space even more quickly. It only had two doors: one leading to the monastery, which he had yet to be given permission to visit, the other to the square outside. He dreaded to think what would happen if a crowd of people followed him out of the baptistery and the hordes in the square noticed. So this was yet another place to be avoided.

The basilica was still his best option if he wished for a change of scenery and some stimulation. It was also a magnificent space in which to pray. Galen spent many hours facing the main altar from his shadowy seat near the doors to the palace, debating and praying to God for further enlightenment on what it meant to be a saint and how he should behave. It had always been an added strain to try and be more saintly, to not have negative thoughts, to not be bad tempered, to not rely too much on the people around him and tie them down, to be at peace with sometimes being the conduit for a miracle and sometimes not.

Aside from that, he still watched and listened to the people around him. He had a vain hope that his family might send more letters and so he always had an ear open for speakers of Englisc. They were few and far between in these masses, although the wide diversity of peoples provided its own interest. The different languages, the different clothes, even their different scents were all fascinating.

'It's been a while since I last saw you, my young friend,' the man with the gravelly voice said as he settled just within conversation distance of Galen. He was still wearing the same cream robes, although, unlike before, his forehead was glistening with sweat. 'It's been a hot summer, no?'

'Very,' Galen said, glancing around anxiously to check whether he was noticed.

'I had no idea I was chatting to such an exalted person the last time we met.'

It was as Galen had feared and made him even check the shadows to ensure they weren't likely to be overheard. 'That is still to be determined.'

'But you don't deny it?'

'I can't really at this point. Please don't do anything to attract the crowd's attention.'

'You may rest easy. I am not one to make a scene. I prefer to work quietly from the shadows.'

'I see. And... what is it that you do?'

'Oh... this and that,' the man said, waving his right hand vaguely. 'You could say I help people out when they are in difficulty.'

'Really?' Galen was surprised because the man didn't give out a particularly philanthropic air. 'What kind of help?'

The man made a hand gesture as if weighing a bag of coins in his hand and said, 'I help them out financially.'

'You engage in usury? Here, in this most holy of basilicas?'

'Money may be the root of all evil, young man, but there's no denying you can't live without it. Even monks, or at least their monasteries, rely upon cash. And while the church can go out and beg for alms, the average subject has no such recourse.'

'That is true... but do you charge interest?'

'I am not a friend to those who need money. If you want money without that extra burden, ask those closest to you, or family. If you can't do that, then you have to go to one who charges interest. But the money that comes back is used for yet more lenders, so that everyone, including me, benefits. I really don't see the evil in that.'

Galen had to agree that it seemed fair. 'I know nothing about money, but I suppose if the interest is only as much as is necessary for the lender to keep going, then it seems fair enough. However, I understand that many of those engaged in usury charge excessive rates.'

'I doubt those who lend the money think so. It's a judgement call after all.'

Galen disagreed, but doubted the man could be convinced otherwise and Galen didn't like confrontations, so he kept his peace.

'If you recall,' the man said, 'the last time we spoke it was about the millennium.'

'Yes, I remember that.'

'Unlike the vast majority of people, you didn't seem perturbed by its approach. It got me thinking, after I discovered what you are, that you have no reason to be worried as one of God's most beloved.'

Galen had never felt that he had a better relationship with God than others. 'God is a benevolent father - He looks upon all His children with equal favour.'

'That is not church dogma,' the man said, his eyes sparking as if he'd caught Galen in a lie.

'I am aware of that,' Galen said, his voice shaking with the strain of speaking up before one who obviously was judging him. 'But I can only speak my truth.'

'Huh,' the man said, eyeing Galen with renewed interest. 'Then perhaps you are the pope's weakness.'

The monastery bell rang for Sext before Galen could even consider the man's words. Galen realised he was running late and Alcuin would be waiting for him so that they could say their prayers together.

'I'm sorry, I must go!' Galen said, springing to his feet too quickly and causing himself a surge of pain.

'Of course you must,' the man said, waving him off. 'We might continue this conversation next time.'

That sounded ominous to Galen as he made his way as quickly as he could to the stairs leading into the palace. He would have to consult with Alcuin over this.

Galen had just arrived at the corridor when he heard running. He stepped back to avoid whoever it was and a girl ran into him, knocking him into the wall.

'Help me! Help me, please!' she said, her breath coming in gasps.

Galen pushed her behind him and threw his cape over her as he backed against the wall without thinking.

'You!' a burly man cried as he turned the corner and ran up, followed by a couple of others.

'M...me?' Galen said, a tremor in his voice.

These men were warriors. There was no doubt about that, despite their clerical robes.

'Yes, you! What are you doing against that wall?'

'I... I heard running. I was getting out of the way.'

'Huh,' the man grunted as he ran a disinterested glance over Galen. 'Have you seen a girl come past this way?'

'No,' Galen said and hoped his own trembling would hide the shaking of the girl whom he could feel through his robes.

'No girl come past?'

'As God is my witness, nobody has passed by me,' Galen said, keeping his eyes fixed on the man.

The soldier sneered in disgust, then turned and said to his men, 'She must have slipped into one of the side rooms. Come on, she can't have got far,' and ran off.

Galen stood stock still, terrified that the men would come back.

The girl stuck her head out and peered around his arm. 'Can I come out now?'

'Not yet,' Galen whispered.

'You lied to those men. You did it very well.'

'I didn't lie. You didn't go past, you stopped.'

'Oh, that's very clever,' the girl said.

Galen nodded, straining his ears to hear the men. Their footsteps had gradually grown quieter and then gone altogether.

'It's hot under this cloak. I don't understand why you are wearing it.'

Galen couldn't explain that the cloak gave him comfort, as it provided a link to home and family.

'It hid you, didn't it?'

'Yes,' the girl said and surprised Galen by giving him a tremulous smile, as if she was determined to look brave. 'But we can't stay here. The soldiers will come back and what will they think if they see you still in the same place?'

'That's true. We need to get some help. Stay under the cloak and move with me,' Galen said as he set off for his room.

Alcuin would know what to do. But as Galen shuffled along while thinking about how he would explain this latest predicament to Alcuin, he was filled with doubt.

He stopped for a moment and a muffled voice asked, 'Are we nearly there?'

'Not yet.'

Galen turned and made his way back to the stairs and up to the third floor. Over the last few months he'd made a slow and detailed exploration of the entire palace. Sometimes on his own, sometimes with Alcuin or Carbo. The top floor was the quietest.

He walked down a dark corridor until he spotted a side door and pushed it open. Inside was a small room he and Alcuin had assumed was used for storage as it had several chairs piled one upon the other. The only light came from a narrow slit of a window in the corner. It was the safest place Galen could think of, so he sneaked in, pulled the door closed behind the two of them and swept back his cloak.

A charming, flushed, heart-shaped faced gazed back up at him. The girl blinked and then cocked her head to examine Galen. He felt himself blushing to be examined in such an unabashed manner by such a pretty girl.

'My name is Cara,' the girl said in a tense and breathless voice. 'Who are you?'

'I'm... I'm Galen,' he said, disconcerted by her directness.

Cara looked around and Galen noted that her trembling wasn't subsiding. 'This isn't your room, is it?'

'No, I just needed to find somewhere to stop and think.'

'You're going to think? Does this mean you'll help me?'

The girl called Cara looked both anxious and hopeful. Galen wondered why. Most people he offered his help to would laugh and turn to somebody else.

'I suppose I will help,' Galen said, so off balance, he wasn't certain his mind was working at all.

'Well, if you are going to help and you need some time to think, you'd best secure the door,' Cara said, glancing at it anxiously. Although her words were practical her face looked tense, with a touch of calculation, which, Galen supposed, was understandable. She was also well dressed, and well groomed which meant she was probably a noble.

'Oh, yes,' Galen said as he turned to the door and scratched his head. 'I suppose a wedge would work.' He grabbed the chair nearest the door and placed it tightly under the latch. 'That should do it.'

Cara nodded in approval and ran her fingers through her hair, straightening out the dusky curls which had got tangled after having been under Galen's cloak. It looked like a nervous reaction.

Galen blushed to see her so engaged and hastily looked away, examining his toes till he judged it safe to look up again. Cara was watching him with wide appraising eyes, her head tilted to the side.

'Um...' Galen cleared his throat, 'you'd better tell me who those men were and why they are after you.'

'Aren't you going to invite me to sit down first?' Cara asked.

'It isn't my room,' Galen said, thrown by the prosaicness of the girl.

'I still think you should invite me to sit. And then you should sit too. But first you should dust the chairs. I don't think anyone has used this room in a long time.'

'No, indeed.'

Galen dusted off two chairs and waited until Cara was seated before he sat down opposite her.

'Well!' Cara said and then paused. She clasped her hands tightly in her lap and said, 'I am the natural daughter of Cardinal Gui.'

'Oh!' Galen said.

Why did it have to do with Cardinal Gui?

'That dismays you,' Cara said tightly.

'The cardinal is a powerful man.'

'Oh, I like you!' Cara said and looked reassured. 'You didn't say that I was born in sin. Everyone always throws that in my face. And all I can say in my defence is that it was beyond what my mother could prevent, and until this pope came to power, hardly anyone at all minded about concubines.'

'True,' Galen murmured. 'But that doesn't explain why you were running through the palace.'

'Well, it does, in a way. You see, my father summoned my mother, and she's a dear, really she is, but she has no backbone at all,' Cara said with a sorrowful shake of her head. 'She always comes when he summons her. Only this time she should have resisted, for he had a terrible reason.'

'You?'

'Usually he doesn't ask her to bring me too, but this time he did because he wanted—' Cara paused, her bosom heaving with indignation and fear. 'He wanted to give me to a friend of his, Bishop Vecchius, as a... as a concubine!' Cara was so angry at the thought that she couldn't prevent a tear from slipping from her eye. 'And he had the nerve to say I was fortunate to find the patronage of such a powerful man. But I could tell he was lying. I think he's scared of the bishop.'

Galen was appalled by the thought of this beautiful girl being given over to a life of little more than slavery without even the security of a marriage. 'But... but surely he can't do that. The pope wouldn't allow it.'

'The pope wouldn't know. And even if he forbade it, my father and this bishop would contrive some way to achieve their own ends.'

'Have you no-one who can help? No family who can protect you?'

'My grandfather. But he knows nothing about what is happening because he lives south of Rome in a villa in the mountains.'

'Your grandfather?'

'Yes, my mother's father. He brought me and my brothers up in his home because my father didn't acknowledge us or make the least attempt to get to know us. And now, when I have some value for him, my father calls for me. I was fool enough to believe that he cared about me and wanted to get to know me better. Never have I been more betrayed by anyone. And my mother didn't do a thing to help me,' Cara said as another tear slipped down her face.

'Please don't cry,' Galen said. 'I'm sure we can come up with some solution to your dilemma.'

'Do you think so?'

'I expect so.'

Cara looked up into Galen's face with such utter faith that he'd come up with a plan that it was disconcerting.

'You mentioned brothers. Can't they help you?'

A surprised laugh was startled out of Cara. 'Of course not, they're both younger than me. Tomas has only just turned six and Julius is eight.'

'Well then, I suppose they are far too young to help.'

'Did you actually have to consider that?'

Galen gave a self-deprecating smile. 'I was making a joke.'

'Oh. Well, it was a very strange joke, for you said it without a trace of a smile.'

'It is the humour of my people. I've noticed that Romans don't understand it.'

'You aren't a Roman?'

'I'm an Anglo-Saxon. Now you surprise me, for I didn't think I looked like a Roman.'

'What's an Anglo-Saxon?'

'We come from a land far in the north. It's called Enga-lond.'

'Oh! I've never heard of it. But don't feel bad. I haven't had much of an education. I can't even read.'

'You can't?' Galen said, while reflecting that the girl must have had some education, as he could understand her Latin, despite it being heavily accented. A very charming accent, as it happened.

'There's no need to look quite so astonished,' Cara said, her colour heightened with indignation.

'I'm sorry. I'm sure there are many other things you can do.'

'Of course. I can sing and play music and dance and embroider, all things a high-born woman should be able to do.

And on top of that, I can cook and manage a great house, for my mother is no good at that either, so I have been doing it for years.'

'You sound very accomplished.'

'You're making fun of me again. Your eyes are gleaming!'

'No, I mean it. You are very accomplished, and you are very charming.'

'Now you're trying to make up to me.'

'I'm a monk. I'm forbidden from making up to women.'

Galen was aware of a twinge of conscience. He found himself powerfully drawn to this engaging girl.

'It hasn't stopped many clerics,' Cara said, and her voice trembled as she spoke.

'Temptation can be a powerful thing.'

Cara heaved a great sigh, then leaned forward as she rested her elbows on her knees, bringing her face dangerously close to Galen's. 'So, have you thought enough yet?'

'You don't have any other family in Rome you can turn to?' Galen asked, making absolutely sure.

'None at all,' Cara said with a firm shake of her head.

Galen didn't want to let Cara down, but it was quite the predicament. Although one thing was clear: if she wasn't to be captured and handed over to Bishop Vecchius, she had to remain hidden.

'I need time to think, and I need to do some investigating. I know something of Cardinal Gui, for he is always very busy in the Lateran, but I know nothing about Bishop Vecchius.'

'He's a pig.'

'No doubt he is, to even consider your father's proposal. But he must also be a powerful man for Cardinal Gui to want to offer him such a great prize as you. It would be unwise to act before we know what power that is.'

'Why?'

'Why?' Galen replied blankly.

'I don't need to know anything about any of them. I just have to escape!'

'But where to?'

'Anywhere. Maybe I'll go to your Enga-lond. It must be very far away. They'd never find me there.'

'What would you do there?' Galen asked, staring in surprise at Cara.

Did she really mean it? Did she even understand what it was like to leave not only your home and family behind, but your entire culture?

'I don't know what I would do.' Cara examined Galen thoughtfully. 'But you could take me, couldn't you? You must have family there who could help me.'

Galen stared at her, aghast. 'You must be in a great deal of turmoil to even consider such a thing. Do you really want to be so far away from your mother and your brothers that you will never see them again?'

'I'm not likely to see them again if I get taken away by Bishop Vecchius,' Cara said, her voice tinged with panic. 'All in all, I'd much rather go away with you.'

'The thing is, the pope wants me to stay here. I can't go back to Enga-lond.'

'Oh.'

Galen nodded and rubbed his hands over his eyes as he tried to think. 'I need time.'

'You could hide me in your room,' Cara said with a snap of her fingers as the idea came to her.

'What?!' Galen jumped at the shock of that outrageous suggestion.

'They'd never think to look for me there, would they?'

'I suppose not. But how would it look if anyone ever found out about it? They'd think you were my concubine.'

Cara suddenly smiled and said, 'I don't think I'd mind that.'

That made Galen's eyes open all the wider. 'We can't do that because I share my room with another monk.'

'Oh, well, that would make it impossible then,' Cara said. 'Then I'll just stay here.'

'In this room?'

'It doesn't look like anyone is using it at the moment.'

'But what will you do, sitting in this room all day on your own?'

'I'm sure I'll think of something. And I hope I won't be alone all the time, for someone will have to bring me food and keep me company sometimes.'

Galen felt as if he was rushing headlong down an unfamiliar path. No, he was being pushed down it. 'I'm not sure I like this idea.'

'I do. I can wedge the door shut and we can invent a secret knock known only to the two of us, so I only let you in,' Cara said, warming to the idea. She saw Galen's dubious look, took his hand and looked imploringly at him. 'Please.'

All of Galen's resistance crumbled as this lovely girl turned her deep brown eyes on him. 'Alright, we can give it a try, although heaven alone knows how I'm going to find food for you.'

'You will come up with a plan,' Cara said.

Galen felt utterly defeated by her belief in him. There was no way he could do anything but go along with all she asked for.

Galen hurried back to his room, his mind seething with thoughts of how he'd get Cara out of her predicament and how he got himself into this mess. Alcuin would know what to do, but his steps slowed as he approached their quarters.

It wasn't Alcuin's mess and it wasn't fair to add this to Alcuin's already sizeable burden. Galen was filled with a resolve to deal with this himself and not involve Alcuin as he invariably did. Perhaps that way, if things turned out badly, Alcuin would be protected through having known nothing. Would anyone believe that? Galen hoped so.

The second problem was how he would get food and drink for Cara. He didn't like the idea of her stuck in that little room all on her own, but for now, it seemed to be the safest place for her. Galen's never very fast pace slowed as he approached the door. Carbo was sitting on the floor to one side, weaving a basket. That was typical of him. He liked to keep himself busy, and he frequently complained that Alcuin and Galen didn't give him enough to do.

'Brother Galen,' he said, turning as he heard Galen's approach. 'I missed you for our prayers.'

Oh dear, he'd been so distracted by Cara he'd completely forgotten about Sext. 'Was Alcuin worried?'

Carbo shook his head. 'He went out to visit the stained glass workshop that's making the pope's window. He's not saying much but I think he's proud to have his design chosen.'

'Ah...' Galen was relieved he wouldn't have to do any explaining to Alcuin, for he would be harder to evade. Besides, his baser instincts told him, this was an opportunity.

'Carbo,' Galen said, a plan starting to form. 'Could you... could you give me some money?'

'You need money, Brother? Why?'

This was what he had no answer to. 'I... I wanted to buy some food.'

Carbo's frown deepened. 'But you don't even finish what I buy for you. Don't you like the food I get? Should I bring something different? Only say the word and I'll make the changes. I have failed in my duty as your servant for bringing you what you don't like.'

'No.' Galen was uncomfortable whenever Carbo called himself a servant. He didn't like the shift from equals to this. 'No, the food is delicious.'

'But why do you want more?'

'It... it isn't for me.'

'Who then? Why don't they have food of their own? Is somebody trying to bully you, Brother? I knew I should go with you when you wander around.'

'No one's coercing me,' Galen said, trying to keep his voice low, because he didn't want anyone to overhear them.

'Are they trying to prey upon your kindness? Is it a beggar or some hard-up pilgrim?'

'No,' Galen snapped, then gasped. It wasn't like him to lose his temper. 'Please Carbo. Don't ask any questions and just give me some money.'

'Is it really food you're after?' Carbo asked, looking hurt. 'You haven't got into trouble, have you?'

Galen shook his head and said, 'It really is food, honestly.'

'In that case, I'll get it for you. Roman shopkeepers are a rough bunch. You will have difficulty dealing with them, especially as their Latin is atrocious.'

Galen didn't want to argue any further, especially since the thought of trying to go shopping was intimidating. It seemed his newfound courage was severely lacking. Galen gave an accepting nod and said, 'Aside from that, have you ever heard of a Bishop Vecchius?'

'Bishop Vecchius?' Carbo said, rubbing his head as he considered. 'The name doesn't ring any bells.'

'Could you ask around about him? Discreetly.'

Carbo's already unsettled expression grew grave, but he nodded. 'I'll see what I can do.'

'Thank you.' Galen took a deep breath for courage and added, 'Please keep this between the two of us.'

'You don't want Brother Alcuin to know?' Carbo said, looking doubly shocked.

'Not yet. Please promise me you'll say nothing to anyone about this.'

'As it's you, Brother Galen, I will. But in return you must promise that if you get into trouble, you'll tell me.'

Relief flooded Galen to have won this concession. 'Thank you.'

'Thank you for what?' Alcuin asked as he rounded the corner from the stairs that led to the palace's front door. 'What have you been up to, Galen?'

'Alcuin,' Galen said and felt his face flush. He prayed his friend had only heard the last part of what he'd been saying. 'How was your day?'

'Fascinating, look!' Alcuin said and held up a tiny golden square as he stepped into the room, turning to wait for Galen to follow him in. 'I visited a glass factory today to see how they make coloured glass. Turns out they make mosaic tiles. They're called tesserae, by the way. Look, it's two sheets of glass with the gold leaf sandwiched between them. See how it glows,' Alcuin said, holding it up to the light. 'It's more iridescent than if you just stick the gold leaf straight onto the wall.'

'So it is,' Galen said, marvelling at this remarkable square glittering in the sun as Alcuin tilted it this way and that.

'How about you?' Alcuin asked. 'What have you been up to?'

It was typical of Alcuin to not forget a question. 'Oh, the usual. People watching in the basilica.'

Today this was a useful lie. He would be going back to Cara, but Alcuin would assume he was still going to the basilica and wouldn't question his absence.

Practising deception against his friend filled Galen with guilt. Still, he was trying to do this for the best, or so he told himself while a barely acknowledged voice deep in his heart wondered if there wasn't something more to the lengths that he was going to, to conceal Cara's existence from Alcuin.

Chapter 15

It took all of Galen's self-control to wait until the middle of the following morning before he dared risk seeing Cara again. He had to check in on her and make sure she was safe. He also needed to take her food, and for that he had to find Carbo.

He'd no sooner had that thought than he spied Carbo coming up the stairs. They met before his and Alcuin's room and Carbo held out a rough sack.

'Are you sure you want to do this?' Carbo said.

'I am certain. Thank you,' Galen said as he took hold of the sack which felt quite heavy. It seemed Carbo had made sure to get plentiful supplies. 'Do you think you can also get me a chamber pot?'

Carbo's head jerked back and he said, 'Seriously? What is going on? Are you setting up house?'

'No questions, please. I will explain when I can.'

'It's going to need a truly amazing explanation,' Carbo said, shaking his head at Galen, but he gave a deep sigh at the same time and muttered, 'I'll see what I can do.'

'I am truly grateful, Carbo.'

'Is there anything else?' Carbo said in a voice that implied there had better not be.

'This is all,' Galen said and nodded that Carbo should leave.

He didn't want the big man to see where he was going, while wondering how the man would feel if he asked for even more food in the future. Thankfully, Carbo accepted his dismissal and stomped off back the way he'd come. Galen wondered whether he'd tarnished the big man's impression of him. Would that be bad? Perhaps not.

There was no time to lose, so Galen hurried through the palace and up the stairs to the top floor, his senses on high alert. He was worried that Cara might have vanished. Some might consider that to be a good thing, but only if she'd decided to leave herself, not if she'd been discovered and hauled away.

That thought made him so anxious his hand was shaking as he reached the room., He double checked that the corridor was empty and knocked on the door in their agreed pattern. He almost couldn't breathe as he waited in an interminable silence for Cara to respond.

'Brother Galen, is that you?' Cara whispered.

'Yes, it's me. Hurry and let me in.'

'Brother Galen!' Cara cried as she flung open the door and rushed into Galen's arms. 'I feared you'd abandoned me!'

He tried to sidestep her, but Cara closed in on him and hugged him.

'Cara, you're not supposed to touch monks!' Galen said, pushing her away. 'And quickly, get back inside. People might see us out here.'

'I'm sorry,' Cara said as she backed into the room and waited for Galen to come inside before she reinstated the wedge under the door.

'Food,' Galen said and put the bag down on a table that Cara must have unearthed from amidst the rest of the furniture. There was also now a neat row of chairs along the far wall. 'I hope you haven't been bored. It looks... it looks like you've been doing some tidying.'

'I'm not very good at just sitting around, so I've organised things. That's where I slept last night,' Cara said, pointing at the row of chairs. Then she reached into the bag and took out a loaf of bread, an entire cheese and two large amphoras of wine. 'Goodness, this is a lot!' Cara plopped herself down before the table and took an enormous bite out of the loaf. 'Mmm, it's so good! I'm so hungry I could eat it all, especially since I haven't eaten in days.'

'Not in days? Why not?' Galen lowered himself onto a facing chair, all the while cursing himself for not having known this sooner and leaving Cara the whole day with nothing.

'I was fasting in protest. It worried my mother to the point of tears, but it didn't move my father's heart in the least. Have you seen him, by the way? Does he look worried or angry that I've disappeared?'

'No, I haven't seen him,' Galen said with a shudder.

Just imagining Cardinal Gui angry was enough to leave Galen feeling sick.

'I'll bet he's grinding his teeth. He always grinds his teeth when he's enraged.'

'Then I don't think I'll try and see him.'

'Were you going to?' Cara asked with interest.

'Well no... that is, not immediately.'

'So, have you thought up a plan yet? Do you know what you are going to do?'

Galen had spent a sleepless night trying to come up with a plan and, frankly, thought he deserved more congratulations than he was getting for having organised breakfast.

'I'm going to try to find out more about Bishop Vecchius.'

Cara sighed but gave an accepting nod. 'Very well. I shall wait here, but I must have something to do. You'd better give me your cape.'

'My... my cape?' Galen was utterly lost over what she could possibly mean.

'To mend, silly. It's very ragged. I don't understand why you've been allowed to wander around the palace in such a threadbare and torn cape.'

Galen looked down at his cape and supposed it did look bad. 'It has been through rather a lot.'

'And nobody has given you a new one?'

'Um... no.'

Carbo had arranged for new habits, and had had their old ones mended by the nuns at the laundry. It was just that Galen wasn't willing to part with the cloak his father had given him, not even to have it washed and repaired. 'I'm sure we would have been given new cloaks if we'd asked, but... we never have.'

'We?'

'Alcuin and me. We travelled from Enga-lond together. We're from the same abbey.'

'So he's a friend of yours?'

'He is.'

'Then perhaps I can meet him.'

'No!' Galen said and felt shame over his actions all over again. He didn't want this charming girl to meet his handsome friend and, he realised with that thought, not just because he wanted to keep Alcuin from any scandal. 'The... the fewer people who know where you are, the safer you'll be. And another thing... you mustn't come rushing out of the room when I arrive. It's far too dangerous.'

'Very well, then I won't. As long as you get me some needles, pins and twine. Oh! And a pair of scissors so that I may mend your clothes.'

'But I need my clothes. I have nothing else to wear.'

'You don't need the cloak. You can leave that with me first, then I'll come up with a plan so that you can give me the rest.'

'But you don't have the needle and thread yet,' Galen said.

'I can use it as a blanket in the meantime. It was cold last night.'

Galen decided it was wisest not to argue, so handed over the cape, while kicking himself for not realising Cara would get cold. He really wasn't any good at looking after others.

'Is there anything else you need? I've already asked for a chamber pot.'

'That's good, because I had to sneak out last night to do my business.'

That sounded dangerous, and Galen could only thank God that Cara wasn't discovered.

'I should go, and leave you to finish your meal,' Galen said.

'Must you leave immediately?' Cara said, resting large, dismayed, beautiful eyes on Galen.

'I can't stay too long or people will wonder where I've gone, and I can't arouse suspicion or that will put you in danger. But I promise I'll be back shortly.'

'Really? Sometime today?'

'If I can get the things you need, then yes, I'll return today,' Galen said and felt even worse seeing Cara's mournful expression. 'I will try my best to get back to you quickly.'

Galen hurried away, filled both with a sense of relief to be away from such temptation as Cara presented and a feeling that he wanted so badly to be back in the room with her. He liked her lively, pragmatic nature just as much as he liked her face. Most seductive of all, he liked the way she treated him like a man, one who could help her. It was a new and exhilarating experience and left him determined he wouldn't let Cara down.

Carbo was at his now familiar post by the door, having made considerable progress on his basket when Galen got back to their room. He'd confessed to Galen that he was selling them to a man in the abitato and putting the money towards their living expenses.

'Not that I need to, mind you. Piccardo gives me more than enough to keep body and soul together. But I like being independent. Who'd have thought this humble skill that I learned at my abbey could be put to such use in Rome?' Carbo had said.

'Is Alcuin in?' Galen asked and felt immediately deceitful, because he didn't want Alcuin to overhear what he was about to ask.

'He went back to the glass factory,' Carbo said.

'I see,' Galen said and sat down beside Carbo, resting his back against the wall. It only felt slightly cool. Summer had been long and hot, but autumn was heading in now, although he hardly noticed. Galen's mind was preoccupied by how he could help Cara. It was dangerous that she was Cardinal Gui's daughter, since that man was out to unseat the pope. If a man the pope was considering as a saint got entangled with the cardinal's daughter, how useful would that be for the cardinal?

A quiver of fear shot through Galen as he realised Cara could be a trap. If Alcuin knew about her, he'd most certainly be suspicious of her.

'Oh, how fortuitous,' he'd say at his most sarcastic. 'She just landed up needing your help?'

Galen shuddered at the thought and yet couldn't bring himself to believe ill of Cara.

'Are you alright, Brother?' Carbo asked, eyeing him anxiously. 'You're not coming down with a fever, are you?'

'I'm fine,' Galen said, and steeled himself for he was doing this for Cara. 'Can you sew, Carbo?' Galen had never felt more deceitful and less like a saint than he did now, and he could feel that his face was flushed with his shame.

'Sew? That's one thing I can't do. My fingers are too thick and clumsy.'

'Ah well, in that case, could you get me some needles and thread? I need to patch up my cape.'

'The nuns at the laundry can also do that for you, Brother.'

'I prefer to do it myself,' Galen said, feeling like he was sinking deeper and deeper into guilt. His behaviour was a puzzle even to himself.

'If that is what you wish,' Carbo said.

'Thank you,' Galen said, grateful that Carbo wasn't questioning him. He felt like the man was holding back, rather than believing him. Perhaps that was because of his guilty conscience. 'It's a good thing you ordered extra clothes for us, too,' he said, almost in a panic at his deceitfulness and spewing nonsense because of it. 'That way I can wear one habit not only when the other is being washed but also while the other is repaired.'

Carbo just grunted, as if he could tell those thoughts weren't worth responding to.

'I asked around about that Bishop Vecchius fellow.'

'Really? What did you discover?' Galen said, surprised at how quickly Carbo had worked.

'He's trouble,' Carbo said, his eyes darkening.

'Why? What did people say?'

'They didn't say anything, that's why I know he's bad. Everybody I asked just shook their heads and told me to stay away from him. If I persisted, they actually walked away, as if people were distancing themselves from me, just in case.'

'Dear God!' This was more serious than Galen had feared.

Galen was so sunk in worries of how he could help Cara that he barely noticed that he'd already arrived at her door. He had to be more careful, he thought, as he looked around. Thankfully, there was nobody in sight. This upper level seemed to be much quieter, but with the type of enemies he now had in Gui and Vecchius, even if they didn't know of his role in their current dilemma, he couldn't be seen doing something unusual, or forming a routine that people would notice.

Cara seemed happier to see him today even than yesterday. It made Galen feel good, even as he worried about what Alcuin would think and whether Cara might be a trap.

'Thank goodness you've come,' Cara said as she reached through the door, grabbed a handful of his habit and pulled him inside.

'Are you alright?' Galen asked, instantly worried.

'I'm fine now,' Cara said, beaming up at him. 'I was just bored and worried. That probably sounds strange. You'd think you can't be bored when you're worried, but I was. And with nothing to do, I was even more restless for I couldn't prevent my imagination from going to all the worst places.'

'I can help with that,' Galen said and held out the sewing paraphernalia Carbo had handed to him in a surreptitious way that had looked awkward and would have drawn Alcuin's attention if he'd been around.

'Wonderful,' Cara said, clapping her hands. 'I'll get to work on your cloak right away.'

She skipped to the row of chairs she used as a bed and shook out the cloak that had been folded at one end.

'I spent some time marking all the bare patches, tears and holes, so I know exactly where I want to start. Now you have to tell me everything that you did since yesterday,' Cara said, looking up from arranging the cloak, thread and needles.

'What I did?' Galen said as he settled opposite Cara, unable to take his eyes off her expressive face.

'Yes, tell me about your day. What do you usually do? Monks live very ordered lives, don't they?'

'Normally we do. Alcuin and I have been trying to maintain that pattern as much as possible,' Galen said and gave a short version of his daily activities. Then, because it was something he had to discuss with Cara, he added, 'I found out about Bishop Vecchius yesterday.'

'But you already know he is a pig for I have told you so,' Cara said, her mouth halfway towards the black thread that she snipped through with her teeth.

'Well, yes, I know, but now I understand better why you think so. Have you ever met him?'

Cara gave an eloquent shudder but shook her head. 'I had him described to me. He is quite old, you know.'

'So I have heard.'

'But now you know more and it strengthens your resolve to help me, no?'

'It does,' Galen said and tilted his head, considering.

Then he pulled his book out of his robe, riffled through it till he found the page he wanted, uncorked his horn of ink and started writing.

'What are you doing?' Cara asked, leaning over her work to get a better look.

'I've been making notes of the different ways in which people speak Latin. Yours is very good. It isn't as debased as most Romans, but now and then you use an expression or word order that is unfamiliar to me.'

'And you write it down?' Cara said, her eyes widening in surprise.

'Grammar and words are interesting to me.'

'They may be, but you are wrong about one thing. You say the Romans have debased Latin, but it is your Latin which is surpassing strange. And you have a funny accent,' Cara said, delivering a final, indisputable fact.

Galen wanted to burst out laughing, and even give her a hug for being so adorable.

He clenched his fists to restrain himself and said, 'You are right, of course. The Latin of my lands is new. The Hibernian monks maintained Latin after the Romans left Enga-lond, and my people only took it up again a long time after that. That being the case, you could argue it is we who have debased it. But you could equally say that we are the ones, taught by the Hibernians, who still speak Latin in its purest form.'

'I couldn't. I know nothing about reading and writing.' Cara stopped to consider the matter, her eyes running over Galen's book. 'Could you teach me how to read?'

'I can.' Galen was pleased there was something he could do for Cara, and something that would be easy for him to do. 'And once you can read, I can give you some books to help you pass the time here.'

'So it doesn't take long to learn to read then?'

'Not very long,' Galen said, although he doubted they'd be together long enough to do more than introduce the basics.

'Good, because I don't want to stay in this room for much longer.'

'Ah... the thing is, Cara, I haven't been able to find a solution to your dilemma yet.'

'Neither have I,' Cara said with a sigh as she rested her hands on her knees, the right one gripping the threaded needle as she stared into space. 'I daren't step out of this place lest my father's men see me, and aside from sending my grandfather a letter begging for rescue, I don't know what to do.'

'Well then, perhaps we should write a letter. But how will we get it to your grandfather?'

'My grandfather usually sends his letters via the tradesmen that go between Rome and our home. If they're very important letters, though, he gives them to some of the lesser noblemen who also go back and forth to Rome. But I think the merchants demand money for carrying the letters, and the nobles, well, they're clients of my grandfather's, so this is a way they can pay him back.'

'Still... a letter would be a good idea. I'll bring some parchment this afternoon and we can compose something together. After that, I can start teaching you how to read. By the way... what is your grandfather's name?'

'It's Bonacorso, Lord Bonacorso.' Cara said.

The confirmation of Cara's nobility didn't come as a surprise. She had the bearing of a noblewoman, and some of what she'd said had implied a degree of wealth for her family. Still, it was useful for that to be confirmed.

Galen never felt guiltier about what he was doing with Cara than when he spoke to Alcuin. It gave him new insight into how Alcuin must have felt when he fell in love with Emma. The only solution for his guilt was to get Cara to safety as quickly as possible. Then he could go back to his ordinary life.

Getting Cara to safety, though, was more difficult than he'd thought it would be. He couldn't tell Alcuin and Carbo because he didn't want to get them into trouble. It was no use knowing that they wouldn't mind, and that they would be upset that he hadn't told them.

He couldn't tell Piccardo or the pope because he worried about what they'd say about him hiding a young woman away and what they would do to Cara. They might use her for political ends or hand her back to her father. It wasn't worth taking the risk. The same held for anyone else neutral.

There was the convent nearby that did their washing. They might take Cara in and hide her. Many a nunnery had been used by women fleeing persecution. But even they couldn't be trusted. Not if they owed allegiance to Cardinal Gui. Or even if they simply feared him.

To know how much of a danger Cardinal Gui and Bishop Vecchius were, Galen needed to know more about them. But that was no simple task. Even with this, he had to be discreet lest word got around that some unknown person was asking after the two men.

Heaven help Galen if Gui put two and two together and realised the one asking was the monk the pope was considering making a saint. Gui didn't like the pope and Galen had heard that he was doing his own research into who was behind the miracle that occurred near the Colosseum. Galen didn't care what the man thought of him, whereas in the past he'd have felt inadequate. He supposed that showed growth on his part.

Having come to that conclusion, and because he had a letter to deliver, Galen made his way to Piccardo's office. He wouldn't tell him about Cara, but the pope's secretary was a discreet man, so he was probably the best to ask about Bishop Vecchius in general and his connection to Cardinal Gui.

'Piccardo, may I come in?' Galen said as he tapped at the secretary's half-open door. In the past it would have taken him days to work up the courage to come to this point, but now he had a greater need that pushed him to not waste time. 'May I ask you a question?'

Piccardo looked up from the pile of papers he was working through methodically and said, 'Brother Galen, you are always welcome. What can I do for you?'

Galen felt doubly guilty because over the last few months, he had found that the reserved Piccardo treated him with extreme respect and now he was taking advantage of that.

'I have a favour to ask, and I wish to find out about somebody.'

'Indeed, a favour? Well, I owe you a lifetime of favours so let's hear it.'

'I was wondering whether you knew a certain Lord Bonacorso?'

Piccardo stared off into the distance in deep thought and looked like he was working his way through a mental list of names.

'Ah yes,' he said after an uncomfortably long silence. 'His daughter is Cardinal Gui's concubine. Although he rarely comes to Rome, so I have never met the man. Why?'

'I need to send him a letter,' Galen said, while keeping his hands tightly clenched in his lap.

'A letter? But why?'

'Please... please don't ask me that. Or mention it to anybody else. Not yet.'

Piccardo arched a sceptical eyebrow at Galen and said, 'If you are in some kind of trouble... If Cardinal Gui—'

'I know,' Galen said hastily. 'I know you would help. This is just... it's something I must do on my own. I have the directions on the letter,' Galen said, handing over the folded and sealed missive. 'It's urgent. How long do you think it would take to get there?'

Piccardo's fingers ran along the edge of the letter as his brow beetled into deeper thought while examining the directions. 'No more than five days.'

'Five days?'

'Two if I send it via a messenger on horseback.'

Galen blinked at Piccardo, touched that he would make such an effort for him. 'There's no need to hurry.'

Although Galen wasn't sure that was true, he didn't want to cause even more upheaval. He was already working out that, at best, Cara's grandfather might get back to them within seven days, hopefully ten at the most. It depended on the urgency he felt over his granddaughter's situation.

'Oh... yes, I asked for a reply to be sent via you. I have not put my name in the letter. I'm sorry, I know that sounds like I am taking advantage of you.'

'On the contrary, at least you are taking precautions, which I find reassuring.' Piccardo sounded tired and a little disappointed. 'Was there anything else?'

Galen thanked God for Piccardo's forbearance that meant he wouldn't interrogate him further. But... was it wise to mention anyone else now? And if not now, when would he have such a situation again?

So, gathering his courage, Galen asked, 'Are you familiar with a certain Bishop Vecchius?'

'Vecchius! Why in all that is holy would you want to know about that raddled old man?'

The description of the bishop alarmed Galen. Despite what Cara and Carbo had told him, Galen had still held on to a slight hope that the bishop was a reasonable person, one Galen could go to with representations for Cara. That hope died with Piccardo's words.

'I just... I was curious.'

Piccardo eyed him sceptically, and Galen, knowing how his face gave him away, fixed his eyes on the motes of dust shining and twirling through the light which pierced the patterned shutters of the secretary's office and tried to think of nothing at all.

'Have you got yourself into trouble, Brother Galen?' Piccardo asked.

'No! That is... I'm fine, really. Why would I be in trouble?'

'Because you asked about Bishop Vecchius and only people who are in trouble speak of the bishop at all.'

'Oh?'

'You don't know who he is, do you?'

'I've only heard his name mentioned.'

'You must hear many names mentioned in the palace. Why come to me over this one?'

Galen stared helplessly at Piccardo, desperate to keep his secrets and not involve this man. 'Please... don't ask me, just... please tell me what you know of him.'

'Ah, Brother Galen, I owe you an unpayable debt for saving my wife and son so, on the one hand, I'm willing to tell you all you want to know. On the other hand, I owe it to you to keep you safe. Telling you about Vecchius, or worse, leading you into the bishop's clutches, would be the worst thing I could ever do to you. But as you ask, I'll tell you. At least promise me you won't get yourself involved with the man.'

'I won't,' Galen said and meant it.

He didn't want to go near anyone Piccardo obviously thought so dangerous.

Piccardo sighed. 'I suppose I've done what I can to warn you. Bishop Vecchius is involved in usury.'

'But that's not allowed,' Galen said, although less surprised by this than he might have been, were he freshly arrived at the Lateran.

'It isn't allowed, but Vecchius is a wily old devil. He's developed methods of lending his money and getting it back with an exorbitant interest in such a way that he hasn't been caught. His corruption has spread its foul tentacles to some of the most respected and influential men in the Holy See. At some point, nearly everyone seems to fall into financial difficulties. It is also rumoured that he had a hand in financing the antipope, John, and may even have been involved in the death of Pope Gregory. I'm relieved to hear that you knew nothing about the bishop's money lending. At least you weren't wanting to see him because you're short of cash.'

'You give Alcuin and me more than enough, via Carbo, and we are both very grateful for your consideration,' Galen said.

Piccardo nodded. 'The bishop's usury is the least of what he's involved in. I have heard rumours, His Holiness and I are yet to confirm, that he is also involved in trafficking people.'

'But slavery is entirely legal,' Galen said, looking puzzled.

'I don't mean the trade of slaves. I mean the kidnap and sale of free young women. Sometimes to order.'

'Dear God in Heaven!' Galen was overcome with dizziness while he contemplated what this meant for Cara. 'He sounds... he sounds very dangerous indeed.'

'He is the kind of man Pope Sylvester is trying to eradicate, but his political power makes it difficult. With so many in the church hierarchy beholden to him financially or through blackmail—'

'Blackmail?'

'Think, Galen. Even if all you did was borrow money from this man, you broke the law. You could then be blackmailed, even after you'd paid the money back, lest your secret came out. That is, if you can even repay the bishop with the extortionate rates he charges. Who knows what he gets his most desperate debtors to do in a vain attempt to pay him back? That's not to mention if the man under the bishop's thumb were involved in the more sordid trade in women and girls, well... his career, not to mention his life, would be over.'

'Oh yes, of course. So Bishop Vecchius is also involved in blackmail?'

'Without a doubt. A powerful and very popular cardinal, one who might have reached the level of pope, is rumoured to have killed himself because Vecchius threatened to expose him.'

'He sounds like an evil man. He... he shouldn't be allowed to continue doing what he does.'

'The pope knows that, but it will be difficult to unseat him with the tentacles Vecchius has woven through the leading men of the church.'

'I see,' Galen said and wondered what he could do now. It was impossible to hand Cara over to her father, knowing what he knew. He prayed the grandfather would take action and soon. 'Thank you, Piccardo. It isn't reassuring information, but important for me to know about it.'

'Brother Galen, if something is bothering you or you find yourself in difficulty, please know that I will always stand your friend and come to your aid.'

Galen felt his face grow hot as he leapt to his feet. He felt so unworthy of Piccardo's friendship, for his entire visit had been filled with deceit, and now he was doubly worried because he was hiding the cardinal's daughter and the situation could easily be misconstrued.

'Thank you, Piccardo. I've taken up far too much of your time,' Galen said, then bowed and hurried away.

Galen had grown dangerously fond of Cara. He'd thought it was because of his innate enjoyment of spending time in the company of women. These had always been his mother and sisters and, at first, he'd felt the same with Cara. He liked nothing better than to sit beside her, taking everything in and allowing all his cares to be washed away by her voice while she sewed and chatted.

He desperately wanted to help her and had risked all to ask Piccardo to deliver his letter. It was the only way he could be sure the letter would reach Lord Bonacorso. It piled even more onto Galen's guilty conscience. Yet his need to help Cara overrode everything else. If it wasn't for that, he'd never even have asked for Piccardo's help nor considered even more extreme solutions.

One solution was so outrageous that it made him dizzy just to think about — that was for him to marry Cara. Just thinking of it made Galen realise that he didn't see Cara as a stand-in for his family or some sort of younger sister, but as something even more important. He dismissed the idea instantly, frightened that it had occurred in the first place, but clear that this wasn't his calling. Even so, at night he lay awake staring at the ceiling, plagued by doubts.

Marriage would solve one problem. If Cara was his wife, she couldn't be given directly into sexual slavery to another. But it would bring a host of additional problems. Most obviously, Galen would have to fight to keep Cara from her family, his family and even the church.

Even if he married Cara, though, he had his doubts that Cara being married would deter Cardinal Gui. He might still sell his daughter off as a concubine. Galen was miserably aware that he had no power to stop Gui from getting his evil way.

How would Cara feel about him then, if he couldn't even protect his own wife? His family would be shocked too, but perhaps the easiest to placate. His father, after all, had once asked him whether he wished to leave the church and get married.

The church, on the other hand, was the most problematic. Monks who seduced women were frequently defrocked, sometimes castrated, and usually sent away in shame. How much more severe would the reaction be if a so-called saint fell from the pedestal they'd placed him on? The thought made Galen shudder.

Still, there was no need to think about this more deeply as he was back to see Cara, and for the hour or so he spent with her, he didn't have to think about anything else. Cara, as always, welcomed him with a big smile. Galen reminded himself that Cara was probably only starved for company and would have welcomed anyone with her sunny smile, but it still made him feel special.

'I have more than usual to report today,' Galen said as he settled on what had become his chair, while Cara sat down opposite him on the row of chairs. Galen had taken to telling Cara everything. Not about his past - that felt like it didn't even exist when he was with her - but about the minutiae of his day, the places he'd been and the people he'd seen.

'I can't wait!' Cara said, clapping her hands together. 'Tell me everything.'

She really was, at heart, a joyful person.

'Well,' Galen said and paused, trying to work out what to say first. 'I have sent off your letter to your grandfather. Hopefully he'll act quickly on it and come to your rescue.'

'Yes,' Cara said, her eyes widening in thought. 'I'm sure he'll send somebody to fetch me.'

'Any day now,' Galen said with a confident nod because Cara looked less reassured by the news than he'd expected.

'What else has happened?' Cara said, smiling again and, it seemed, more interested in news about Galen than her own concerns.

'Oh... well, that history of my life that I had been writing... I handed it over to the pope.' While Galen had told Cara about his day-to-day work, he'd not explained anything about being a saint and she, thankfully, hadn't asked why he was working on such a strange commission for the pope.

'How exciting,' Cara said, clapping her hands as her face lit up. 'You must be very clever indeed!'

This was such a different reaction than he got from everyone else.

Alcuin had smiled and murmured, 'Congratulations. I'm sure the pope will be impressed.'

He had only mentioned it to Carbo in passing and the big man had expressed his fervent belief that Galen was surely very clever. Piccardo had been even more low-key, just nodding. It felt like for him it was simply something else on the long list of jobs Piccardo had to monitor.

'This is the second work I've done for the pope,' Galen said, and it was obvious he was bragging, not that he could stop himself.

'Oh... what else have you done for him? Cara said.

Galen blinked because he hadn't thought this far and suddenly realised he was about to speak about love poetry. Galen hadn't even shown the manuscript to Piero and Bosso, for he was unsure the racy nature of the poems would be appropriate, especially for one as young as Piero. How much more shocking to tell a young woman like Cara about such things.

'Um... how old are you?' he asked, suddenly more self-conscious.

Cara laughed and said, 'I'll tell you my age if you tell me yours.'

'Me? I've just turned nineteen.'

'Oh... you're older than I thought,' Cara said as she seemed to be analysing his appearance.

'That's because I'm small,' Galen muttered and felt his face grow warm. 'Now you have to tell me your age.'

'I'm fifteen,' Cara said. 'Which was why I thought my father summoned me - to bless the marriage my grandfather had arranged for me.'

Galen nodded, although he thought Cara was far too young to get married, but he'd thought the same for his sisters. Then again, noblewomen were often married off young, to secure connections with other powerful families.

Cara, in the meantime, cast sparkling eyes at him and said, 'Can you recite one of the poems to me?' as she reached across and held his hand.

Galen always avoided her touch, as his order demanded, and twisted away this time too.

'My version, the version I've memorised, is in Englisc, so you wouldn't understand it,' Galen said and then felt himself blushing at the thought of Cara hearing any kind of love poetry at all.

'I don't care, I just want to hear what you sound like speaking your own language,' Cara said. 'I'm sure it's wonderful.'

Everything she said filled Galen with exquisite joy. How could such happiness even exist?

'Alright, let me see,' Galen said, running through the poems in his head until he came to the perfect one. Thank goodness there were some poems that had little to do with love.

'This is about a poet who is lamenting that everyone thinks he should give up what he loves to do something useful.'

This poem had spoken to Galen far more than the rest, probably because he understood that situation better than most of the rest. Although, now that he'd met Cara, the poems had new and often uncomfortable meanings to him.

'Here goes:
Unrelenting Envy, reproach not my loafing life:
Why call the work of my genius wasteful song?
Is it that I don't follow the custom of the country,
seek the grubby reward of army life in my youth?
That I don't study logorrheic laws,
or prostitute my voice in the forum?
Mortal is the work you seek. I seek eternal fame,
throughout the world, forever to be sung.'

Galen stopped and watched Cara, waiting for a reaction, expecting just bemusement on hearing something she couldn't understand.

But Cara clapped her hands enthusiastically and said, 'It sounded wonderful. You have such passion when you narrate! What does it all mean?'

Galen recounted it in the Latin and Cara nodded along and at the end said, 'That's just like you, isn't it?'

'Well... I'm not a poet, although I enjoy writing poetry from time to time. I think, if anything, I'd like to be a chronicler and tell the tales of people's lives.'

'Saints?'

'Not only saints; other important people too, and maybe some of the day-to-day issues that trouble ordinary folk.'

'That's a wonderful idea,' Cara said. 'I'm sure you would do it well.'

Galen felt like he might burst from pride as he grinned so widely at Cara his cheek muscles ached. 'I hope His Holiness likes it half as much.'

'I don't see why he wouldn't.'

Galen loved Cara's uncritical, sunny attitude. It would be a terrible shame if this young woman were to fall into Bishop Vecchius's clutches, for he'd surely drive the innocence out of her.

Chapter 16

'Galen,' Alcuin said as they took the short walk back to their room from the chapel where they'd just said Terce together.

He'd deliberately waited until Carbo had left for his combat practice before saying anything, because he wanted to give Galen space to talk freely. Over the last few days there had been something different about Galen. Not the change he'd seen with Bregowine, where he'd been more at ease with the man and then happy to finally get a letter from home. No, Galen was happy, but in an awkward way.

When they'd first arrived at the Lateran, Galen had been filled with gloom and uncertainty. But a while back, it was as if he'd found some peace, yet he wouldn't discuss it with Alcuin. In fact, it felt like Galen was avoiding him, but in such a subtle way that at first he hadn't even noticed.

He'd encouraged Alcuin's outings to meet with craftspeople, saying he had his own work to do. True, he had the pope's translation, and, in between that, the letter home, and finally the work detailing his life, but Alcuin was certain there was more to it. That had been confirmed a few days earlier when he'd noticed Carbo surreptitiously slipping a heavy-looking sack to Galen who'd whipped it behind his back and hurried away.

Alcuin was tempted to ask him about it when he returned much later than usual, but his premonition was that Galen would evade the question. Since he didn't want to put Galen in an awkward position, he had merely joined him in the chapel for prayers, and then they'd gone to bed.

'Mmm?' Galen asked because they'd come to a stop in the middle of their room.

'Ah...' Alcuin said, embarrassed that he'd got too absorbed in his own thoughts. 'I'm going to visit a weaver today to see how they create their intricate patterns with thread. I can wait until you've finished your lessons with Bosso and Piero if you'd like to join me.'

Galen looked tempted for a moment, but then a shadow of an emotion Alcuin couldn't put his finger on crossed his friend's face and he shook his head.

'I should stay here and wait to hear from the pope.'

'About your life story?'

'Yes,' Galen said and blushed. 'At least His Holiness didn't make me stay in his study when he read it. It was hard enough when he read my Ovid translation with me in the room. But he might... he might have changes and corrections he wants me to make.'

'He probably realised you'd be curling up like a crisp leaf if he did the same with this work. Not that you have anything to be ashamed of,' Alcuin added hastily. 'And it's a considerably longer read so it will take two or three days to get through it.'

'I was surprised I had so much to say,' Galen said, flushing a deep red.

'It's a well written and thought-provoking read,' Alcuin said, and even though he knew Galen thought deeply on things, even he was surprised by the depth to some of his ruminations on his life and what it all meant, and what it taught him. Less surprising was that Galen's thoughts weren't entirely orthodox doctrine. Alcuin wondered what the pope would make of that. It was no wonder Galen thought he might be called upon to make changes.

'If you're not coming with me, I may as well head off straight away,' Alcuin said as he packed his new pattern book into a small sack, along with a couple of quills and a travelling pot of ink so that he could make sketches not only of the patterns he saw, but also the women hard at work.

It had taken considerably more effort to enter this domain of women than it had to see the work carried out by male artisans. If he had Galen with him, it would have been easier. Men might not warm to Galen, and sometimes judged him harshly, but women seemed to take to him almost immediately. It was as if they could see that he valued them and saw them as equals.

'Are you sure you won't change your mind?' Alcuin said, giving Galen one last chance as he made for the door.

'I'm certain, thank you,' Galen said with a smile and a nod.

'Make way, make way,' Bosso said, approaching from the other end of the corridor, 'Important Arabic language scribes coming through!'

Piero was grinning beside him and Alcuin also couldn't help laughing. He was imitating a recent guest to the palace. Usually, he and Galen had the whole wing to themselves. But for about a week a delegation from the Kingdom of Swabia had shared their wing, and the bishop representing them had his servants sweep through the halls, pushing everyone out of the way with a similar proclamation. It wasn't surprising from a powerful man, but that same bishop had been curiously tall, with stalk-like arms and possibly the same type of legs hidden under his long cassock that had made him look preposterous as he walked. Ever since, Bosso and Piero had been pushed aside, they'd started mimicking the Swabian bishop.

'Enough of that,' Galen said, his eyes gleaming in amusement. 'Come in and get some work done.'

'Of course, Brother,' Bosso said. 'What would that snobby bishop do, do you think, if he'd known he was pushing a saint out of his path?'

'I'm sure he'd be mortified,' Piero said, beaming at the idea.

'Really, enough,' Galen said with a laugh, waving the two boisterous monks in.

Alcuin watched his friend with an appreciative smile and wondered when Galen had become so comfortable with those two. He was almost able to engage in banter, and didn't even look intimidated.

Alcuin clattered down the stairs to the Lateran's front door, reflecting that Galen had grown a lot. Had he done the same? He felt as though he was more set in his ways than Galen and less willing to change. He was finding the art and craft of Rome's people fascinating, but his mind continually drifted to how he would be able to tell his brothers in Yarmwick one or other anecdote.

He sighed deeply as he wondered whether he would ever see them again. He'd become Galen's companion and support and it had changed how the world saw him. Before, he'd been Alcuin of Yarmwick, the great illustrator. Here in Rome he was Alcuin, support to Saint Galen.

Sometimes he resented that. Then he'd chide himself for being so mean-spirited. He'd fight anyone who tried to take his role as friend and support to Galen away from him, so why did he sometimes wish to rebel against the situation? It was because he was contrary, he decided, again, for this wasn't the first time he'd considered this dilemma.

'Ah, Brother Alcuin,' Piccardo said, heading into the Lateran as Alcuin headed out. 'Good morning.'

'Good morning to you too. Are you after Galen?'

'I am indeed. The pope has arranged a date for the interrogation over sainthood.'

'Oh yes, when is it to be?'

'In a fortnight. That will give Cardinal Gui sufficient time to go through all the evidence His Holiness has gathered, but not enough time to dig up or, more likely, fabricate anything against Galen.'

'Ah...' Alcuin said, his heart beating in nervous anticipation.

Once this matter of sainthood was decided it would mean change for both him and Galen, but hopefully an end to the limbo they'd been dwelling in.

'Tell me, has Galen been out meeting people?' Piccardo asked.

'Meeting people?' Alcuin said and considered. 'He frequently goes to the basilica, but aside from Bregowine, who has long since returned home, I don't think he has got to know anybody else.'

'That is also what I assumed,' Piccardo said, 'which makes me wonder all the more how he knows Lord Bonacorso?'

'Who?' Alcuin asked while searching his memory for the name.

'Lord Bonacorso, who doesn't even live in Rome, but in a town south of here.'

'I've never heard of him.'

'And yet your friend asked me to send a letter to him.'

'He did?'

'And, owing Galen as much as I do, I complied. Your reaction tells me Galen's behaviour is unusual.'

Alcuin nodded, feeling like he no longer knew Galen at all. 'I don't think he has ever lied to me or kept anything from me in the past. But lately, he has been a bit more evasive.'

'I see. Well, don't confront him about anything yet or mention that I saw you. I assume this is something he wished to do on his own. You trust your friend, don't you?'

'Completely,' Alcuin said, for that would never change. 'But I worry for him because of his innocence.'

'In that we are of one mind,' Piccardo said. 'I suppose it is a reflection of his saintliness that he gathers people who wish to protect him and who trust him without doubt.'

'I suppose so,' Alcuin said and headed off down the road that led to the abitato. He barely noticed a thing on his walk though, as he was more bemused than ever about what Galen was up to.

Galen was having a hard time concentrating on his work because his mind kept drifting to the image of Cara's face, or lingering over the things she'd said whenever they met. Nearly a fortnight had passed since he'd sent his letter to Lord Bonacorso and they had yet to get a response.

Galen worried the letter had been intercepted, or that Lord Bonacorso had dismissed it as coming from a crank. Galen had told him that his daughter was in hiding and needed his help, and that he, an unknown monk, was helping her. Did that sound credible?

If Cardinal Gui or Cara's mother were asked about the contents of the letter, they could have sent reassurances back that Cara was fine. Worse than that, they would then know that Cara was still in Rome and might increase their efforts to find her.

Because Galen worried about such outcomes, he had asked Carbo to find out more about Vecchius, who did indeed seem to have a sinister ability to keep himself out of harm's way when his machinations infected so many. But he was no nearer to discovering why Cardinal Gui was beholden to Vecchius, for surely the man had to have some sort of grip on him. Anyway, knowing what that grip was probably wouldn't be a help, for Galen had no way of offering a better alternative.

He was also running out of time. The date had been set for the hearing as to whether or not he was a saint. There was no way that he could still be keeping her company by that time.

Galen felt himself slipping into depression as he headed to his rendezvous with Cara. In fact, he felt deceit piling upon deceit and that, combined with his love for Cara, was leading to many a sleepless night. Thankfully, Cara showed no sign of seeing the disquiet she caused Galen.

'Brother Galen,' she said, giving him a glowing smile, 'I'm so happy you're back!'

'More food,' Galen said, handing over the sack. 'Carbo even managed to get some apples. They're delicious.'

Carbo had stopped arguing with Galen about this secret food buying. He'd even stopped looking disappointed in Galen. Now he was simply resigned. It made Galen feel worse.

'Oh, apples, yum!' Cara said, and her face glowed even more brightly.

She took out an apple and bit into it, giggling as the piece was too big to fit in her mouth and juice flowed down her chin.

'I was able to memorise all the letters of the alphabet,' Cara said, as she wiped her hand across her mouth. 'I think your handwriting is easier to read than any of the others I've tried.'

'So I've been told,' Galen said and tried to fix everything about Cara in his mind so he would never forget her. 'And you are an excellent student,' Galen said. 'I've taught one other to read and it took him longer.'

'Maybe that's because I have more time to practise when you're gone,' Cara said, twinkling up at Galen.

Galen nodded and said, 'But we can't remain this way and I... I may have come up with a plan, but first I have to ask you a few more questions.'

Galen wasn't even sure why he was bothering with the questions. It was obvious what he had to do, but perhaps he just needed to go through these steps.

'Ask me anything,' Cara said as she drew her legs up, pulling her bare toes in under the hem of her skirt.

'I'm not sure why your grandfather hasn't come to find you, but it seems, from everything you've said, that he does care for you, and it also sounds like he's the only one who can help us. Do you think he will?'

'I'm sure he will.'

Galen nodded. 'I was uncertain whether he had sufficient power.'

'Well,' Cara said thoughtfully, 'on his land, Grandfather's word is law. He also arranged a marriage for me with another local noble by the name of Pandolfo. That was one reason Mother could bring me here. She said my father should give his blessing to the marriage. Grandfather didn't like the idea. Cardinal Gui seduced Mother into becoming his concubine after all, but in the end, Mother won him round.'

'Do you... do you like the man your grandfather chose for you?'

Galen regretted the jealousy that filled his breast to hear of the man. He would have a lot to repent of once all of this was over.

'He seemed nice. He's young and handsome. Oh, and he has a scar across his cheek from when he was in a battle.'

'Would you mind marrying him?'

'Does that mean you won't marry me?' Cara said as she took Galen's hand.

His fingers tightened around hers as he looked away. 'Cara... I can't.'

'Why not?'

'Because... because I'm a monk, and I can't support you and I can't protect you.'

'Yes, you could,' Cara whispered as she raised his hand to her lips and kissed it gently.

'Please,' Galen said. 'Don't.'

'Don't you love me?' Cara said in a little voice.

Galen looked up into her shining eyes. 'Yes, oh yes, I love you so much it hurts. But I can't. You know I can't.'

'At any rate, we won't talk about it now, for you said you had a plan, so we should talk about that instead,' Cara said, because she'd learned not to push Galen when he was unwilling.

Galen was relieved that he wouldn't have to say out loud all the reasons he'd rehearsed over and over since he'd got to know Cara why he couldn't be with her. His resolve always crumbled when he stood before her.

'If your grandfather is a powerful man and has found a husband for you, then we should get you back home so that you may have his and your husband's protection.'

'I don't want his protection. I want yours.'

'Cara, look at me!' Galen grabbed both her hands and held them up before him. 'Can you not see how small and weak I am? Can you not see that I'm no warrior? My heart shakes in my body merely contemplating trying to get you out of Rome. I dread letting you down because I am too frail to get you all the way to your grandfather's. Can't you see that? Can't you see how useless I would be as a husband?'

'No,' Cara said.

Galen looked down at that lovely, inviting face, her lips wet and shiny from the apple juice. Her breath smelled sweet and her expression was so inviting that he felt an overwhelming urge to plant a kiss on her lips. They looked soft, yielding and smooth as silk. Passion rolled up from his heart and suffused his body, almost robbing his mind of control.

'Oh Cara!' he muttered.

It took all his self-control not to wrap his arms around her and squeeze her tightly to him. His passion burst through him like an unstoppable wave, growing and reaching his groin, which quivered in response. Blood flowed downwards, driving him on. Pain blossomed. The usual dull ache grew claws and stabbed through him. Galen screamed and collapsed into blackness.

'Galen! Galen, wake up!'

Galen blinked and looked about in confusion. Cara was slapping his cheeks, a look of terror on her face.

'I'm on the floor?'

'You passed out,' Cara said. 'Are you alright? Please tell me you're alright.'

Galen felt awful, sick and in excruciating pain, a worse pain than he'd had to deal with in a long time.

'I'm fine,' he said and forced a smile, which he hoped was reassuring.

'What happened? I don't understand.'

'It's complicated,' Galen said and hoped that he didn't faint again. He was feeling so dizzy it was making him nauseous, but he didn't want to explain to Cara what had happened, nor dismay her any more, for she clearly hadn't been convinced by his reassurances. 'I shouldn't have hidden you away for so long. I'm a monk and not supposed to associate with women.'

'Are you saying you were punished? But no, you were just helping me.'

'Not a punishment, never that,' Galen said as he gingerly pushed himself upright and prayed he wouldn't start bleeding again, because it was so painful it felt like a possibility. That would be a disaster. He forced another smile and said, 'I don't know why I never mentioned it before, and surely you could see it in me, but I'm a sickly person. I'm just ill. I'm sorry I distressed you.'

Cara clutched his hand and said, 'You won't desert me, will you, Brother Galen? You're the only friend I have.'

'Don't worry. I will stand your friend, and I will still try to help you out of your dilemma. Although, truth be told, I am at a loss to know what to do to help you. I can't understand why your grandfather has taken no action. But you've been hidden for a long time now, and maybe your father has had a change of heart.'

'Never. He'll never change his mind. You don't know him. He'll be even more vindictive now that I've evaded him for so long. He might even try to kill me,' Cara said, her voice dropping to a frightened whisper.

'I won't allow that,' Galen said with far more bravado than he felt. 'But now I really have to go. I have to do some proper thinking.'

'You will come back, won't you?' Cara said as she helped Galen to get up.

'I will never abandon you. I give you my word before God.' Galen was trying to look calm and reassuring as the world faded in and out before his eyes. God help him, he couldn't pass out before Cara again. 'Now I must go.'

Galen walked to the door, checked that nobody was in the corridor to see him leave, and gave Cara another quick smile as she shut herself back in. She looked more upset than he'd ever seen before.

The moment the door was closed, Galen buckled over with a grinding groan as he gave in to the pain. It had taken all he had not to show his weakness to Cara. Now sliding along the wall to keep himself at least on his feet, he groped his way downstairs towards his room.

'Vecchius, what are you doing here?' Galen froze at the sound of Cardinal Gui's voice coming from the hall beyond the stairs.

'I came in search of you, Gui,' a familiar, rough, gravelly voice replied.

Galen leaned forward, peeking around the wall at the bottom of the stairs.

Cardinal Gui had his back to Galen. The other man was all too familiar. Short but powerfully built, black hair peppered with grey, stubble and deep-set eyes, wearing a plain cream-coloured robe. It was the man who'd debated with him in the basilica. This was Bishop Vecchius?! Had he deliberately sought Galen out? If so, what was he after? Another pawn?

It also made no sense that this man looked normal while Gui was as hideous as before. Was it possible that Gui was even more corrupt than the deceitful, money-lending, people-trafficking bishop?

'I grow impatient, Gui. You promised me your daughter and yet I have still not seen her,' Bishop Vecchius said.

'The little fool has run away. That's the problem with leaving a woman to bring up children. Eufimia has exercised no control over her daughter and that wild girl has escaped.'

Galen's heart filled with rage to hear Cara described in this way by her own father. Any hope he'd harboured of appealing to the man's conscience evaporated with those words.

'That is not my concern. You must find her and hand her over,' Vecchius said as his tongue flicked across his lips, leaving a moist smear.

'I'm doing all I can to do just that. I have sent people back to her grandfather's house to discover whether by some chance she has managed to get back to him, especially as I took such pains to separate her from him, but with no luck. She hasn't been back.

'Lord Bonacorso asked several searching questions of my messenger and I've had reports that he also sent his own people to Rome to look into things. I know for certain that somebody contacted her mother, but she knows nothing,' Gui continued. 'I also have men posted along the road and outside the lord's house in case she goes back home and I'm making discreet enquiries at all the convents in the city to see if she has taken refuge there. But all of this takes time.'

'Time you are fast running out of,' Vecchius said. 'If I don't have my hands on that delightful young flesh by the turn of the year, then all my patience will have run out as well.'

'You have never explained to me why you want her,' Gui said, his voice harsh with irritation.

'Let's just say I need some insurance come the millennium. And I can't imagine a better way to spend New Year's Eve than blooding a virgin. So you'd better pray your daughter hasn't found herself a man to hide her who is even now despoiling my prize.'

'She isn't with a man,' Gui snapped. 'And I assure you, if she is, he will have a very short life indeed.'

'That is of no interest to me if he has already deflowered your girl.'

'Would no other virgin do you well enough? I can find you any number of them.'

'I can find those without your help,' Vecchius said disdainfully. 'What I need at the turn of the millennium is the virginal daughter of a highly placed church official. If the pope had a daughter, that would be ideal. As he doesn't, and as he appears intent on being a virtuous pope, I'm having to look lower.'

Gui's face twitched in disgust as he said, 'You're working hard to undermine his reputation.'

'Do you never feel the irony of your own words, Gui? Just who is working harder in this endeavour? And this after what you did to Gregory. But there is nothing harder to assail than a virtuous pope. However, I am making progress. The hints I've dropped that all his interest in numbers and mechanical contraptions indicates a connection to the hairy one is affecting his reputation.'

'Already I've heard whispers in the markets that he practises sorcery,' Gui said.

'There you are. Add that to devil worship and the coming millennium, and we'll quickly have him off his pedestal.'

'Let's hope you are right.'

'And let's hope you find your daughter in unblemished condition,' Vecchius said silkily as he turned and walked off.

The moment he was gone, Gui cursed under his breath and stormed off.

Galen sank onto the lowest step, his knees pressed up against his chest. He wrapped his arms around his legs, hugging himself to get the shaking under control. Added to his pain was an overwhelming sense of doom.

It had been bad enough when he'd assumed that Gui wanted his daughter to barter as a concubine, but this… what had they been talking about? Vecchius hadn't made it clear and Gui obviously had no appetite to find out.

That man, who had been circling Galen, was pure evil. Under no circumstances must Cara fall into his hands. And he was threatening the pope, too. Was there some way in which Galen could mould those two dilemmas into one? Could Vecchius do the same to him? Make use of his unguarded words in the basilica to undermine the pope? He tried to think, but his mind wouldn't co-operate. Pain shot through his legs in protest at being folded up, so Galen flopped over till he was on his hands and knees and then slowly and painfully pushed himself to his feet.

Alcuin dipped his brush into the blue paint and trailed it along the edge of a wave. He was working on a full page illumination of a ship at sea. It was more use of the blue paint that Galen had teased him about a couple of days ago. That had been an increasingly rare moment when Galen had seemed relaxed and lowered his guard.

Alcuin was still at a loss to understand what was troubling Galen, and doubly so since he'd spoken to Piccardo. The usual reasons he'd been downcast before were considered and discarded. The idea of being heralded as a saint was clearly on Galen's mind. He also missed home, and had read and reread the letter from his family every night. But there was something more. Galen was happier and yet also weighed down by guilt and less inclined to go on excursions with Alcuin or even speak to him.

What was even more infuriating was that Carbo seemed to have more of Galen's confidences than he did. Why did Galen trust Carbo and not his best friend? Alcuin had tried to tackle Carbo on the matter, but the big man had turned red, uttered something incoherent and quite literally run away. Since then, he'd been jumpy around Alcuin too.

Alcuin hated to put Galen on the spot so had been waiting for his friend to come clean. He'd believed it would only be a matter of time, but he was reaching the point where he had to say something. More because he worried about his friend and not, he kept telling himself, because he was feeling left out.

He would say something the moment Galen got back, Alcuin decided, glancing at the door. It was time he reappeared, anyway. Seconds later, Galen staggered through the door. Alcuin opened his mouth to speak, then clamped it shut. Galen was paler than Alcuin had seen in a long time.

He gave Alcuin a vague smile, probably intending it to look as though he was fine, when he was curled over more than usual. As Galen realised Alcuin was still watching him, he straightened out and walked with slow deliberation to his bed.

'What's wrong?' Alcuin asked as he swished his brush in the water to get it clean.

'Nothing,' Galen said, but his voice came out as a whisper. 'I'm just feeling a bit under the weather. A little rest will soon restore me.'

That wasn't true, Alcuin thought, as Galen cautiously lowered himself onto his bed.

'Something is wrong. You're unwell, sneaking about, sharing secrets with Carbo, keeping me from everything,' Alcuin said, his voice rising, even as he was regretting how much he sounded like a petulant child.

'No,' Galen said as he pulled the blanket up to his ears, despite the heat, and rolled over to face the wall.

'Yes.' Alcuin pushed aside Galen's obvious attempt to forestall his questioning as he stoppered his paints and crossed to Galen's bedside. 'I came upon Piccardo the other day and talked as if you were still going to the basilica, only for him to tell me that you haven't been near it in weeks. So where have you been going instead?'

Galen screwed his eyes shut and looked like he would have liked to do the same for his ears.

'You've never kept anything from me before, Galen. I don't understand what's happened. Have I done something to offend you?'

'No.'

'Then what? Remember, we're family. If you're in trouble, you know you can rely on me.'

'I know,' Galen muttered. 'There's nothing to worry about.'

'I'd like to believe that. I'm just finding it difficult when you won't speak to me, or even look at me.'

'Please, Alcuin, I'll... I'll explain eventually,' Galen said, keeping his eyes screwed shut.

It was obvious that whatever Galen was dealing with, he still wasn't ready to talk about it and, unusually, Alcuin doubted he'd be able to force it out of him. Not that, in his current condition, Alcuin would want to.

'Alright,' Alcuin said and went to get Carbo who would arrange some boiling water for them.

Alcuin had long since realised that Carbo could get far more out of the palace kitchen staff than he could. Besides, the big man lived to serve Galen.

'Is he unwell?' Carbo said as he returned, holding a pot of steaming water with a thick rag.

'I'm afraid so, and he'll want to be left alone.'

Dealing with one hurt person was Alcuin's limit, but it looked like Carbo was also suffering under a load of guilt. If he couldn't find out from Galen what was happening, Alcuin thought, as he brewed a healing tea, he was going to tackle Carbo next.

Galen was still in that miserable curled up posture Alcuin hadn't seen in a long time when he took the steaming mug over.

'Here,' Alcuin murmured. 'You might not listen to what I have to say, nor share your troubles with me, but at least drink this tea. It will make you feel better.'

'Thank you,' Galen whispered as he wiped an arm across his eyes. 'You are a true friend and more than I deserve.'

Alcuin shook his head. 'I'll remain that, no matter what's going on, and maybe you'll remember that in time and tell me what on earth has got you so filled with despair.'

Galen gave a quick nod but couldn't meet Alcuin's eyes as he pushed himself upright, struggling more than usual. He took his herbal tea and slowly sipped it.

Chapter 17

All Galen wanted was some peace and quiet and some relief from the pain so that he could think. Thankfully, Alcuin had shown truly saintly forbearance and left the room after he'd handed Galen his tea. The guilt over how he'd treated his friend would have to be dealt with later.

Now Galen had to find a way out for himself and for Cara. Despite the urgency of the matter, though, another thought kept pushing its way in. One thing had become blindingly, painfully obvious: he'd never be able to unite with a woman.

It wasn't as if he'd wanted to or planned to. In the past, he'd wondered whether the motion of love making might damage his fragile wounds. Now he'd discovered that even a powerful desire could bring him low with nausea-inducing pain.

Why would God do that to him? Why would He shut this one door so firmly in Galen's face? It was as if He'd taken all free will from Galen. He was going to be celibate, whether he liked it or not. His rage and frustration brought bitter tears to his eyes, which squeezed through his eyelids and soaked into his pillow.

It was a few hours before dawn when Galen rose. He hadn't been able to sleep anyway. Pain, fear and anger kept him up as thoughts chased one another through his mind. At least

Alcuin's tea had helped to ease his pain and take the panicked edge off his mind. Now he had a plan.

He scribbled a note for Alcuin by the light of an almost full moon, pinned it to his desk, gathered his spare habit and slipped out.

His senses were on high alert as he closed the door with infinite care so as not to make a sound and wake Alcuin. Then he stood for a moment, gathering himself, back against the door, waiting for his eyes to adjust to the almost pitch-black corridor so that he didn't accidentally trip over and wake Carbo. His guts still hurt tremendously, which made it difficult to focus, but he had no choice - both he and Cara were running out of time.

Galen was about to take his first cautious step out, feeling ahead with his toes, when he heard running. Carbo emerged out of the gloom and almost punched Galen as he made to grab the door to the room, and only realised at the last minute that somebody was standing there.

'Who the hell are you?' Carbo growled as his fist wrapped around Galen's habit and hauled him upwards.

'Wait! Carbo, it's me!' Galen whispered frantically.

'Brother Galen what are… did you hear them too? Have they already come this way?'

'Who?' Galen gasped, thankful that Carbo had at least eased, if not released, his powerful grip. 'Who are you talking about?'

'There's men lurking about these corridors,' Carbo whispered. 'Piccardo warned me to be extra vigilant. He said that accursed Cardinal Gui might try something. Looks like he has.'

'No!' Galen gasped. He was certain the men weren't after him, but Cara. 'Carbo, quickly, I need your help.'

'Well, of course,' Carbo said, finally letting go of Galen. 'You step inside, Brother, I'll take care of these miscreants.'

'No,' Galen said and laid his hand on Carbo's arm. He'd been a fool to think he could do this on his own. Especially with his body in its current state. 'There's somebody else we need to rescue.'

Although Galen was most worried for Cara's sake, he'd also realised, long ago, that if she'd been found in that little room, his involvement was bound to come out. Cardinal Gui and Bishop Vecchius would inevitably have used that fact, and Galen's dubious conduct, to bring down the pope. He couldn't allow his foolishness to lead to all of that.

'We have to hurry, Carbo!' Galen said and staggered forward.

'May the Lord have mercy upon my soul,' Carbo muttered before asking, 'Where to?'

'Upstairs,' Galen said.

His eyes had adjusted so that Carbo was now a dark lump amongst the darkness and that was probably as good as it could get in this space.

'Alright, let's go.'

Carbo took a firmer hold on Galen's arm than he usually did and hoisted him half off his feet.

It hurt so much it was all Galen could do not to cry out, but it also enabled Carbo to walk the two of them along at speed. Thankfully the big man seemed to know the palace well and he made unerringly for the stairs. The sound of footsteps could be heard coming along the corridor and then a door was opened with what sounded like great care. It squeaked and Galen recognised it as the chapel door that was beside their room.

They'd be in his and Alcuin's room soon. Galen prayed to God that they didn't do anything to Alcuin. At least they were working slowly and carefully which gave him and Carbo a chance to outpace them.

Carbo shot around the corner, his face momentarily lit a burnt orange in the light of the flickering votive candle placed on the altar at the end of the corridor. Then he plunged back into the darkness and to the stairs.

'Thankfully they haven't placed any guards here,' Carbo murmured in Galen's ear. 'But they have them at the front door.'

Galen's stomach clenched with fear to hear that as he struggled to keep up with Carbo's pace as he hauled him up the stairs.

'Where now?'

'To the corner room,' Galen muttered.

Thankfully his dread of getting caught had taken away any reticence about Carbo meeting Cara.

'Here,' Galen whispered as they reached the right door and Galen knocked in their agreed pattern. His heart felt like it was hammering even more loudly. He was aghast at the drastic action he was about to take, but he couldn't think of anything else that he could do.

'Galen, what's going on?' Cara asked, rubbing the sleep from her eyes. She was dimly lit by the lamp Galen had provided for her when she'd first arrived. 'Are you alright? Have you recovered from yesterday?'

Then she jerked back as she spotted Carbo.

'Don't worry, he's a friend, and I'm fine,' Galen whispered. It took some effort because he was so out of breath. 'But we need to go.'

'Has my father discovered my hiding place?' Cara said, suddenly anxious and peering down the dark corridor.

'I think so,' Galen said, pushing her inside as he whispered to Carbo, 'Guard the door, we'll be quick.'

'I brought you this,' Galen said and shook out a black habit.

'You got that for me? Why?' Cara asked, while at the same time she took the robe and started to pull it on over her clothes.

'Your father is searching for you in the palace and he's watching the road to your grandfather's house, but he's looking for a woman. If you put that on and keep the hood well down over your face, then you'll look like a monk, and nobody will think anything of seeing two monks on the road. I can lead you and if anyone asks, I'll tell them you've taken a vow of silence, so you won't be expected to speak.'

'That's very clever!' Cara said, her voice muffled as she pushed her head through the garment and then popped back into view. It was just as well the two of them were practically the same height. The loose-fitting garment also did a good job of hiding Cara's admittedly not very prominent curves.

Galen was unable to suppress the gratified flush at Cara's words and was glad for the darkness. 'My plan depends on you, though,' he said. 'Do you know the way back to your home?'

'But of course. It's very easy. We just take the Via Labicana out of the Porta Maggiore, and we stay on that same road up into the hills and my grandfather's town. We will have no difficulties with that.'

'Good. Then gather up the food; we have to get out of here now.'

Cara hastily packed everything into the sack and handed it to Galen. Galen flung the sack of supplies over his shoulder, while trying his best to make it look like it weighed nothing at all, and cautiously opened the door. He assumed there'd be a racket if Carbo was spotted, all the same it was best to be careful.

'Now what?' Carbo asked, his voice flat.

Galen couldn't miss the disappointment in the man's voice, along with the resignation.

'We have to get out of here, and out of Rome,' Galen whispered.

Carbo took the sack out of Galen's hands as he took his arm again. 'I assume the little miss is able to walk undertake such a long journey without assistance?'

'Yes,' Galen muttered and was glad the darkness hid his embarrassment that he was not similarly capable.

'We'll have to go via the basilica if we need to get out without being spotted,' Carbo said.

Galen nodded agreement.

'You, miss,' Carbo said, 'stick close behind me.'

It was hard to tell in the dark, but it seemed that Cara drew slightly closer as Carbo once again hoisted Galen so high that his feet barely touched the floor, and then they hurried back to the stairs. Carbo stopped at the top and listened intently before he swooped down, rounded the bend on the first landing, stopped to listen again then headed towards the stairs that would take them into the basilica. Galen prayed that they weren't locked at night.

A bell rang out into the cold night air, making Galen jerk with fright.

'It's Nocturns,' Carbo muttered, using the ringing of the bell to cover his voice.

Thank you God, Galen prayed, for now the basilica door would be open. Alcuin had told him that the basilica was opened for the hour of prayer.

'Hey!' a voice shouted behind them.

Carbo muttered a string of curses under his breath as he threw Galen over his right shoulder, then grabbed Cara around her waist and threw her over his left shoulder then ran full tilt down the stairs.

'Out of my way,' he bellowed to the guard who was stood at the bottom of the stairs, slowly opening the door, like one still half asleep.

Carbo kicked the half-open door wide with a bang that reverberated around the basilica and shouted, 'Don't let anyone through!' as he barged past the startled guard.

A row of monks was coming from the monastery through the opposite door, and a dozen or so pilgrims, who were on their knees or prostrate on the floor of the basilica, all turned to watch as Carbo, with a monk over each shoulder, sprinted to the entrance, out into the square and skidded to a halt behind a statue at its edge. He eased Galen off his shoulder while Cara hopped off.

'Made it,' he said, huffing like a charging bull.

Galen fought to get his own breathing under control as he anxiously looked about. It was hard to tell what was going on because the only lights were the two large lanterns at the entrance to the basilica.

'Where to now?' Carbo asked.

Galen was grateful that he was just accepting the current situation and seemed to be willing to follow his lead.

Chapter 18

Guiltily aware that he'd been cursing Him only a few hours before, Galen prayed his apologies and begged God to help him, Cara and Carbo get to her grandfather's house. They hurried through the disabitato to the Via Labicana and from there, the short distance to the Porta Maggiore. The lightening of the sky was the only indication of the approaching dawn, yet the streets were already alive with merchants getting their produce into the city for a day of trading.

It was therefore easy to slip through Rome's Porta Maggiore against the traffic flowing in. The sight of two monks barely registered with the guards, although they did pause to take in the burly servant. But overall, the guards were more interested in inspecting and taxing incoming goods.

The crowd of vehicles and people heading towards the city, some carrying great baskets on their backs, some with laden carts or pack mules, remained heavy till midday when it started to thin as they increased their distance from Rome.

It was strange to Galen how it could still be so hot in autumn. Grasshoppers created a lethargic buzz that rose from the sunbaked grass all around them and filled the valley. It was a distinct contrast for Galen, who was used to almost permanently green fields. Here, the lack of summer rain left the land parched and the grass bleached to a straw-like colour while the leaves of the shrubs and trees took on a deeper green hue that was now starting to turn brown.

When she thought there were no people about, Cara grumbled under her breath about the fact that the robe, with its hood pulled up, was unbearably hot.

'Where did you get it?' she asked.

Galen bit his lip guiltily and said, 'It's one of mine. The spare I have for when the other is being washed.'

'I'm wearing something of yours?' Cara said, and the white of her teeth flashed in the shadow. She tilted her head to sniff the hood and said, 'It smells like you.'

'I'm sorry. I'm sure you'll get used to it eventually,' Galen said.

'I like it,' Cara said, as she wrinkled up her nose in that charming way of hers.

Despite the agony he was in, and the fact that Carbo was half carrying him and therefore listening in to this conversation, Galen couldn't prevent himself from smiling back which, as Cara couldn't see him, went unnoticed. He was trying to act brave but, while it was a relief to escape that tiny room, Galen was jumpy. He was terrified they'd be discovered or chased down at any moment.

He scanned the faces of everyone they passed to check their expressions. They must have looked out of place, but the passersby barely gave them a first glance, never mind a second. He also searched the faces of anyone who looked to be loitering on the side of the wide Roman road.

There were few people. Some farmers with their wares laid out on straw mats for passing traffic to look and buy, children from nearby villages playing, the odd cart or train of mules heading to Rome and, once, a monk standing as still as a post at a quiet intersection. But nobody looked like they might be a soldier or henchman of Cardinal Gui. Not that Galen knew what a henchman would look like, but all seemed safe enough.

'I think we should stop,' Carbo said as it approached late afternoon.

It was the first time he'd said anything. Galen had worried at first that Carbo would tell him off for his wildly inappropriate behaviour and order him back to Rome. Or at the very least, demand an explanation and grumble about what Galen was doing. He was convinced he'd deeply disappointed the big man. Perhaps that was also why he'd not said a word all day.

'I think I can keep going,' Galen murmured.

Carbo turned sharply to glare at Galen, examining his face minutely.

But before he could say anything Cara said, 'Galen, my legs are getting tired and my feet are killing me. I'm certain I've developed blisters.'

'Oh,' Galen said, giving Carbo a guilty look. Had the big man realised that Cara needed a rest too? 'Well, I suppose we can stop here.'

Galen was more relieved than he was going to show that Cara also wanted to take a break. He felt as though he was stumbling along. After the attack that brought him low, a sleepless and interrupted night, and a longer walk than he'd taken in a long time, he was struggling but unwilling to stop before the girl did.

'Are we going to spend the night in a hostelry?' Cara asked.

'We can't.'

Galen's mind boggled at the idea of walking into an inn with a young woman dressed as a monk. They were ignored on the road when everyone was going about their own business, but hostelries were places of rest where people shared stories to pass the time. They would wonder about two monks and their mountain of a servant showing up and would ask far too many awkward questions.

'Why should we not?' Cara asked, sounding plaintive for the first time on their journey. 'Plenty of monks and priests stay at hostelries, you know.'

'I don't have any money.'

'You went out without money?' Cara said and turned wide, amazed eyes upon him.

Galen hadn't even considered taking money with him. People were usually willing enough to provide alms when a monk asked for it.

'Keep your head down,' Galen hissed and looked about quickly to make sure they hadn't been spotted.

'We aren't going to stay in a monastery, are we? Because I couldn't deceive them there.'

'I didn't think you would. I just thought it would be safest if we avoided people and slept out in the fields.'

'In the fields? But there are bandits and wild animals out here.'

'If there are bandits, they will have very little interest in two penniless monks. And we've got Carbo. If he gets himself a big stick or a club we'll be able to see off any wild beasts. We'll be alright.'

'Humph,' Carbo grunted and steered his two charges to a clump of low, flat rocks underneath a tree.

'I've never slept outside before,' Cara said unhappily.

'I'm sorry,' Galen said, feeling inadequate. 'Carbo... you don't happen to have some money on you, do you?'

It was a pertinent question, because while he and Cara might be able to survive for five days on the food in Cara's sack, a big man like Carbo would need more.

'Of course I have money on me,' Carbo said, sounding less angry than he should have.

'I see... thank God,' Galen said and gave the man a wry smile. He hadn't wanted the big man to be pulled even deeper into his sinful actions.

'Here,' Carbo said, handing the sack over to Galen, now that he was seated on one of the flat rocks in the shade.

Galen noted that Carbo had taken them around the back of the tree where they were no longer visible to the road. It was warm and dry, so Galen reasoned, as he had before his flight, that shelter wouldn't be necessary.

'Now, Brother Galen,' Carbo said, settling himself on the ground opposite Galen and Cara who were sitting side by side, 'would you please explain to me what is going on?'

'Ah yes, you deserve that much at least,' Galen said and explained how he'd met Cara, why he'd hidden her away and why they were now on this desperate dash, with Cara adding in detail wherever she felt it was needed. 'And to top it all, I overheard Cardinal Gui saying he has men stationed all along the route back to Cara's home, so I fear being found out by them, especially if the men we managed to give the slip, send word about our escape.'

'Dear Lord in Heaven,' Carbo said, shaking his head, 'you do find yourself in quite a few muddles, don't you, Brother Galen?'

Galen felt himself flushing as he hung his head and nodded.

'It isn't his fault,' Cara said. 'He saved my life. I fear what my father and Bishop Vecchius might do if they catch me.'

'But why not just tell the pope?' Carbo asked.

'Because I wasn't sure what he would do for Cara,' Galen said, turning beseeching eyes upon Carbo, hoping he'd understand.

The big man rubbed his hand over his head, considering, and then grunted, 'Fine, not the pope, but why not Brother Alcuin?'

'I didn't want to drag him into this mess.'

'You little fool, Brother,' Carbo said. 'Brother Alcuin will be so hurt that you wished to exclude him when you needed his help more than ever.'

His words pierced Galen's heart and filled him with a greater pain than that already in his guts. All he could do was nod.

'Humph,' Carbo said and got back to his feet. 'I'm going to go back a short way. There was a crossroads leading to a small town. I'll get us some more supplies. You two stay here and have something to eat and drink while you wait. You look like you need it.'

For a heart-stopping moment, as he said he was going back, Galen had feared Carbo was going to head back to Rome. Thank God that wasn't so.

'We will wait here,' Galen murmured. 'Thank you, Carbo.'

The man left, shaking his head, which filled Galen with even more guilt.

'Don't feel bad,' Cara said and gently patted his arm. 'He isn't that angry with you.'

Galen nodded for he knew it was true. He hadn't completely destroyed Carbo's faith in him, but it was shaken.

'He's right that we should eat. It's been a very long walk and we haven't had a single drop to drink or crumb of bread,' Cara said and fished out the food she'd brought from her room.

Galen forced himself to eat because he knew this was going to be a difficult journey for him. It would have been hard even if he were in his best condition, but to have fled when his injury had flared up was doubly challenging.

Carbo didn't return even as night descended and Galen's fears grew. Cara also looked more and more anxious.

'You must sleep,' Galen said as they huddled among the stones. 'Tomorrow will be another long day of walking.'

'But where is Carbo?' Cara asked and shifted herself so that she was right up against Galen.

'I'm sure he will be back soon,' Galen said, and he really was.

The only thing that might keep the big man away was if he was captured. Galen prayed that wasn't the case, and then prayed some more that God would watch over all of them.

Cara pulled Galen's arms over her shoulders and clung onto his hand with both of hers. Galen would have remonstrated but for the fact that he could feel her shivering with fright. So he gave her a quick, reassuring hug and tried to get as comfortable as possible for the night's watch.

Galen felt numb from exhaustion and pain. His back and arms ached as much as his legs from a day of walking. It made him realise, once again, how lucky he'd been to have Carbo carrying all their goods and providing him support. But as Cara was relying on him, he was determined not to say a thing or slow them down. He didn't dare to anyway, lest Cardinal Gui found them.

His intention had been to stay up all night on watch, but somewhere along the way, after Cara's head had slipped down onto his shoulder, Galen also fell into sleep.

Cara woke him with a nudge in the ribs and said, 'Have some breakfast, sleepyhead,' as she held some fresh bread and cheese in front of him. She appeared far happier now that it was dawn again.

Galen was relieved to see Carbo sitting on the ground before them, also eating breakfast, a new and chunky staff resting on the ground beside him.

'Did you end up keeping watch all night?' Galen asked.

Carbo grinned at him. 'When I eventually found you again. All the damn trees along this road look alike.'

Cara gasped at his remark and then gave Carbo a big grin. 'Thank goodness you did find us.'

It seemed she'd taken to the big man. That was understandable - he was far more reliable than his own scrawny self, Galen thought, mournfully.

Chapter 19

It took five long days to reach the outskirts of Cara's hometown by which time Galen could barely hold back the tears because he was so exhausted and in such pain. He would have given anything for one of Alcuin's reviving teas, but suppressed that wish and held back from complaining because he didn't want to disappoint Cara.

She was also looking tired. Young noblewomen didn't walk all that much and she'd developed serious blisters. Galen probably had too, although his other aches and pains meant he didn't notice.

The only one who was still fine was Carbo who'd fallen back into his usual respectful manner and simply did all he could to help Galen.

Three days into the journey he'd even said, 'Let me give you a piggyback, Brother Galen.'

Galen was too embarrassed by the suggestion to accept, and said, 'You should give one to Cara, she's also looking tired.'

'Not as tired as you.'

'I'm fine,' Galen had assured him, although five days later he was regretting it.

'Well... we're nearly there,' Carbo said, looking down at the footsore, dusty, exhausted pair limping alongside him.

Cara always stuck to Galen's side, which seemed to indicate that she still preferred him over Carbo.

They hobbled up a gentle slope into a shaded town square surrounded by stone houses with thatched roofs. A fountain took up a prominent place at the south end of the square and its trickling water sounded loud in the silence since it was the hottest part of the afternoon and most of the residents had taken refuge indoors.

'Keep your eyes open, especially you, Lady Cara,' Carbo said. 'You know who's a local and who isn't.'

Ever since Galen had told Carbo and Cara that there might be people looking for her, Carbo had kept an eye out for anybody suspicious and had even pointed out a couple as they walked.

'Although our disguise seems to work,' Carbo had said, 'since nobody is taking any notice of us.'

The square in Cara's hometown was deserted save for one old woman sweeping the porch before her house, a trio of dogs lying in the fountain's shadow who only had the energy to raise their heads and examine the newcomers before going back to sleep, and a pair of men playing dice on a bench under a tree.

'I don't recognise those men,' Cara said.

'And here they might be suspicious of anyone, including monks,' Galen said, because in his letter to Lord Bonacorso he'd told him that a monk had hidden Cara away.

'But that's my grandfather's house,' Cara said as she pointed at a large three-storey building opposite, painted a dusty ochre. The windows on the ground floor had solid iron bars protecting them, the windows on the two upper floors were shuttered. Cara made to push back her hood and Galen grabbed her hand.

'No!' Galen and Carbo said simultaneously, and Carbo pulled them both down a side track.

'What are you doing? My grandfather's house is just on the other side of the square. We can reach it before those men even notice.'

'Your father said he was watching your home and those burly men are suspicious. They could be your father's spies,' Carbo said.

'So how do we get in?' Galen asked.

'Do you know of any secret ways into your house?' Carbo asked. 'Things maybe known only to the children of the house.'

'Of course,' Cara said, perking up. 'We can go in through the back. I'll call to Julius and he'll open the low window.'

'Good, let's do that.'

They circled round the outside of the town and through an apple orchard, their habits catching on the scratchy, dried-out weeds, before they came to the paved back yard of the ochre house.

Cara stopped below a large balconied window the size of a door. She put her hands together and blew between her thumbs, producing a cry like a dove. They waited, the backs of their necks tingling in anticipation of being found out. The sound of someone coming through the bushes behind gave them a fright and Cara put her hands together and gave another cry.

The window swung open and a slim boy with curly black hair leaned out to take a look.

'Julius, thank God!' Cara said. 'Quickly, give us a hand up.'

'Cara?' the boy said in surprise.

'Quickly, I'll explain everything later,' Cara said, holding her hands up to her brother.

Julius hoisted her up effortlessly and as she landed lightly in the room she said, 'Quickly, help me get Brother Galen in.'

The sound of someone breaking into a run came to all their ears. Julius grabbed one of Galen's hands as Cara grabbed the other and as they heaved, the two men who'd been sitting in the square came into view.

'I can't do it,' Galen said, trying his best to help as Cara and Julius pulled on his arms. It was all he could do not to black out, never mind get onto the balcony.

'Hang on, Brother,' Carbo said as he wrapped his arms around Galen's waist and launched him into the air.

Galen flew up, helped by Cara and her brother, and rolled over the railing before landing hard on the floor. It robbed him of breath, but he scrambled up, shaking his head to clear his vision as the two men charged at Carbo, both armed with short daggers,

'Close the shutters!' Carbo shouted as he turned to meet the men, his thick staff held out in front of him in both hands. 'I'll deal with these two.'

Galen helped the brother and sister slam the heavy wooden shutters just as the men roared and closed in on Carbo with colourful and very loud curses.

'Quickly, Julius, where's Grandfather?' Cara said breathlessly.

'Where he always is, in his study. Cara, what has happened to you? Why are you dressed like a monk?'

'Go and tell the guards about the intruders and get them to help Carbo, little brother. I need to tell Grandfather what's happening,' Cara said and took off at a run.

Galen hobbled along behind, using the last ounce of his strength to keep up. Cara stopped at a heavy wooden door, knocked forcefully and pushed her way in.

'Cara!' a white-haired, but still very athletic-looking man said as he started up from his desk.

'Grandfather!' Cara cried as she ran into his outstretched arms and burst into tears.

'Hush now. What is the meaning of this? And why are you wearing monks' robes?' Lord Bonacorso asked as his eyes flicked from his dusty, dishevelled granddaughter to Galen, who'd stopped in the doorway.

Galen propped himself up against the doorframe, trying to gather himself. He had to stay alert, although now that Cara was back in her grandfather's embrace, thankfully looking like he did care greatly for her, there wasn't much else Galen could do for her.

'What is going on?' Lord Bonacorso said, looking from Cara to Galen and back to Cara. 'First, I get a message from some unknown monk, presumably that fellow,' the lord said, pointing at Galen, 'telling me he was keeping you safe and that your father was up to no good. Then your mother sent me a message that you'd vanished, obviously written by your father. But the men I sent to Rome to find you came up empty-handed, and now you turn up like this? What am I to think?'

'Oh, Grandfather, I'm in terrible trouble—'

'Not because of this monk, I hope!' Bonacorso said as his brows snapped together into an angry frown.

'Oh no, not because of Brother Galen. He rescued me. It was Father. He wanted me to become the concubine of Bishop Vecchius. That's why he asked for me to go to Rome.'

'The Devil he did!' Bonacorso said angrily.

'He did, and he's furious that I ran away. He's been watching your house. Galen and I had to sneak in through the back and even then these two men tried to catch us. And Carbo... he's still fighting them.'

'Carbo?' the lord said, looking confused.

'I told Julius to get our knights to help him.'

'Good God in Heaven, what chaos,' Lord Bonacorso muttered. 'Let's hope we capture the two who dared to chase after you. I need answers.'

'They'll probably have run away by now,' Galen said quietly.

There would be no point in them staying and risking injury when they'd already lost their prey. They'd also have to report back to their employer. Although, hopefully, they'd think better of that and just slink off.

Bonacorso looked Galen over again and said, 'So you are Brother Galen?'

'Yes, my lord,' Galen said with a bow.

It was almost too much to have to straighten up again, but straighten he did and went back to the solemn examination of Cara's grandfather.

'You don't happen to be Galen of Yarmwick, do you?'

Galen's eyes widened in surprise. 'How could you know that?'

'There has been some gossip that the pope has found a new and learned saint.'

Galen flushed and gave an uncomfortable shrug. Cara cast a surprised look from her grandfather to Galen and back again at that news.

'So you don't claim to be a saint then?' Bonacorso asked.

'There have been some miracles I can't deny,' Galen said, shifting awkwardly on his feet, more because he was embarrassed that Cara was finding out. He'd never wanted her to treat him like a saint.

'Mmm, well, you'll have to tell me about it later,' Bonacorso said as Julius arrived at a run, tailed by a younger, remarkably similar-looking boy, a couple of sturdy henchmen and a somewhat flustered Carbo, who had a slight cut to his cheek that was beaded with blood.

'Tomas,' Cara cried and wrapped her little brother in a hug.

'Cara! We missed you,' he said with an enormous grin.

'Carbo, are you alright?' Galen asked.

'It's just a little scratch,' Carbo said with a grin. 'But the bastards... oh, beg your pardon for my language... the criminals got away.'

'You did well seeing off two of them,' Lord Bonacorso said, looking Carbo up and down. 'Now, you all look like you could use a bath and a rest. And Cara needs to put on some decent clothes.'

'Yes, sir,' the travel-worn trio said.

Galen hoped it was safe to relax his guard and then decided it made no difference. He had no strength left and could neither run nor fight at this point. Thank God he still had Carbo, who'd stepped over to provide Galen with the support he'd been gaining from the doorframe up till now.

Chapter 20

Galen was led to a decent sized room with a large bed in the centre and a washstand. As with the rest of the house, the shutters were almost closed, letting in only a sliver of bright light so the room felt shaded and cool. Galen barely had the energy to say to Carbo, 'You should also go… get that cut seen to.'

After Carbo left, looking reluctant, all Galen did was wash his hands and face before he crept onto the bed, curled up on his side and closed his eyes. His whole body ached, and the pain in his guts was so severe that if he were to eat anything, he'd probably throw up. That last mad dash and being hauled over railings had been the final straw.

Despite all that, he was relieved that Cara was safely delivered and that her grandfather was trustworthy after all. That had been worrying Galen throughout their journey. A burden had been lifted from his shoulders that he hadn't been aware he'd been carrying and he finally felt that he could rest.

The light had a dusk-like quality when Galen's sleep was interrupted by a low-voiced conversation taking place somewhere nearby. Aside from opening his eyes a crack, Galen had neither the strength nor inclination to move. The one voice he recognised immediately was Cara's. The other sounded like her grandfather.

'Don't you think you've hovered around him enough?' Lord Bonacorso said.

'I'm worried. He looks so unwell.'

'He'll recover,' the lord said. 'Tell me about this Brother Galen.'

'Isn't he wonderful?'

Cara's voice was filled with such admiration that Galen felt a twinge of embarrassment. Nobody had ever described him in this way, let alone a beautiful woman.

'He looks more dead than alive,' Bonacorso said. 'But all the same, I'll keep my men watching his room to make sure he stays there till I know what he's up to.'

'Oh, Grandfather, you don't need to be so suspicious. Galen is an honourable man, although I didn't know he was a saint. He didn't mention it to me.'

'Didn't he?' Bonacorso said dryly. 'So what *did* he mention to you?'

'He was teaching me how to read,' Cara said proudly.

'To read! Now that is unexpected. Do you love him, child?'

'I do, and he loves me too.'

It didn't come as a surprise to Galen to hear Cara say that - she'd said as much to him on their long journey to her home. It still caused a pain in his heart to hear it though. He loved her back, of course he did, but that was immaterial.

'So you want to marry him?' Bonacorso said and his voice turned harsh. 'No, I won't allow it!'

'I don't want to marry him,' Cara said, her voice soft and sad. 'Or rather, I would marry him if he asked, but he won't. He says he's taken a vow of celibacy and he won't break it. He brought me back here to help me escape from my father and so that I could marry Pandolfo.'

'Now I am confused. He helped you even though he doesn't know you, has no family ties with you, and even though he loves you, he's willing to see you married to another man?'

'I ran into him when I was fleeing my father and had no choice but to beg for his help, and he gave it.'

'Odd,' Bonacorso said and got his granddaughter to explain her entire tale again, frequently interrupting for clarification.

Sometime during the tale, Galen drifted off again.

He was shaken awake several hours later, with a candle burning in a now darkened room.

'You're little more than skin and bone beneath this habit,' Lord Bonacorso said, lifting the hand that had gripped Galen's shoulder. 'And even in sleep, you seem to have a great weight hanging over you.'

Galen stifled his nerves and, with great difficulty, pushed himself upright. He was about to climb off the bed, to give his host a bow, but Lord Bonacorso shook his head and waved for him to stay down as he fetched a chair.

'Forgive me for waking you when you are so obviously tired, but I must ask you some questions.'

'Is Cara alright?' Galen asked before he could stop himself.

'She's fine. I do want to know why you took such an interest in her, though.'

'She needed help,' Galen said softly. 'And she has a good heart.'

'According to her, you are the one with the good heart, and so it would appear.'

Galen pushed himself further upright. He felt at his usual disadvantage facing this man, but just that movement left him feeling so weak and dizzy that he didn't go further.

'My lord, I didn't know how to help Cara for a long time, and even though she told me you could protect her, I had my doubts.'

'You had your doubts about me? Why?'

'Well...' Galen said, giving him a dubious look, uncertain of how his words would be taken, 'you didn't respond to my letter and you didn't protect her mother... She became Cardinal Gui's concubine and apparently remains so.'

'I found Cara a safe husband,' Bonacorso snapped.

Galen gave a slight nod. He had no wish to offend the man, but he needed to know that Cara would be safe.

'He can keep Gui away, can he?'

'He is from a powerful family. She will be safe. Far safer than her mother. Cara doesn't know the whole story about what happened to her mother, for we have kept it from her. Better for her to think her mother loved Gui. But the truth is that Gui murdered the man I found for my daughter on her wedding night. Then he stole her away and deflowered her.

'After that, well, nobody else would have her. Gui then came to me and offered a great deal in reparation and an alliance with his family, who are also very well connected. I didn't like it, but I had little choice, especially when it became clear that she was pregnant by him.'

'Thank you for telling me. It can't have been easy. But why did you ignore my letter?' Galen asked. 'We waited for so long to hear from you.'

Lord Bonacorso hung his head and said, 'Forgive me for that. The letter came via the pope's office and... ever since my run-in with Gui, I have mistrusted the church and its clergy. I was worried that the pope was involved. That was why I dispatched my people to investigate and see if they could find you.

'They discovered they weren't the only ones looking for her, that Gui's men were also on the hunt, so they came back to report to me. I also considered... that if Cara was already safe, it was best to leave her where she was. Had I known the full situation, I might have done more. And then you and Cara turned up here.'

'The full situation?'

'You kept your letter vague. I don't blame you. It was best in case it got intercepted, but it made things trickier to understand.'

Galen nodded and fell into silent contemplation. It was strange that he had the courage to challenge this noble lord. It had to be the power of love driving him to confront somebody he normally never would.

'I am relieved you have found somebody to protect Cara, for she is in very grave danger,' Galen said. 'What I couldn't put in the letter was something I overheard. It was a conversation between Cardinal Gui and Bishop Vecchius that disturbed me profoundly. The bishop was after a virgin born of a priest for some rite he intends to hold on the eve of the millennium. I don't know what exactly it entails, but it filled my heart with fear for your granddaughter.'

'Heaven's Blood,' Bonacorso muttered. 'Gui has ever been willing to sacrifice anyone for his ambition, but to go so far, no! It's too much!'

Galen nodded. 'Did you catch the men who were watching the house?'

'I'm afraid they're long gone. But I've sent for Pandolfo. It is clearly a matter of the utmost urgency to get my granddaughter safely married and over the wedding night.'

Galen grimaced as he gave a quick nod. 'If she is no longer a virgin, then she will hold no further interest for Bishop Vecchius. I don't know what he will do to Cardinal Gui for failing to deliver though.'

'I have no interest in what happens to that man,' Bonacorso said, 'but I hope it all ends badly for him.'

Galen felt the same but was in no position to say so.

Alcuin stared out of the window and watched the swallows dart around the arches of the aqueduct. It had been five days since his friend had disappeared and he was so worried that he couldn't think, let alone do his illuminations.

And right now, now that his stained glass window was finished and about to be installed. Alcuin had wanted to share the moment with Galen, and now he couldn't.

'Damn you, Galen, where have you gone?' he muttered for the hundredth time under his breath.

Piccardo knocked at the open door and gave Alcuin a slight nod. 'Pope Sylvester wants to see Galen.'

This was the moment Alcuin had been dreading. 'He can't.'

'What?' Piccardo reacted like a man who was rarely turned down, especially when he summoned someone before the pope.

'Galen's gone.'

'He's gone? Gone where?' Piccardo asked, shaken out of his usual calm.

'I have no idea,' Alcuin said and waved a note at Piccardo. 'I woke up and found this pinned to my desk.'

Piccardo took the note and scanned it, frowning over the words. It wasn't Galen's normally neat script, so Alcuin had struggled over the words too, and then worried the note had been written under duress. He still wasn't sure which and that had eaten at him all this time.

'*Alcuin, I've gone away for a bit. Don't try to find me. I'll be back soon, Galen*. What does that mean?' Piccardo said as he handed the note back.

'I have no idea. Galen's never done anything like this before. He's never even kept a secret from me before... Well, only once, and only for a short while.'

'What am I going to tell the pope?' Piccardo asked. 'When did he disappear?'

'It's been five days now. At first I didn't look, but I have over the last couple of days, as discreetly as possible, so that I didn't raise any suspicions.'

'He hasn't run away, has he?'

'He left his notebook, which he wouldn't do if he'd run away. But he took both his habits,' Alcuin said, reluctant to share this information but relieved to finally have somebody sensible to share it with. 'He may not like where he is and what he is expected to do, but he doesn't run.'

'I'm sorry, I didn't mean to offend you, but I still have the problem of what I tell the pope.'

'You don't really have a choice, do you? You have to tell him the truth - that you don't know where Galen is. Unless of course, you can stall the pope? Give Galen another couple of days to reappear.'

'Do you think that's likely?'

'Honestly, I don't know, but I'm worried sick. I'm keeping myself awake at night thinking he's run into trouble, or fallen ill, and I'm not around to help him.'

'Might somebody else know? Carbo, for example?'

'Ah... Carbo, he disappeared on the same night,' Alcuin said.

This was what he felt most bitter about. If Galen had gone off on his volition, it looked like he'd taken Carbo with him. That hurt more than if the two of them had been left behind. Why Carbo and not him? That had been bothering him too. It had also been tremendously inconvenient, since Carbo provided all their meals, and Alcuin had had to make do with a combination of begging for alms, raiding the Lateran's kitchen and trading some of his art for food. All this to hide that Galen had disappeared. His friend surely did owe him for all that.

Piccardo blinked at Alcuin and said, 'You're being remarkably calm about all this.'

'Do you think so?' Alcuin said with a laugh. 'Honestly, Galen had been acting strangely, even before he disappeared, and I saw Carbo pass him a sack of goods once. It's so damned confusing.'

'What was in the sack?' Piccardo asked.

'I have no idea.'

'You didn't ask... you didn't confront your friend with all these questions?'

Alcuin sighed as he shook his head. 'Galen's under enough pressure as it is. And I know... eventually he will tell me.'

'But whatever he was given by Carbo... he brought nothing new back to his room?'

'He didn't,' Alcuin said and wondered why he'd never considered what happened to the sack and its contents.

'So he must have been giving it to someone else,' Piccardo said.

'Most likely, but who?'

'A woman?' Piccardo asked.

Alcuin had been wondering the same thing. 'Not, perhaps, for the reason you might be thinking. He wouldn't have set up a lover.'

'Are you sure?' Piccardo asked and his expression hardened.

'I know Galen better than anyone and I'm certain. But if somebody was in distress, he would help. That's the kind of man he is.'

'Without telling his friends?' Piccardo said, looking dubious. 'Look, Brother Alcuin, I'm not judging Brother Galen. I gave up my calling for my wife, so I am not one to cast stones. But Galen is only human, after all.'

'No,' Alcuin said.

'Very well, there's no point in arguing about this anyway. But the reason the pope wanted to see Galen was to prepare him for his meeting with Cardinal Gui to determine the sainthood question. This vanishing act will hardly stand him in good stead. Are you sure he hasn't run away? Maybe to avoid the meeting?'

'I already told you, Galen doesn't run away. And if he was doing it to avoid the meeting, he'd have left a day or two before, not a fortnight.'

'Very well,' Piccardo said with a sigh. 'But I will have to tell the pope that he's missing. I think it's time we started looking for him properly too, don't you?'

'Probably.' Alcuin was relieved that the decision had been made for him. 'Can I go with you to see the pope?'

'That may be best,' Piccardo said as he waved Alcuin out of the room and the two of them took off at speed to the council chamber.

Sylvester was standing before his brand new stained glass window admiring the effect of the coloured light spread across the council chamber floor when Alcuin and Piccardo arrived.

'Galen, come and look it's—' He stopped and raised an enquiring eyebrow.

'Brother Galen has vanished, Holiness,' Piccardo said as he handed over Galen's note.

'Is this genuine?' Sylvester said, once he finished reading the note.

'It is Galen's hand,' Alcuin said, 'if somewhat more cramped than usual.'

'But why would he go off?'

'I don't know, Holiness. But I've felt that Galen was keeping something from me. It is uncharacteristic of him to be so closed off.'

'This is unsatisfactory! My saint can't just fall off the face of the earth. Piccardo, do you suspect foul play? I wouldn't put it past some of my more scheming cardinals and bishops to try something like this.'

'I don't know, Holiness,' Piccardo said slowly, 'although Galen did ask me about Bishop Vecchius.'

'What?!' Sylvester roared. 'That evil, scheming travesty of a churchman! What was Galen doing even knowing about that man?'

'Whatever it was, it had nothing to do with money. Galen knew nothing of his usury.'

'Do you know why he was asking about the bishop, Brother Alcuin?'

Alcuin blinked in surprise and shook his head. 'I've never even heard the man's name before.'

'Long may it remain that way, my boy,' Sylvester muttered. 'But it still doesn't explain… Damn it, the hearing is in five days.'

'Strictly speaking,' Piccardo said, 'he doesn't actually have to be present, does he? All we need is the evidence and the witnesses.'

'That may well be, but it's undermining of his position and would be an inauspicious start to his sainthood. No, Galen must be found before that. Piccardo, Alcuin, do what you must to make sure that Galen is present for the hearing. But be discreet, I don't want Cardinal Gui hearing about this.'

'But... is this Bishop Vecchius so dangerous?' Alcuin asked, his alarm over Galen growing because Piccardo and the pope were both looking unusually grim.

'More than you can imagine,' the pope said. 'Let us pray Galen hasn't fallen into his clutches.'

Chapter 21

Galen's gaze drifted over a ceiling which was painted with an image of a blue summer sky dotted about with puffy white clouds, trying to work out where he was.

'Pandolfo arrived this morning,' Cara said.

Galen jumped, for he'd assumed he was alone, but Cara was sitting on the edge of his bed, watching him. 'Cara, what are you doing here?'

'I came to make sure you were alright. The journey was difficult for you, wasn't it?'

Galen felt the usual blush of shame warm his face. 'I told you I was a weakling.'

'You are no weakling,' Cara said with a decisive shake of her head. 'You are very brave and I will never forget you, never in all my days, even if I live to be one hundred years old.'

'I'll never forget you either,' Galen said softly. 'I pray you will lead a happy and fulfilled life.'

'I'm sure it will be fine,' Cara said, looking far more mature than usual. Before he could stop her, she swooped down and gave him a quick kiss on his forehead. 'Thank you for agreeing to stay for the wedding. We've had word from Pandolfo and his family. They will be here this evening.'

Galen took a long, slow breath to steady himself and said, 'So the wedding will be held here?'

'It's going to take place in my grandfather's chapel first thing tomorrow morning. He's already fetched the local priest to come and bless the union and he's not allowing him to leave the house until the wedding is over and the marriage confirmed to the world.'

'I see. Well, I too will play my part,' Galen said, although he doubted he would enjoy seeing Cara being given to another man.

'If you are there, I know I will be strong. Now I have to go and get ready. Here's the habit you lent me,' Cara said, pointing at a neatly folded black square at the foot of the bed. 'It's been laundered,' Cara added before she gave a quick, forced smile and ran away.

'Wait,' Galen called after her. 'What happened to Carbo?'

'I'm here,' Carbo said, appearing in the doorway. 'I've been waiting here for you to recover. I only wish you'd also taken some of the medicine Alcuin keeps for you. You've looked like you need it.'

'I'll survive,' Galen said and looked back up at Carbo who'd developed a melancholy air. 'Have I disappointed you?'

'A little... at first. But then I realised... you're only human. And even so, even though I can see how much you like little Lady Cara, you didn't break your vows.'

Galen felt his face grow warm merely remembering how close he'd come to doing just that. 'Being with Cara... that's not my calling. I sometimes feel rebellious towards Him, but for the most part I have accepted the path God has laid out for me.'

The Bonacorso family chapel took up an entire wing of the house. Before he'd come to Rome, Galen would have been astonished by such a thing. But now he was living in a palace which was five times grander than this mansion. Not that the chapel was a trifling affair. The ceiling was at the full three-storey height of the house. The walls were painted with scenes from the life of Christ and the apse was tiled in gold mosaics with an edging of purple, lilac and white tiles in a twisted rope pattern. The altar was of white marble and had gold candelabra set upon it.

Galen spent more time than usual examining the surroundings because it was difficult to look at the bride and groom, although he couldn't stop himself from time to time. Cara was wearing a dusty pink dress, covered by a lighter pink, diaphanous outer garment that matched her soft pink veil.

The bridegroom, Pandolfo, was tall and fair. The scar across his right cheek made him look dashing and fierce rather than hideous. Galen felt his heart twist with envy every time he looked at Pandolfo. He was a powerfully built, handsome man.

Galen stood no chance in comparison and he couldn't understand, watching that bronzed, god-like figure, how Cara could have even given him a second glance. Still, she had, and it had been wonderful.

The wedding ceremony was a simple one. Few of the bride's or bridegroom's family were there, given the fact that it was being carried out in a hurry. There were only two men of importance from the town, one being the mayor, plus Lord Bonacorso, Julius and Tomas for Cara. On the groom's side was a woman Galen gathered was the groom's mother, her brother and three of the groom's brothers, one with his wife.

Galen and Carbo sat on the bride's side of the church, the only two other guests. Galen clenched his fists tightly in his lap as the priest blessed the newlyweds. As the priest's sermon continued, Galen prayed to God for His understanding of Galen's envy under these difficult conditions.

It was over now. Cara was now completely beyond his reach and it was all his doing. If only he could feel happy about that.

Lord Bonacorso stood up and said, 'Thank you, Father Titus, for that wonderful blessing and thank you to all the guests who could make it on such short notice. I will host a proper banquet soon to mark this significant union. Now, I believe it would bring the happy couple good fortune if the saint, Brother Galen, were to bless them too.'

Galen looked up in surprise, aware that his eyelashes were damp with tears. Lord Bonacorso was smiling at him and the rest of those present had turned to examine him, many with more thoughtful expressions than before, for he hadn't been introduced when they'd arrived.

He forced a smile and said softly, 'Of course.'

Carbo helped Galen to stand and then he held his hands up in blessing as he said, 'Cara and Pandolfo, may your union be happy and fruitful and may you both prosper till the ends of your days.'

'Nicely put,' Bonacorso said.

Galen hardly heard him. He was watching the tear that had slipped from Cara's eye as it traced down her face. The pain of it was almost more than he could bear.

'Now, we should go,' Lord Bonacorso said as he made his way to Galen and Carbo's side.

'Now?' Galen said, shaken by the sudden declaration. 'What about the wedding breakfast?'

'That will proceed without us. It is urgent that I get to Rome and deal with Gui, and you have your own important reason for making haste back to the Lateran, not so?'

'Well... yes,' Galen said.

Carbo must have told the lord about the sainthood hearing, for he'd not mentioned it himself, although he had been keeping count of the days and was feeling anxious about how long it would take to get back.

'I have ordered that a breakfast be packed for our journey,' Lord Bonacorso said. 'I intend to get to Rome in two days.'

'Two days?' Galen said, feeling stunned as he cast a glance back at Cara, who was still watching him. 'How?'

'I have a carriage, of course. And I would be honoured to have you, a saint, travel with me.'

The news that they had a carriage to take them back and it would take a mere two days should have come as a relief to Galen who had been worrying, when he wasn't thinking about Cara, about the effect his absence was having on Alcuin.

'My horses are fast and my carriage is modern,' Bonacorso said as he took Galen's elbow and led him out of the chapel.

Galen had only a moment to turn and wave to Cara. This was probably for the best. A long, drawn-out farewell would have been too painful.

She waved back, suddenly more animated as she shouted, 'I'll write to you!'

Chapter 22

Due to a broken wheel, Galen, Carbo and Lord Bonacorso were considerably delayed and only arrived back in Rome on the day of the hearing. The thought of being so late terrified Galen and meant he'd become monosyllabic in response to Lord Bonacorso's questioning.

It had turned out that the lord was a quietly persistent interrogator and had whiled away the time on their journey finding out all he could about Galen, particularly what it was that made him a saint. But he'd been fair, too, and answered Galen's questions about Cara's life, and the politics of Rome, in exchange.

Galen had finally worked up the courage to ask whether Lord Bonacorso knew what Bishop Vecchius might hold over Cardinal Gui.

'In my opinion,' the man had said, 'it's most likely to do with the death of Gregory, the last pope.'

Galen had been less surprised than he might have expected, but it sounded right to him. It also tied the different way Galen saw the old pope to how he saw the cardinal. Perhaps God was sending him a sign. He had no way to verify it, though. He was also distracted by his concern over the time the journey was taking and glanced at the sun every few minutes, agonising over the passage of time on the day of the hearing.

'I will help you get to the hearing,' Lord Bonacorso said.

'That is my role,' Carbo rumbled.

'And I will explain that it's my fault that you were delayed,' Lord Bonacorso said with a slightly irritated smile at having been cut off.

'Oh... but it isn't really,' Galen said as he was filled with relief to see the Lateran roll into view.

'We're almost there, so let's not argue about this,' Bonacorso said. 'Allow me to do this one thing to repay all you have done for me and my family.'

Galen nodded acceptance, but he was nearly jumping out of his skin with impatience as the lord dismounted from his carriage, and then waited as Carbo helped Galen out and took his arm in a strong supportive grip.

'Where to?' Lord Bonacorso asked.

'The pope's council chamber, in the palace,' Galen said, half dragging Carbo to the entrance of the palace and up the stairs in his anxiety to get there. 'We're late,' he murmured to Carbo when the big man tried to slow him down.

'In that case,' Carbo said, hoisting Galen up so that his body took most of his weight, 'let us hurry. I will lead the way.'

They rushed through the palace, Galen ignoring the pain, up the stairs and past the half dozen guards standing to attention at the council chamber doors, who thankfully recognised Galen and did nothing to stop him, Carbo or Lord Bonacorso.

They were late. Galen looked about anxiously to guess what had already happened. The pope was seated on his throne, the cathedra, wearing a white cassock heavily embroidered in silver and gold. To his right, in even more splendid red robes than usual, was Cardinal Gui.

He was waving a handful of parchment clutched in one hand, saying, 'While this is all very interesting reading, and would make for an evening of entertainment beside a fire, the tales herein are too fanciful to be believed.'

'But we have witnesses,' Pope Sylvester replied. 'We have letters from the King of Enga-lond, and his courtiers, confirming two of the miracles. This isn't mere hearsay.'

'But how convenient, they are so far away,' Gui murmured with a sardonic smile.

Galen looked around, searching for Alcuin, and found him seated at the end of a row of chairs, alongside several red-robed cardinals and white-robed bishops and, surprisingly, a skeletal-looking, black-robed Fra' Martinus, accompanied by Brother Iacopo the Armarius.

At the other end of the row was Piccardo, and a woman Galen assumed was his wife. She looked so different to the last time he'd seen her that it was hard to tell. She had a healthy glow, which was augmented by the coloured light that fell across the congregated people from the stained glass window of Saint Luke that Alcuin had designed. It was so new that the ramp they'd used to install it was still in place.

'Your Holiness!' Galen said, softer than he'd intended as he staggered deeper into the throne room, closely followed by Lord Bonacorso.

'Galen!' came a cry from more than one person, and Alcuin ran to his side.

Galen smiled up at Alcuin, trying his best to look unperturbed, then turned back to the pope and gave a deep bow.

'Holiness, I... I'm sorry I am so late.'

'Late? My boy, I feared you'd been done away with.'

'No,' Galen said, pausing to catch his breath. 'I don't know how to tell you this...'

'Just come straight out and say it, Galen. And after you have relieved yourself of whatever burden you are labouring under, you can explain why you thought you could go off without a word of explanation.'

'Yes, Holiness,' Galen said, flushing with embarrassment.

'Out with it then,' Sylvester said in a considerably softer tone, aware that his mild reproof was taken more seriously than he'd intended.

Galen took a deep breath and said, 'Holiness, Cardinal Gui and Bishop Vecchius are involved in a plot that I inadvertently got tangled up in.'

'What is this?' Gui said, his voice nasal and harsh. 'This so-called saint who didn't even bother to turn up on time for his own hearing has the nerve to lay the blame on me and Bishop Vecchius? What audacity! He should be thrown out and excommunicated, rather than be adjudicated as a saint.'

'You would say that,' Lord Bonacorso said as he strode towards Gui, his back stiff, his fists clenched by his side. 'You who have schemed to sell your own daughter to Bishop Vecchius as a concubine to be used for some God-forsaken ritual. How you can even pretend to be a man of God is beyond me.'

'How dare you?!' Cardinal Gui roared, having to raise his voice, for the assembled men in the audience had erupted into questions of their own and loud remonstrances.

'This is a hearing,' one of them shouted. 'Show some decorum.'

'That man has no business deciding on the sanctity of another,' Lord Bonacorso said, making sure he was heard over all the rest.

A bang, bang, bang echoed through the hall and everyone turned to face the pope who'd just hammered his crosier into the marble floor with all his might.

'What Cardinal Gui may or may not have been up to can be discovered on another day. I would prefer to hear how our dear Brother Galen is involved in all of this.'

All eyes turned to Galen, who staggered back at that, and was thankfully kept on his feet by Alcuin and Carbo.

'I would like to know that too,' Alcuin murmured.

It filled Galen with relief to see his friend again and to know, by his wry expression, that he wasn't angry for having been left behind.

'I... I came upon Cardinal Gui's daughter when she was fleeing for her life and I... I hid her away.'

'Ah,' Pope Sylvester said and waved his hands to indicate to Carbo and Alcuin to step away from Galen, which they both reluctantly did, taking two steps back but hovering in readiness should they be needed. 'So there was a woman involved in your disappearance.'

'Yes, Holiness,' Galen said as he stepped closer to the pope so that he could speak more privately, without all those in the room being able to hear him. It was a futile attempt.

'So,' Cardinal Gui said, pushing past Lord Bonacorso's strenuous attempts to stop him, 'this so-called saint of the pope's has been spending time with a woman. A very young, virginal woman at that. This calls into question not only the saint, but Sylvester's right to remain as a pope.'

'How quick you are to leap to judgement, Gui. Let us hear the rest,' Sylvester said. 'What happened to the girl, Brother Galen?'

'I... I took her home to her grandfather,' Galen said, pointing to Lord Bonacorso. 'She is safely married now to a man from a good family.'

'That is true,' the lord said. 'And I can verify that she was not touched by Brother Galen, for she told me herself, and I watched the two of them. There was nothing between them other than a wish to get my beloved Cara to safety.'

'Now you surprise me,' Sylvester said, turning back to Galen. 'I assumed you'd fallen in love with the girl.'

'I did,' Galen muttered and couldn't look Lord Bonacorso in the eye.

'But you took her home?'

Galen nodded, his gaze now fixed on the floor.

'You continue to surprise me, Brother Galen.'

'Whilst all he does is annoy me,' the gravelly voice of Bishop Vecchius said as he stepped into the throne room accompanied by a dozen soldiers, their swords held at the ready. The pope's soldiers surrounded them, and moved when they moved, but made no attempt to stop them.

'Vecchius, what is the meaning of this?' Sylvester asked.

'It's about revenge! That creature you call a saint robbed me of my rightful property and my chance of safety come the millennium.'

'You're mad!' Galen gasped, unable to understand how this man could come so boldly before all these men of the church to utter such depravity.

'I'm mad? I'm enraged, boy! You will pay for what you did and none will save you!' Vecchius moved like lightning past the pope's guards and past Alcuin and Carbo. He grabbed great bunches of Galen's robe in his fists and hoisted him clean off his feet. 'Let's see God save you now, saint!' he bellowed as he ran Galen backwards up the ramp. Everyone clamoured at him to stop as Alcuin and Carbo ran after the bishop. With a heave, Vecchius threw Galen through the stained glass window.

The glass shattered and everything froze. Galen hung suspended in the air, his arms reaching desperately into the room, the glass fragments scattering a flickering light which burned brighter than the sun, radiating from two golden figures to either side of Galen, while the air was filled with the sound of massive beating wings.

'Help,' Galen whispered.

Alcuin flew forward, braced his legs against the wall and grabbed Galen's wrists.

The golden figures vanished, glass crashed to the ground and Galen fell, his full weight pulling on Alcuin's arms. He hit the stone wall and clung onto Alcuin, his nails biting into Alcuin's skin. Carbo rushed to his side and his enormous hands closed around Alcuin's.

'Hang on, we'll get you in,' Alcuin said as, with a mighty heave, he and Carbo pulled Galen back into the room.

Galen collapsed to the floor under the shattered window and curled into a ball. 'Ang... Ang... Angels!' he said and burst into jagged sobs.

He was alive. He was alive thanks to the grace of God.

'It's alright, Galen, you're safe now,' Alcuin said as he patted his friend's back.

His hands were shaking and his face was pale. Alcuin abruptly stopped patting Galen and pulled at his robes, lifting the cloth at the back. Galen was barely aware of what he was saying as he struggled to regain his composure. How could he after what had just happened? He was shaken to the core of his soul.

'Look at this!' Alcuin gasped. 'The cloth is burned through and Galen's skin is marked with a white handprint over each shoulder blade.'

'Angels!' Sylvester said. His voice sounded faint and distant and his eyes were round in wonder. 'They burned through his clothes where they grabbed hold of him to stop him from falling to his death.' He turned to Bishop Vecchius who stood frozen to the spot, a look of horror on his face. 'Vecchius!' Sylvester said loudly.

The bishop swayed then dropped to the floor, prostrating himself.

'Have mercy,' he wailed. 'God have mercy!'

At the same moment, Cardinal Gui toppled over and hit the ground with a loud crack. Piccardo rushed to the man's side and felt for a pulse.

'He's dead!'

'The shock must have carried him off,' Sylvester said as he surveyed the room.

Everyone looked as stunned as Galen felt. Half the soldiers were staring at him as he struggled to get his sobbing under control. They looked to be in a trance. The other half fell to their knees and were praying and crossing themselves over the miracle they'd just seen.

'What did you have on Gui, Cardinal Vecchius?' the pope asked the still prostrate man.

'I lent him money; money he used to do away with Pope Gregory.'

'I see,' Sylvester said. 'Guards, arrest this man. And take Gui's body away. The rest of you,' he said, taking in the ring of shocked and flustered onlookers, 'can there be any doubt we are in the presence of a saint?'

Galen gulped in the last sob, fighting for control as a murmur of agreement went around the room.

'Even I, the Devil's advocate,' Fra' Martinus said, 'am convinced.'

So that was why he was here, Galen realised. How ironic that he'd pronounced so clearly on Galen's side.

'Then this hearing is at an end,' Sylvester said. 'I believe we all need a period of rest and reflection after witnessing such a stupendous miracle.'

There was a murmur of agreement and the crowd slowly trooped out, all of them casting backward glances at Galen, still collapsed on the floor.

Sylvester knelt beside Galen and Alcuin, with Carbo hovering behind, and gently felt over Galen's body.

'Nothing broken, and only minor cuts. You and Carbo should take him to bed, Alcuin. You know best how to look after him.'

'I do, Holiness,' Alcuin said, his voice also holding a tremor.

The pope smiled sympathetically at him and Galen, whom he was patting reassuringly on the shoulder. 'We've just witnessed a miracle beyond anything I have ever seen. To glimpse angels, and to know they supported Brother Galen for those crucial seconds, is incredible even to such a believer as myself. But now I have said enough. We will talk about this again later, once we have all regained the balance of our minds.'

Chapter 23

Alcuin administered a powerful sleeping draught to the overwrought Galen and contemplated taking one for himself and giving another to Carbo, who hadn't stopped crossing himself since they'd got Galen back to the room. He was now kneeling beside Galen's bed, praying, but thankfully Galen didn't notice, for he'd have been uncomfortable with such open adoration. The draught had worked its magic and Galen dropped into a deep and dreamless sleep.

'You should try to get some rest,' Alcuin said.

'Later,' Carbo said, his gaze not wavering from Galen's face.

Alcuin understood, and spent the hours until night deep in his own prayers, for himself and for Galen, whose life would never be the same again. The hearing was a foregone conclusion before the miracle of the angels, but how much more powerful a saint was Galen now?

The questions plagued Alcuin for the rest of the day and for a restless night. His mind was filled with whispers and flashes of glowing wings. Despite everything he knew about Galen, he'd never expected to see such an overt show of God's hand and it shook him to his core.

He pushed his blankets off with a sense of relief, the moment dawn sent out the first blush of light. He no longer had to work at trying to sleep. It seemed Carbo, too, had finally dropped off and was slumped in the corner beside Galen's bed. Galen was awake, his eyes staring blankly into nothing.

Alcuin took the mug of now cold tea that he'd prepared the night before and crouched beside Galen's bed.

'Here, you'd better have this.'

'Thank you,' Galen whispered and pushed himself upright before taking hold of the mug with both hands.

Alcuin watched him for a bit. He seemed very down.

'So you fell in love?'

'Yes.'

'Is that why you kept it from me? You didn't want me to know you'd fallen for a girl?'

'No,' Galen said, and, for the first time, he made eye contact with Alcuin. 'I don't know what I would have done if... if I'd fallen in love first, but... Cara was fleeing for her life when she asked me for help and I... I feared it was going to bring down trouble. I didn't want you to be implicated in what I was doing.'

'You were trying to protect me? You little fool, Galen,' Alcuin said with a wry smile as he settled on the foot of the bed.

'The thing is, you see... Cara... she treated me like a man. She... behaved as though I could rescue her. No-one else has ever behaved in that way to me. And I tried... I tried to show her that I was too weak, too frail, but she... she never believed that.'

'And she was right,' Alcuin said softly. 'For you did rescue her, didn't you?'

'I suppose I did,' Galen said as a tear slipped from his eye.

'You couldn't have married her.'

'No,' Galen said sadly. 'She wanted to but... I couldn't.'

'It hurts, doesn't it?' Alcuin said sympathetically.

'It is almost unbearable,' Galen whispered.

None knew better than Alcuin how true that was. 'Where did you go when you took Cara home?'

'It's a little village to the south of Rome in the mountains.'

'How did you get there?'

'We walked... disguised as monks, lest we be discovered.'

'Monks!' Alcuin said with a delighted shout. 'What ingenuity. You'll have to tell me all about it one day, for I believe it will make a wonderful illustration. And then you came back, looking utterly haggard. Did you walk all the way back too?'

'No, Lord Bonacorso brought us in his carriage. He wanted to make things right between me and the pope and he wanted to fetch Cara's mother back in case she was in danger from Cardinal Gui.'

'I expect the coach was travelling as fast as may be.'

'Yes.'

'No wonder you looked so ashen yesterday. All that jolting must have been a severe trial for you.'

Galen nodded and flicked an uncertain look at his friend. 'Alcuin the... the angels.'

'Ah yes,' Alcuin said with a sigh. 'I was afraid we'd have to talk about them sometime.'

'They were very frightening, weren't they?'

'Terrifying. Nobody should ever be that close to the Glory of God.'

'They... they whispered in my ear.'

Alcuin took in a hiss of breath. 'What did they say?'

'That I shall never die by the hand of man.'

'That much is clear enough. This is the second time, after all, that a man has tried to kill you and failed.'

'The third time,' Galen said softly and looked down into his empty mug.

'Septimus?'

'Yes. They said... they said the price I will pay al... always is the pain.'

'Oh,' Alcuin said. It seemed unnecessarily harsh that his friend would be doomed to suffer for the rest of his life.

Galen nodded and said, 'I had so hoped that one day... one day I would be healed.'

'Was there any explanation?'

'It was not because of the rape,' Galen said, sounding more thoughtful. 'I always wondered about that. But because of my silence. I said nothing after I was raped and two others died because of that. I have always felt guilt over it and it seems this is to be my punishment. I suppose that now I know, there is no point in praying for relief anymore.'

'Did you?'

'Every day.'

'Well, it's no wonder. I prayed for you every day, too.'

'Thank you.'

Alcuin gave Galen's arm an encouraging squeeze and said, 'I will continue to pray for you. If not for the pain to go away completely, then for it to be reduced, just like when Hatim saw to your wounds. They've never bled again, have they? And you hit the wall with quite a thump after you were thrown out of the window.'

'And was rescued by you again,' Galen said as his shy smile twitched his lips.

Alcuin laughed and said, 'A paltry service, that.'

Galen gave a deep, relieved sigh and smiled up at Alcuin. 'It's good to be back. Thank you for waiting, my friend.'

Enjoyed this book? You can make a huge difference
If you enjoyed the book please take a moment to let people know why. The review can be as long or short as you like.
Thank you very much!

Get my short story collection Shorties for FREE!

Sign up for my no-spam newsletter that only goes out when there is a new book or freebie available and get my collection of short stories for free, at: https://substack.com/@marinapacheco

Find out more about me and all my books: www.marinapacheco.me

ALSO BY

Get all my books here:

MEDIEVAL HISTORICAL FICTION ePub, paperback, hardback and audiobook (narrated by Jacob Daniels)
Fraternity of Brothers, *Medieval Mysteries of Galen, Book 1* – Cast out for a crime committed against him, his future looks bleak. Until an unexpected visitor gives him hope for justice. A fight for acceptance, absolution and friendship in Anglo-Saxon England.
Comfort of Home, *Medieval Mysteries of Galen, Book 2* – Proven innocent, he's returned from exile. Can he recover all that he lost? A tale of friendship and return to a family he thought he'd lost, set in Anglo-Saxon England.
Kindness of Strangers, *Medieval Mysteries of Galen, Book 3* – Trapped in a land plagued by vikings, can one small miracle be all they need to survive? A tale of miracles, betrayal and friendship while under viking siege.
The King's Hall, *Medieval Mysteries of Galen, Book 4* – As if being commissioned to create a book to turn back the Apocalypse isn't enough, intrigue and romance threaten to

destroy everything he's come to rely upon. Friendship, love and intrigue at the court of King Aethelred the Unready.

Restless Sea, *Medieval Mysteries of Galen, Book 5* – Just when they thought they could go home, they're thrust into an adventure at sea. A journey that tests the bonds of friendship.

Friend of My Enemy, *Medieval Mysteries of Galen, Book 6* – Captured by an implacable enemy, their future looks bleak. Will escape even be possible?

Road to Rome, *Medieval Mysteries of Galen, Book 7* — A journey across a turbulent continent. Will Galen find the answers he seeks?

Eternal City, *Medieval Mysteries of Galen, Book 8* — Galen and Alcuin delve into the secrets of the corrupt and decaying city of Medieval Rome.

Path of Sainthood, *Medieval Mysteries of Galen, Book 9* — Miracles, schemes, and a perilous journey to truth in the heart of Medieval Rome.

HISTORICAL ROMANCE: ePub, paperback, hardback and audiobooks with AI narration

Sanctuary, *a sweet Medieval mystery* – He needs shelter. She wants a way out. Will his brave move to protect risk both their hearts? An optimistic tale of redemption with heart-warming characters and feel-good thrills.

The Duke's Heart, *a sweet Victorian romance* – His body may be weak, but his dreams know no bounds. Will she be the answer to his prayers? A disabled duke, a strong and determined woman and a slow-building relationship.

Duchess in Flight, *a swashbuckling romance* – She's on the run from a deadly enemy. He lives in the shadows of truth. When their lives merge, will their battle for survival lead to love? A reluctant hero, a woman and her children in distress, a chase to

the death.
What the Pauper Did, *a body swap mystery romance* – How do you define yourself? Is it through your appearance, your memories or your soul? Intrigue, murder and romance in an alternate Lisbon of 1770.

CONTEMPORARY ROMANCE ePub, paperback, hardback and audiobooks with AI narration
Scent of Love – *Loves of Lisbon, Book 1.* Can two polar opposite perfumers overcome their differences and create a unique blend all of their own? Love, intrigue and clashing values in the perfume houses of Lisbon.
Sky Therapy — A detective and the son of a serial killer. Is it safest to stay apart, or will they risk everything for love?
Terapia Celeste — My first novel to be translated into Brazilian Portuguese.

SCIENCE FICTION/ FANTASY ePub and paperback
City of Night, *Eternal City, Book 1* – World-threatening danger, a female demonologist, an unwitting apprentice, a city in a single tower, a satisfying ending.

SHORT STORIES: ePub, paperback, and AI narration
Living, Loving, Longing, Lisbon, Vol 1 & Vol 2 – A collection of short stories inspired by the city of Lisbon, written by people from around the world who live in, visited or love

Lisbon.

Christmas of Love – *A Loves of Lisbon short story collection.* Christmas advent calendar of 24 short, sweet romances of the intertwining lives of the residents of Lisbon.

FREEBIES: ePub and AI narration

Shorties – My shortest works: futuristic, contemporary and historical available for free when you sign up to my newsletter.

ABOUT AUTHOr

Marina Pacheco a binge writer of historical fiction, sweet romance, sci-fi and fantasy novels as well as short stories. She writes easy reading, feel-good novels that are perfect for a commute or to curl up with on a rainy day. She currently lives on the coast just outside Lisbon, after stints in London, Johannesburg, and Bangkok, which all sounds more glamorous than it actually was. Her ambition is to publish 100 books. This is taking considerably longer than she'd anticipated!

You can find out more about Marina Pacheco's work, and download several freebies, on her website:
https://marinapacheco.me
Website: https://marinapacheco.me
   Sign up to Marina's newsletter via her website or on Substack to keep up to date on all her writing activities, get early previews of covers and first chapters, short stories and freebies.
Follow me on substack:
https://substack.com/@marinapacheco
email: hi@marinapacheco.me

Printed in Great Britain
by Amazon